Praise for Sarah E. Ladd

"A sweet Regency romance about grief, forgiveness, and being true to one's gifts. Ladd is a master of the genre, and she shines in this tale filled with intrigue, gentle manners, and lots of heart."

—Anna Lee Huber,
USA TODAY bestselling author

"Sarah Ladd deftly weaves her charming, rivals-to-lovers romance with antiques-filled intrigue, wonderful Regency-era detail, and an intelligent heroine who beautifully comes into her own strength. Add in a house party set in atmospheric Yorkshire and The Cloverton Charade is a gentle Regency romance that's an absolute delight to read."

—Celeste Connally, author of
ALL'S FAIR IN LOVE AND TREACHERY

"A sweet, enjoyable second-chance-at-love Regency romance with a strong heroine, a steadfast hero, a dash of suspense, and elegant descriptive prose. I rooted for this well-matched couple from the very first page!"

—Syrie James, author of THE MISSING MANUSCRIPT OF JANE
AUSTEN, for IN THE SHELTER OF HOLLYTHORNE HOUSE

"The Regency has found a gifted voice in Sarah Ladd, who spins magic from windswept moors and romance from a love separated but not forgotten. In the Shelter of Hollythorne House is a beautiful tale of lost love finding its strength again when all hope seems lost. Atmospheric and lush, readers will find themselves swooning in the manner of Jane Austen."

—J'nell Ciesielski, bestselling author of THE
BRILLIANCE OF STARS and THE SOCIALITE

"The swoon-worthy romance of Jane Austen meets the suspense of Charlotte Brontë in Sarah Ladd's enthral‌
Park. As Cassandra navigates the mystery c

T0205028

clear that family—either of blood or heart—are where she, and we, ultimately find our home."

—Joy Callaway, international bestselling author of *The Fifth Avenue Artists Society* and *The Greenbrier Resort*

"The Light at Wyndcliff is a richly atmospheric Regency novel, reminiscent of the works of Victoria Holt and Daphne du Maurier. The storm-swept Cornish coast is a character unto itself, forming the perfect backdrop for an expertly woven tale of secrets, danger, and heartfelt romance. A riveting and deeply emotional read."

—Mimi Matthews, *USA TODAY* bestselling author of the Parish Orphans of Devon series

"[*The Light at Wyndcliff*] expertly deploys elements of gothic mystery . . . The descriptions of the dilapidated property add dark, delicious atmosphere . . . The atmosphere and intrigue keep the pages turning."

—Publishers Weekly

"[Ladd] faithfully depicts the rough Cornish coast of the 1820s, with its rocky coves and windswept moors, the slow-simmering romance between the attractive principals is skillfully done, the suspense is intriguing, and all is brought to a satisfying conclusion . . . This charmingly written, gentle tale of manners and romance hits the right notes."

—Historical Novel Society for *The Light at Wyndcliff*

"Fans of Julie Klassen will love this."

—Publishers Weekly for *The Thief of Lanwyn Manor*

"Cornwall's iconic sea cliffs are on display in *The Thief of Lanwyn Manor*, but it's the lyrical prose, rich historical detail, and layered characters that truly shine on the page. Fans of Regency romance will be instantly drawn in and happily lost within the pages."

—Kristy Cambron, bestselling author of *The Paris Dressmaker* and the Lost Castle novels

THE
CLOVERTON
CHARADE

ALSO BY SARAH E. LADD

THE
CLOVERTON
CHARADE

SARAH E. LADD

THOMAS NELSON
Since 1798

The Cloverton Charade

Published in Nashville, Tennessee, by Thomas Nelson. Thomas Nelson is a registered trademark of HarperCollins Christian Publishing, Inc.

Published in association with Books & Such Literary Management, 52 Mission Circle, Suite 122, PMB 170, Santa Rosa, California 95409–5370, www.booksandsuch.com.

Thomas Nelson titles may be purchased in bulk for educational, business, fundraising, or sales promotional use. For information, please email SpecialMarkets@ThomasNelson.com.

Publisher's Note: This novel is a work of fiction. Names, characters, places, and incidents are either products of the author's imagination or used fictitiously. All characters are fictional, and any similarity to people living or dead is purely coincidental.

Any internet addresses (websites, blogs, etc.) in this book are offered as a resource. They are not intended in any way to be or imply an endorsement by Thomas Nelson, nor does Thomas Nelson vouch for the content of these sites for the life of this book.

Library of Congress Cataloging-in-Publication Data

Names: Ladd, Sarah E., author.
Title: The Cloverton charade / Sarah E. Ladd.
Description: Nashville, Tennessee: Thomas Nelson, 2024. | Series: The House of Yorkshire Novels; 3 | Summary: "A long-held family feud reignites when two rival antiquities brokers arrive at the same house party in Regency England"—Provided by publisher.
Identifiers: LCCN 2024009350 (print) | LCCN 2024009351 (ebook) | ISBN 9780785246862 (paperback) | ISBN 9780785246879 (epub) | ISBN 9780785246701
Subjects: LCGFT: Christian fiction. | Novels.
Classification: LCC PS3612.A3565 C56 2024 (print) | LCC PS3612.A3565 (ebook) | DDC 813/.6—dc23/eng/20240301
LC record available at https://lccn.loc.gov/2024009350
LC ebook record available at https://lccn.loc.gov/2024009351

Printed in the United States of America

24 25 26 27 28 LBC 5 4 3 2 1

This novel is dedicated to RG—with friendship and gratitude

Prologue

"DO NOT GO to the dock alone. It's dangerous."

Olivia's father's warning rang in her mind. He was right, of course. Violence ran rampant along this bustling stretch of the Thames River. More than one tale circulated of an unsuspecting soul disappearing from this dock, never to be heard from again. But the sun had not yet set.

Surely a closer look wouldn't hurt.

Fourteen-year-old Olivia Brannon exited the rear entrance of the Flanner Auction House onto the hectic landing and into a vibrant world that she knew all too well. Sailors and merchants milled about, no doubt eager to make use of the day's fading light, and the noisy white seabirds dipped low and wove among the masts of the tall ships. Curious scents of fish and cumin, of wood and tobacco, perfumed the dank, hazy air, and the revived excitement of things new and unexplored enveloped her.

She wanted to see everything. Know everything. And not just about the treasures brought in on the East Indiaman ships. She wanted to know the stories about the exotic lands from which they came and the people who made them.

She lifted to the tips of her toes and pressed her hand against her forehead to shade her eyes against the golden setting sun as it reflected off the choppy water. Through the throng of sailors, discarded nets, and coiled ropes, she spotted it.

A large wooden crate stamped with the words *Live Animal*.

"Olivia."

The tenor of the familiar masculine voice squelched her anticipation, and annoyance crept in. She glanced over her shoulder.

Lucas Avery, tall, gangly, and three years her senior, stood just behind her with a bulky leather satchel slung over his wiry shoulder. The riverside wind tousled his tawny hair, which appeared to have lightened by time spent in the sun, and his usually ruddy complexion was far tanner than she recalled.

"It'll be dark soon." He nodded toward the Thames. "It's not safe here after the sun sets."

His warning was valid, but she'd not give him the satisfaction of thinking he'd told her something she wasn't already aware of. "I know."

"What are you doing out here anyway?" He fell into step with her as she walked along the wooden planks.

"If you must know, a tiger came in on the *Belletrue* yesterday. It's bound for the Royal Menagerie at the Tower of London. I was hoping to see it," she stated, proud to share new information and determined to gain control of the conversation. "What are you doing here? I thought you were in the Orient."

"I was." He paused to allow two men carrying a large trunk to pass between them. "We returned only yesterday."

She bit her lower lip and looked out at the masts and rigging. Oh, how she envied him.

Timothy Avery, Lucas's father, was a purveyor of antiquities, just like her father. Lucas traveled extensively with him in pursuit of rarities—to India, Egypt, Italy. Her father traveled as well, but she was never permitted to join him. Ever since her mother had contracted diphtheria and died on a sea voyage to Italy, her father deemed both his daughters too delicate to travel—a sentiment Olivia ardently challenged, but to no avail.

An arresting roar, unlike anything she'd ever heard before, reverberated near the bolts of stored sailcloth and brick buildings lining the docks. Shouts and shuffling erupted. She whirled to see two sailors securing a gray canvas tarp over the crate. Other sailors joined them to push the crate away from the landing's edge and toward the buildings.

Crestfallen, she felt her shoulders droop. "I'm too late."

"Perhaps the tiger will still be here tomorrow," Lucas offered.

He was trying to be kind, she knew. Still, his conciliatory comment irritated her. Lucas Avery had always been kind—it had been his most admirable trait when they were playmates as children. But now it hardly seemed warranted—or even appropriate. How could he talk to her so casually as if their fathers were not enemies? As if his father had not betrayed hers?

"Maybe." She turned back toward the auction house's dock entrance.

"I'll escort you back inside."

"That's not necessary." Her words were sharper than she intended.

"I know. I'll join you just the same."

When they reached the entrance to the auction hall, Lucas opened the door for her. Oppressive heat pressed against her as she entered the hall, and the overwhelming odor of too many bodies in a stuffy space burned her nose. She slowed her steps just long enough for her eyes to adjust to the dim light before she turned back to Lucas. "As you can see, I'm inside now and quite safe, so I'll bid you good day."

But he ignored her dismissal and leaned closer to be heard over the chatter. "Is that the Cavesee Vase?"

Olivia followed his gaze to where she'd left her father earlier. Edward Brannon and his brother, Thomas, were unpacking the imposing blue-and-white porcelain Chinese vase—a celebrated relic from the Ming dynasty—from the straw of its shipping crate.

Relief rushed her. It had arrived. Her father had endeavored for years to secure its purchase, and they'd waited more than fifteen long months for the piece to arrive on England's shore. As with any such critical transaction, fear that it would be damaged or lost at sea in transit had hovered.

But here it was: large, intact, and stunning.

She lifted her chin and seized the opportunity to gain an upper hand over the Averys. "Yes, my father acquired it on behalf of Mr. Francis Milton's chinoiserie collection at Cloverton Hall."

She knew the effect that name would have on Lucas, and she paused dramatically to let it penetrate and have its full effect. "I must be going. My father will require my assistance."

Not waiting for a response, she curtsied and wound her way through the onlookers to where her father and uncle were uncrating the massive *tianqiuping* vase, which was nearly two feet in height and required both men to safely lift it.

Perhaps it had been an exaggeration. Her father did not *need* her help. But how else was she to learn everything there was to know about evaluating antiquities if she did not participate as much as possible?

As she drew closer, the details became more obvious: the unmistakable cobalt-blue hue on the bright white background. The fierce, five-toed dragon circling the globular base—a symbol of the emperor. Lotus flowers embellished the columnar neck, and *lishui* waves circled the base and upper rim.

Overwhelming pride engulfed her, and a grin quirked her lips. Brannon Antiquities had done something Avery & Sons would never be able to do: supply priceless pieces to the famed Milton chinoiserie collection. The Averys might have bested them on other fronts, but renewed determination fired through her. This would be the first of many instances in which the Brannons would prevail. It might be wicked to hold bitterness toward the other family, but surely there was nothing wrong in celebrating this hard-won victory.

Chapter 1

OLIVIA COULD HARDLY believe the proposition that had just been presented to her. This was the opportunity she'd imagined only in daydreams.

Giddy anticipation mingled with intoxicating disbelief, and for a brief moment, a dazzling glimpse into an entirely new existence glistened—one where she was independent. Self-sufficient. Needed. Valued.

She looked to the elegantly clad woman in front of her: Mrs. Agnes Milton, the widow of her father's most influential client. "You'd like for *me* to come to Cloverton Hall to evaluate your collection?"

Mrs. Milton shifted the fluffy Pomeranian in her arms before nonchalantly adjusting the jade kid-leather glove on her hand. "Yes. My husband told me of you—a young woman who assisted with her father's appraisals and knew more about antiquities than any purveyor he knew. Now, I find myself in a peculiar situation and require assistance from one knowledgeable on such matters."

Summoning fortitude, Olivia glanced at her uncle Thomas, who was, at present, the only other person in the receiving room of the Brannon Antiquities warehouse. Thomas Brannon had assumed full ownership of their business after her father's death four years prior. Never would he openly display disapproval in front of a client, but his hooded left eye twitched, and his lips had flattened to a thin line.

Olivia returned her eager attention to the petite, plump woman in front of her. "And your collection—are these chinoiserie pieces?"

"There are a few, but mostly it consists of jewelry, shells, and gems. I inherited them directly from my grandfather, an East Indiaman captain. All the items are separate from the Cloverton estate holdings. I would require you to catalog the pieces and estimate their value and, if all goes according to plan, discreetly identify buyers."

Olivia gripped her hands behind her to contain her mounting enthusiasm. Was her dream about to be realized? Was she being sought out for her professional reputation?

Dozens of questions rattled in her mind, but her uncle's sharp stare reinforced her place. Since her father's death, she'd been reduced to little more than an assistant at Brannon Antiquities & Company, and he was keen that she should not forget it.

"Perhaps my uncle should join us," she suggested reluctantly. "He's well-versed in the—"

"That will not do," Mrs. Milton snapped, her sky-blue eyes sharp and direct. "My nephew, the new master of Cloverton Hall, has recently taken up residence there, and he must know nothing of this. I've no doubt he'd attempt to challenge my claim to my collection and acquire it as his own. If your uncle, a known antiquities purveyor, were to arrive at my invitation, tongues would wag, whereas no one would question your presence."

Fearing the offer might vanish straightaway, Olivia blurted, "I'd be honored to join you at Cloverton Hall at such a time that is agreeable to you, Mrs. Milton. I know you would not be disappointed with my work."

Mrs. Milton pursed her narrow lips and stroked the little dog's fur with her free hand, as if completely accustomed to others acquiescing to her will. "I'm glad to hear it. My nephew's to host a house party to introduce his companions to Cloverton Hall, and he has requested that I act as his hostess. Normally I'd refuse such a ridiculous display, but I see it as an opportunity. You shall attend as my guest."

Olivia had heard about these gatherings—where wealthy members of society descended upon a grand country house and indulged in lavish entertainment for a fortnight or so. Never in her wildest imaginings did she think she'd ever be invited to one.

"We shall depart next Wednesday. While there, you'll participate in the entertainment and activities to avoid raising any speculation, but you can conduct your evaluations during the morning hours and as time permits."

A dozen concerns bombarded Olivia. She did not possess the proper attire. How was one to behave in such a setting? But those issues could all be addressed. She owed it not only to herself but to her younger sister, Laura, to seize every opportunity to advance herself.

"As for a fee," Mrs. Milton continued, "I assume it will be as any other such transaction—you'll receive a percentage of the purchase price once it is sold. In the meantime, I'll provide your board and proper attire for your trouble."

Olivia ignored the stab at the simple charcoal-gray printed muslin gown that currently adorned her frame, for it didn't matter. Nothing mattered more to her than securing this opportunity. "Yes, ma'am."

"Good. My maid will contact you with other pertinent details and make arrangements for my modiste to visit you. I'll apprise her of the clothing you'll require. Remember above all, this must be done with absolute discretion. To everyone else present, you will simply be my guest."

Mrs. Milton bid them a staunch farewell, exited their modest shop, and accepted the help of her liveried footman to reenter her carriage. Only after the ornate vehicle lurched into motion and plumed a trail of dust into the thick afternoon air did Olivia dare to move a muscle.

The sense that her life was about to change flared within—and she was eager to begin.

Chapter 2

OLIVIA HAD OVERSTEPPED a boundary. A significant one.

The herbaceous scent of Mrs. Milton's lily of the valley perfume lingered even after her departure. The mantel clock's steady rhythm seemed unusually sharp in the otherwise still silence, as if it, too, was anticipating her uncle's censure.

"So, you've made a decision, have you?" Thomas Brannon grunted at last, his baritone voice uncustomarily tight and gritty. "Without consulting me?"

The question was a legitimate one, but how long had she waited for something—anything—that would offer any sort of autonomy? She turned to face the man who, in appearance only, was so like her father. "I assumed you'd be pleased that such an esteemed member of society would trust us with such an assignment."

"Pleased?" He scoffed and propped his thick fists akimbo. "As I've told you countless times, you are not an agent of this company, Olivia."

His argument stung. In truth, she was little more than the daughter of a once well-respected purveyor, and she should be eager to make an advantageous marriage instead of pursuing professional recognition. Yet she'd spent most of her life in this shop at her father's side, learning the nuances of antiquities and other such artifacts. It was a significant aspect of who she was and how she lived her life.

Unwilling to let the topic drop, she trailed Uncle Thomas as he stormed from the receiving room into the warehouse. The familiar scent of dust and disuse tickled her nose as they entered the humid, dimly lit space. "No, I'm not an agent, but I know just as much, if not more, than most. And this is a good opportunity."

"Opportunity for what?" Thomas stopped at the desk where one of their agents, Russell Crane, was seated and lifted a stack of unopened letters. "I've never heard of her *collection*. I doubt anyone has. This scheme is likely a desperate attempt to claim whatever money she can, now that Francis Milton is dead. It's probably not even worth the trip, but instead of consulting me, you reacted based on emotion."

Olivia clamped her teeth over her lower lip and resisted releasing the sarcastic retort simmering on the tip of her tongue. She despised this feeling—of her knowledge and experience being devalued . . . of not being considered a significant contributor simply because she was not the son who could ensure the business's future. She might be a woman of two and twenty, but she was still at her uncle's mercy in many ways. After all, he was the de facto owner of their business, and as such, he provided the roof over not only her head but her younger sister, Laura's, as well.

"Need I remind you that when Edward died, he asked me to care for you until the day you meet a man I feel is worthy enough to be your husband?"

An uncomfortable tightness pinched in the pit of her stomach as she recalled the conversation at her father's bedside, hours before his death. "I remember it."

"Your father thought me the best person to help guide you, which I've attempted to do. Now you've committed yourself to traveling hundreds of miles to a home where you know no one to evaluate a supposed collection. And what do you know of Mrs. Milton's nephew? Anything?"

Olivia remained silent.

"I will enlighten you, then. The ears of every purveyor, seller, and collector perked when word of Francis Milton's death became public. By all accounts young George Wainbridge is a wild young man with a dubious reputation. Who knows what manner of person will be present at this so-called house party?"

Olivia's defenses—and confidence—faltered. She suddenly felt quite small, like a child reprimanded for impulsive behavior. "Mrs. Milton will be there, and surely—"

"We've worked with Mr. Milton, not Mrs. Milton," he countered. "And now that her husband is dead, who is she?"

The holes he was attempting to poke through her plan were widening. Perhaps her excitement had trumped her sense of reason, but she could not back down. Not now. Her pride would not permit it.

She forced aplomb to her tone and straightened her shoulders. "It's widely known that Mrs. Milton is one of the most prominent women in polite society. You've said yourself that such clients are the exact foothold we need. What's more, she'll be my chaperone. Honestly, I don't see what harm could be done in such a short time."

"You don't see what harm could be done in a country house?" Thomas jeered. "That's the precise reason I should forbid it."

"I'm a grown woman, Uncle, and I'm not a fool. I know exactly what sort of people could be in attendance. But it is for a fortnight at most. The assessment aside, I have spent my entire life within London's city limits, and I might very well spend the rest of my life here without seeing any other part of the world. You know full well that Father always promised that when I came of age, he'd take me traveling. He's gone, but he always made his intentions clear. Give me credit, at least, for having a sensible head on my shoulders."

At this, Thomas fell silent.

Her words had landed with some effect. Maybe it was the reference to his late brother. Maybe it was the fact that he himself had a role in her isolation.

Thomas folded his arms across his barrel chest and stared at her for several seconds. He narrowed his deep-set, coffee-hued eyes, and his tone grew curt. "Very well. Do as you wish, then. You are, as you have said, a grown woman. But by doing so, you accept responsibility for the possible ramifications. I'll have no part of it."

He tucked the stack of letters beneath his arm, snapped up a small crate from Russell's desk, and stomped back toward the receiving room.

Olivia inhaled a shaky breath.

She had not won that argument. Nor had she lost it.

Russell's weighted gaze bored into her. Undoubtedly he'd side with her uncle.

The lanky man had begun working for her father eleven years prior. At thirty-two he was a full decade her senior. His mild manners and straightforward disposition made him easy to interact with, but in moments like this, when professional and family matters intertwined, their unique relationship could be difficult to navigate.

"Go on," she said at last, reaching for the linen work apron she had slung over the chair when Mrs. Milton arrived. "I know you're champing at the bit to share your opinion."

He let out his typical good-natured chuckle, abandoned his chair, and stepped around the desk. He wore no coat, a bottle-green corduroy waistcoat hugged his lean torso, and his blousy linen shirtsleeves were rolled to his elbows. He leaned back against the edge of the desk and crossed one booted foot over the other. "He's right, you know."

She turned to face him. His curly, straw-blond hair seemed to always be in need of a trim. "I thought you'd say that."

"I'm serious. I've heard the stories about George Wainbridge. A wealthy heir with too much time and money on his hands. Do I think you'll be safe with Mrs. Milton as your chaperone? Yes. Do I think it a good idea to get involved with fops like George Wainbridge? Probably not."

Olivia shrugged the apron over her shoulders, annoyed that his assessment of the situation did not match her own. "It's a good thing I'm going for Mrs. Milton, then, and not Mr. Wainbridge."

"Oh, come now, Olivia, don't get testy. I'm only looking out for you, 'tis all. I'd hate to see you get yourself into a difficult situation."

She hastily secured the apron strings behind her back and avoided looking in Russell's direction. An odd dynamic had existed between them ever since her father died. It had been born out of the need for them to work together to keep the business strong, but beyond that, she did consider him a friend, and as such, he knew far more about her personal life than he should.

"But"—he lowered his voice as if taking her into his confidence—"to ease your mind a bit, I know of that collection."

She jerked her head up. "You do? Mrs. Milton's collection?"

He nodded. "Do you recall when your father and I escorted the Cavesee Vase to Cloverton Hall after its arrival? We spent two nights there before returning to London. I didn't actually see her collection, mind you, but old man Milton told us that his wife had an astute penchant for oddities and antiquities, even superior to his own. He said it consisted of a great deal of items in their natural form—shells and gems and the sort."

"Well, that's encouraging, I suppose." She sank into the chair next to his desk, rested her elbows on the desk's edge, and cradled her chin in her hand. "Regardless, I've committed myself. I couldn't go back on my word now. I only hope the collection's value is enough to justify the journey. I hate to give my uncle the satisfaction of being right."

"You mean *you* don't want to be *wrong*, more like." Russell smirked before fixing his bright blue eyes on her. "I know you're frustrated with the state of things, but I do wonder if traipsing all the way to Yorkshire is the best way to go about proving your point."

"If I don't pursue it, another opportunity will not come. You know that."

He shook his head and straightened to his full height. "I'm not entirely sure what it is you're chasing, but I wish you could accept things for how they are. I really do."

Olivia longed for contentment too. But how could peace be found here? Now that her parents were dead, she was subject to her uncle's whims. What was more, her uncle was turning her father's dream into something unrecognizable. She hated it. She wanted freedom to continue her father's work and passion on her own terms, but her options and resources were sorely limited. Any opportunity, no matter how small or unlikely, needed to be explored.

"I'll support whatever you want to do." Russell rounded the desk and sat down at his ledger. "If you want to go to Yorkshire, then go to Yorkshire. But be careful. People who go to those parties are different than the people we associate with."

Russell's warning echoed as she stood to collect the paperwork she'd been reviewing upon Mrs. Milton's arrival. Olivia did believe that Russell had her best interests at heart, and yet he could never truly understand her reasonings. Time would tell if she was on a fool's errand, but this was something she had to do—if only to prove it to herself.

Chapter 3

BROOKS'S GENTLEMEN'S CLUB. No matter how many times Lucas Avery stepped through these doors, he was in awe.

Candles were suspended from the ceiling and hung in wall sconces to illuminated the space, and once inside his eyes quickly adjusted to the smoky haze and flickering light. The low, energetic hum of male voices, broken by the occasional bout of spirited laughter, met his ears. Men from the highest echelons of society were gathered here for an evening's entertainment and camaraderie, but he was not here for such pursuits. Indeed, his goal for the night was infinitely more significant. In fact, this might be his last opportunity to salvage what was left of Avery & Sons.

Lucas accepted a small glass of port from a footman's tray and began his search for William Tate, his friend and his business's only remaining investor. He found the sandy-haired dandy quickly, seated at a gaming table engaged in a rousing round of faro. Card after card signaled Tate's impending fate, and once the game ended in his defeat, Tate muttered undecipherably, slapped his cards down, and shoved his chair away from the table.

It was then he took notice of Lucas. "Not my night, I'm afraid." He stood, pulled his gilded box of snuff from his pocket, popped it open, and extended it toward Lucas. "Took you long enough to get here."

Lucas raised a hand in refusal. "Sorry. Didn't get your message until quite late. What did I miss?"

Tate snorted. "Only my complete degradation at the card tables, and the billiards table before that. If I'd not been so bored waiting for you to arrive, I might have avoided that nasty business altogether. In all reality, my loss is on your shoulders." Tate pinched the black powder between his thumb and forefinger, quickly inhaled it, and returned the shiny box to his pocket.

"That's an interesting assessment," bantered Lucas. "I suppose you could have been doing something productive and followed up with Mr. Chalton over there to gauge his interest in selling me that German silver wine cistern he's been hinting he might want to part with. Don't you?"

Tate grimaced, then scoffed dismissively. "You know me better than that, old friend. Come on. Wainbridge is still here, but we must hurry. This might be your only chance to meet with him. He's quitting London on the morrow."

Lucas scanned the crowded chamber. Over the last few months he'd heard the name George Wainbridge more times than he could count, but he'd yet to meet the fellow. Fortunately for Lucas, Tate and Wainbridge had a longstanding friendship from their time at Cambridge.

As they wove their way through the throng of formally clad men toward the billiards room, Lucas nodded to those members who were familiar, but as he did, he was equally aware of the stares pointed in his direction. Several of the men had, at one point or another, been clients of his father's—which meant they also knew of the scandal that emerged just days before his death.

Lucas had perfected the mask of holding his head high and returning every glare with a smile and a nod. He'd give no indication of discomfort or, worse, embarrassment. If he wanted to reestablish the name Avery as the most important name in antiquities, he needed to make good on his goal for the evening: establish a relationship with the new master of Cloverton Hall in order to gain access to the famed chinoiserie items housed within its walls.

"I spoke with Wainbridge just yesterday," Tate explained as they traversed the lush Persian rug beneath them. "He's ready to sell the bulk of the collection, but he's been inundated with brokers and buyers vying for his attention. He came to me, of course, knowing that I dabble in such things, and after discussing it, he's agreed to meet with you. A word of caution, though. Wainbridge is a proud man, and I'm told Milton left the estate's finances in a bad way. He obviously wants that kept quiet."

This, Lucas could understand. He'd been in the antiquities business long enough to know that if a man wanted to sell an item of high value, it was usually because he needed the money. Public knowledge that an item was for sale would create every manner of speculation—speculation, Lucas could only assume, that would interfere with Wainbridge's efforts to establish himself as an influential member of society.

"There he is"—Tate pointed him out—"in the green coat."

Wainbridge was standing in the corner next to a mantelpiece, engaged in a lively conversation with an older gentleman. His intricately tied cravat and expertly fitted velvet tailcoat were a testament to his valet's skills, and the jewel-encrusted watch fob dangling from beneath his waistcoat glittered in the dancing fire's light.

Wainbridge took notice of them as they entered the billiards room, excused himself from his conversation, and approached them. At first glance the man appeared in his prime, but as he drew nearer, Lucas could see dark circles beneath his eyes, and in spite of the man's broad, easy grin, a tightness firmed his jaw.

"Tate! There you are." Wainbridge flashed his white smile in the low light. "I was beginning to think you forgot our meeting."

"No, no. Nothing like that. This is Lucas Avery, the man I told you about."

Lucas gave a slight bow.

"Good to know you, Avery. Come, let's sit." Wainbridge motioned to a footman for drinks and then led the way to an empty table in the corner. Once they were settled, he leaned back in his chair and fixed his unusually dark eyes on Lucas. "Your reputation precedes you, Avery."

Lucas quirked an eyebrow. "Does it?"

"You're the expert of all things antiquated and valuable, as I understand it," Wainbridge declared, a hint of amusement brightening his tone.

Lucas ignored the subtle air of condescension and chuckled. It was hardly the first time he'd encountered it, and yet, somehow, the simple fact that he knew this man needed his expertise overshadowed any offense. "Expert? Yes, I like to think so."

Wainbridge laughed good-naturedly and leaned back to allow the footman to place three full glasses on the table and then sobered again as the footman departed. "I don't mind saying it, Avery. I don't like this situation I'm in."

Lucas matched Wainbridge's casual posture and leaned back. "And what situation is that?"

"Not being the expert." Wainbridge simpered smugly and draped his arm over the back of his chair. "It guts me, but I'm not too proud to admit that I'm up against my match. Tate swears you'll know what to do with this whole messy business. Tell me, did you know my uncle?"

Lucas nodded and wrapped his fingers loosely around the glass in front of him. "I met him when I was a boy. He traveled with my father on an explorative expedition to Cairo."

Wainbridge raised his dark brows. "Cairo?"

"Mm-hmm. But that was nearly two decades ago. He was well-known in certain circles for his vigor in amassing the odd and the unusual, especially in the area of chinoiserie porcelain."

"Chinoiserie?"

"Decorative items that depict Chinese and Japanese motifs," Lucas explained.

"Ah, well." Wainbridge indulged in a drink. "There is plenty of that at Cloverton. At least I think that's what it is. Have you been there? To Cloverton Hall?"

"No."

"It's brimming with every sort of trinket one can envisage. Large and small. Beautiful and gaudy. One cannot turn a corner or enter a chamber without being stared at by this statue or tripping over some useless table. It's quite vexatious."

Lucas could only imagine what sort of artifacts were tucked away within Cloverton's walls, but he also knew how overwhelming such things could be to those who weren't familiar with them. "So clearly you have no affection for your uncle's collections."

"Affection?" Wainbridge snorted. "On the contrary! I never want to see or hear the words *antiquity* or *porcelain* ever again. I desire nothing more than to have every single piece banished from Cloverton. I'm told some of them are quite valuable, but to me one bauble is just like the other."

"You're hardly the first man to inherit a collection and have no idea what to do with it. One man's passion can quickly become another man's burden."

"Exactly!" Wainbridge threw his hands up, as if relieved to finally be understood. "You see my quandary, then. When I think about the fortune he wrapped up in those useless things, it sickens me. For all of my uncle's grandiose reputation, he was flat broke. In debt up to his gills. Does that surprise you?"

Lucas shrugged. "Not in the least. I'm aware of numerous investors and enthusiasts who allowed their passions to destroy them. Amassing the rare and unique can be just as addictive as gambling." Lucas saw his opening to recommend himself. And he was going to take it. "Tell me. What is it I can do for you?"

"I want to sell the blasted things. Every single one of them. And I want to make as much money as I possibly can. But to do that I need someone I can trust. Tate says you're the best."

Lucas took a swig of port to hide any trace of the optimism budding within him. This was exactly what he wanted—needed—to hear. "If I may be so bold, you need to identify a buyer who is willing to pay a premium for such pieces. Fortunately, that is my specialty."

"Meaning?"

"Meaning I've spent my entire life studying every sort of antiquity, and items from the Far East are my prime interest. I maintain integral relationships with several collectors whose tastes are comparable to your uncle's. It's a matter of matching the piece with the buyer. It's as simple as that."

Wainbridge's affable smile had faded, and now his long fingers tapped rapidly against the table. "I see. How long would all this take?"

Lucas intentionally kept his voice low. Calm. Trustworthy. "Well, that all depends on how quickly you need the money and how much you're willing to accept. You could sell them tomorrow, I've no doubt, but it would be at a loss against their value. If you want to make the most money, your best bet is to look overseas."

"Overseas? Where?"

"America," Lucas clarified. "People there are eager to display wealth, and at this point in time, they're willing to pay for the privilege."

Wainbridge forced his fingers through his thick ebony hair. "How does this begin?"

"A full assessment of your uncle's possessions would be necessary to determine values, and once you and I agree on what items are to be sold, then I begin my work."

"For a fee, of course."

Lucas smirked, folding his hands before him. "Of course. But the more profit we realize, the more that lines both our pockets. And don't forget Tate. As one of my investors he'll profit as well."

Tate's chortle rent the somber tone that had enveloped the conversation. "It's a beautiful arrangement really."

"But those are all details to be sorted later," added Lucas. "Do you know if Milton had a collection log anywhere? Insurance policies? Anything of the sort?"

Wainbridge shook his head. "My uncle was not an organized man. Papers and portfolios are strewn all over the library and in his study. There's little rhyme or reason to it."

"I can review them if you'd like," Lucas offered.

"I'll take you up on that, and I have just the idea for it." Wainbridge shifted eagerly in his chair. "I'm hosting a house party at Cloverton in a little over a week to introduce a small group of friends to my new home. That would be an ideal time for you to visit. The both of you."

"Am I to understand that you've planned a house party and I'm not already on the list of guests?" Tate gaped, aghast. "Why was I not invited?"

Lucas ignored Tate's complaint to focus on the task at hand. "Normally for a project of this magnitude, I'd require the assistance of at least one of my agents and days, if not weeks, of dedicated work."

"No, no," protested Wainbridge. "This must be done surreptitiously, for I have yet to share with you my biggest hindrance yet—my uncle's widow."

Lucas drew a deep breath in response.

"Aha!" Wainbridge's vibrancy reappeared, and he pointed a finger in Lucas's direction. "I see your expression. So you know her reputation then, do you?"

Just as Mr. Milton had notoriety, so did Mrs. Agnes Milton. But hers was of a very different nature.

Wainbridge leaned forward and lowered his voice. "When my uncle died, I inherited not only Cloverton Hall and its properties, but a small estate farther north—Windhurst Manor. He included the smaller property in the will under the condition that I provide for his widow and permit her to live out her days on Cloverton property. As a self-made man, he had the authority to leave any stipulation in his will he chose, and I'm forced to abide by it. If I fail to uphold this condition, Windhurst Manor will pass to another cousin. The issue therein is that Cloverton Hall, which appears to be the jewel in the Milton crown, is in deep debt, and the smaller estate is the only one earning an income."

"Enlighten me," encouraged Lucas. "Surely any rights to the Cloverton collection were solely in her husband's name. What does Mrs. Milton have to do with her late husband's collection?"

"She's mad!" Wainbridge cried out. "She knows full well that I must allow her residence at Cloverton, and she spends her days lording over all as if she is still the mistress of the house. She refuses to allow anyone to touch a single thing that belonged to her husband. I've tried to be patient, but this cannot continue. Our best bet is to make sure she knows nothing of these plans until we are ready to act."

Lucas exchanged glances with Tate again. This opportunity was unlike any other he'd encountered. It seemed almost too fortuitous. Just a few pieces from the famed Milton collection would not only save his business financially but also firmly re-establish him as one of the premier antiquarians in London.

"Well, then," Tate exclaimed as he lifted his glass in a toast. "To a great party, to the old man, and to making lots of money."

Chapter 4

OLIVIA DIDN'T NEED to actually see the expression of utter indignation on her sixteen-year-old sister's face to feel the full brunt of her contentious frustration.

Laura Brannon sank onto the bed in their shared chamber with a huff, lifted the new ivory silk gauze gown that Mrs. Milton's modiste had fashioned for Olivia, and dropped it on her lap. "It's not fair. Why should you get to go while I have to stay here in this prison?"

Olivia shook out a linen nightdress and draped it over her arm. "A *prison*? That's a bit dramatic, don't you think? Besides, I'll be *working* while I am there. You despise all things old and dusty. Remember?"

Laura rolled her amber eyes and fell back against the bed. "If learning to love porcelain was what such an adventure would require, then I'd devote my life to it. You'll meet new people. See new places. I only ever experience Kingsby Street. There is so much beyond this dreary bit of London, and I'll never get to see it!"

Olivia understood her sister's desire to see more, but whereas Laura's main concern was expanding her social life, Olivia wanted to expand everything. She wanted to see China. One day she hoped to visit Rome and see the Nile, just as their mother had traveled with their father before she died. No, Cloverton Hall was not India, but as a step out of London, it was better than nothing.

In a flounce of satin ribbons and pale mauve jaconet, Laura flipped over to her side and propped her head up with her hand. "If you're smart, you'll take advantage of this situation and set your sights on the *other* opportunities. Perhaps you'll meet a wealthy man, someone who can take you—and me—away from this place."

Olivia stiffened, unsure of what to do with her sister's intense desire to leave their home. Ever since their bachelor uncle became their guardian, Laura's sights had been fixed on leaving London entirely. Whereas Olivia had been able to find solace, even comfort, in certain aspects of life remaining the same, Laura had not. The relationship between her uncle and her sister was unarguably tense. He refused to allow Laura the freedom a young woman required to blossom. She needed to be out among society, but their uncle's mismanagement of their father's business and its effect on their financial situation had crippled both their prospects.

Olivia took the gown from Laura, gently folded it, and added the garment to the pile before returning her gaze to her rosy-cheeked, chestnut-haired sister. The two of them could not vary more in tastes and personality, but at times, looking at Laura was like looking into a mirror—same straight nose, same arched eyebrows, and the same dimple in her left cheek.

It would be a lie to say Olivia was not interested in the idea of meeting new people. To Laura's point, Olivia's life did not fluctuate—every day ushered in the same tasks, people, and routines. The only aspect that varied was the antiquities that passed through their warehouse.

Olivia desired what every woman desired—security. And she ardently wanted to believe that she could find security in a manner other than marriage. As much as she prided herself on her knowledge and expertise, she had to be practical. One day she'd probably marry, but it wouldn't happen today. In the meantime she was determined to establish herself as a legitimate antiquarian, and performing this task for Mrs. Milton was an excellent first step.

Olivia forced a smile. "I think you may be getting ahead of yourself, dearest. It's one journey—it is a rather lofty expectation to assume that I'll meet my future husband there."

Laura lifted a loose bit of discarded pale pink ribbon and absently wound it around her fingers. "Maybe not on this excursion, but it's only a matter of time. You *will* marry. Then what will become of me? I'll be left behind here with Uncle Thomas."

Olivia placed a reassuring hand on Laura's thin shoulder. "It's two weeks, love. And then I'll be home, and everything will return to normal."

Heavy footsteps sounded on the corridor's creaky wooden floor just outside their room, and her uncle's bulky frame stepped through the chamber door. His candle's light wavered on the hard angles of his face and his graying side-whiskers and emphasized careless wrinkles on his sloppily tied linen neckcloth.

Thomas motioned to Laura. "I need to speak with your sister. Privately."

A flash of indignation darkened Laura's chagrined expression. She cut her eyes in Olivia's direction, huffed, stood, and tromped from the chamber. When all was again quiet, their uncle crossed farther into the room and stood next to the dark hearth.

Olivia's nerves tightened as she waited for him to address her. The week since Mrs. Milton's visit had been fraught with curt exchanges and aggravating silences, but despite his obvious displeasure, he'd stopped short of forbidding her from going.

She wasn't exactly sure of the true root of his opposition. He might be concerned for her safety as he'd indicated, but Olivia surmised it had more to do with his wounded pride than her reputation. Perhaps he begrudged the fact that Olivia was consulted and he was not.

"I leave tomorrow at dawn for Devon," he blurted as an awkward start to their conversation.

She blinked at the bluntness. "Devon? Why?"

"To visit Walter Sutherland at Cottetham Park. He has Delft he wishes to part with. Bowls and plates and the sort."

She stiffened at the reference to the valuable Dutch pottery. He didn't know nearly enough about the style of art to accurately assess them, let alone to suggest or make a purchase. "Is Russell to accompany you?"

"No. Russell will stay behind and tend to things here."

Something akin to guilt crept over her. If she were to stay at home, then Russell would likely go with him and advise. The thought of her uncle making imprudent purchases was unsettling. He might be the owner of Brannon Antiquities, but with the decisions he'd been making as of late, they would not be able to stay in business long.

"You're certain you'll be all right without me here?" she asked.

"As I've told you numerous times, you're not an agent here." His words were flat, almost to the point of coldness. "Crane and I will manage quite well."

She nodded but said nothing. The suggestion that her contributions were not valued stung. At present she would have to be satisfied with the truth—her absence would be felt whether he acknowledged it or not.

He shifted, and the planks beneath him groaned once again. "I'll see you when you return. Keep on your guard. Remember the people at this gathering are not like you. They're different— their motives. Their designs."

It would be easy to take offense to his tepid words. She might not be as worldly as some, but she wasn't naïve. The memory of the two years she had spent at a girls' school following her mother's death flared. The experience was over a decade ago, but how vividly she recalled the cruel whispers and harsh stares of the girls from more elevated stations.

He motioned toward the gowns. "If nothing else, it appears you will be dressed the part."

She tensed at his sarcastic lilt. "Fine gowns or not, I'm attending to assess the collection. These gowns are to please Mrs. Milton. Nothing more." Unable to resist a last retort, she lifted her chin. "But before I forget, I do intend to take Father's Vinci jewelry with me. Unless you object, of course."

Confusion flashed, and a grim frown quickly followed. "No, no. Get Russell to fetch them for you."

The satisfaction of knowing that he hadn't a clue what she was referring to sizzled through her. She'd always admired the Italian necklaces. They were constructed of naught but pinchbeck and glass, not of gold and gemstones as they appeared, but they glittered with all the beauty of the finest jewelry.

Night's darkness had completely fallen by the time Olivia finished her packing, and as the clock marked the hours, her anticipation intensified. By this time tomorrow, she'd likely be stopped at a travel inn for the night. She'd never stayed at a travel inn before. The idea excited her.

Across their bedchamber, Laura was curled in a chair in her wool dressing gown with a book, her wavy hair woven into a single thick plait, her body angled toward an oil lamp for light.

"I'm going to the storeroom to gather some supplies."

Laura nodded her acknowledgment, and Olivia lifted a chamberstick and made her way from her upstairs bedchamber, down the narrow back stairs, to the storeroom.

After her father's death, their comfortable family home had been sold, and she and Laura moved to live with their uncle in the modest living quarters above the warehouse. This residence was much smaller and far less fine than what they'd been accustomed to. Even after four years, the low-ceilinged rooms and dark, narrow halls still did not feel like home. The entire space had a transient feel, as if any day they'd abandon it and return to something more suitable.

Once she entered the storeroom, Russell, who was seated in his usual spot behind his desk, glanced up and removed his wire-rimmed spectacles. "I don't usually see you down here at this late hour."

"I don't mean to disturb you." She stepped around a small table and headed toward the armoire. "I just need to gather a few supplies."

He closed his ledger. "Need help?"

She placed her candle on the table next to the cabinet. "Yes, if you don't mind. Will you fetch the Vinci pieces for me?"

"The Vinci?" He frowned. "I haven't heard those mentioned in a while. Why?"

"I'm taking them with me. I thought I might use them instead of their just sitting in a box gathering dust."

Russell did as bid, and Olivia opened the armoire door and gathered a blank ledger, a box of pencils, quills and ink, soft cloths, a magnifying glass, and brushes. Russell returned with the jewelry case, and Olivia packed all the items in a small crate. Once finished, she propped the crate on her hip and turned to leave, but then paused. "When did Uncle decide to go to Devon?"

"Hmm?"

"He told me he was departing for Devon first thing in the morning."

"Oh, that. As far as I know he just decided today."

She frowned. "That's odd. Delft is hardly his area of expertise."

Russell grinned lopsidedly. "You know your uncle. What he doesn't really know he makes up."

"I don't know why you're smiling about it," she scolded. "It's really quite serious."

"I'm only teasing, Olivia."

She glared at him for several moments. Her uncle's incompetence had always been a source of amusement between them when her father was alive, but when her father's death put Thomas at the helm, it suddenly wasn't as comical—not when all their livelihoods depended on him.

"Besides," she continued, "if Delft is the item in question, why aren't you going to Cottetham Park? Aren't you always telling me you know more about Delft pottery than anyone else in London?"

"I would, but the shipment for Mr. Beckam is due to arrive at the end of the week. Someone needs to be here to receive it, and your uncle is above such menial tasks."

"Oh." She adjusted the crate in her arms, refusing to feel any sort of remorse for her impending travel. She quickly changed the subject. "I'll see you when I'm back in London, then."

She headed toward the door, but his words stopped her. "It will be odd without you here."

"Gracious." She pivoted to face him, smiling to keep the conversation light. "Everyone acts as if I'll be gone for a year. I'll be home by Michaelmas."

"Will you?" His unusually somber tone caught her off guard.

She blinked. "Why wouldn't I?"

He shrugged his narrow shoulders and folded his arms over his chest. "There'll be a great many distractions at Cloverton Hall. New people and the lot. You might decide you prefer their company to ours. To mine."

Olivia inhaled a sharp breath. "I'm going to help Mrs. Milton. Nothing more."

The hard-set lines of his long face were unmoving. "I hope you know what you're doing, 'tis all."

"No one seems to believe it, but I am a grown woman, completely capable, Russell."

"I know you are." He relaxed his stance and gripped the back of the chair in front of him. "Forgive me. I suppose I've grown used to the way things are. The way *we* are."

The words, and the meaning behind them, froze her.

He offered a half smile. "You could always refuse to go. Or tell Mrs. Milton you've changed your mind."

"Why would I do that?"

"Because part of me hopes that you would see that you have everything you need here. Your uncle and I were talking about your future earlier today. He said that he thought it folly that you would seek out a new situation when you have an opportunity already in front of you."

Heat suffused her face, and she was grateful for the low light, for surely a blush was coloring her cheeks.

It must seem like a natural progression for Russell to marry his superior's ward and secure his place in the business. After all, she had no other suitors, and as far as she knew, he'd never courted a woman. And yet in all the years Olivia had known Russell, he'd never said anything that would suggest he considered her in a romantic way. Perhaps it would have been easier if he had, or even if he'd acted flirtatiously. Then she'd have a reason to dislike him or, at the very least, to discourage him.

But regardless of all, the truth remained: this might be the life he wanted, but it was not the life she wanted.

This storeroom, and the relics in it, would not be her life.

She *would* journey to faraway places. Eat exotic food. Inhale the scent of sandalwood incense in an Indian temple or spy a gibbon in China's woodlands.

If she died tomorrow, what had she really done? What had she accomplished?

He must have interpreted her silence as a refusal to discuss the topic further. A nervous chuckle rumbled from his throat, and he whirled back around to his desk. "After you return from Cloverton, I'll be eager to hear your thoughts on the Cavesee Vase. It really is quite remarkable."

In that moment she almost felt sorry for Russell. She did not doubt his sincerity. He'd always been very cordial to her—helping her, teaching her—and she supposed that given her circumstance, he'd be a good match for her. But if she accepted him or indulged his attentions, then she'd be accepting that this way of life would be her future.

The options for her future would soon be exhausted, and this offer from Mrs. Milton was a miracle—a once-in-a-lifetime opportunity to step out of her world and into one more affluent, where she'd be treated differently. Have a new routine. Interact with elegant people.

Maybe when she returned she would see things from a fresh perspective.

But then again, maybe she would not.

Chapter 5

TODAY WAS THE day Olivia's entire life was going to change.

She could feel it as surely as she could feel the misty rain clinging to her eyelashes and the fine wool of her new traveling gown against her skin. Inside, her nerves were trembling, but she was not frightened. It was the anticipation of something new—the anticipation of an adventure.

Colorless daylight crested over the London rooftops as a carriage turned down Kingsby Street. Four black horses, sleek and glossy from precipitation, effortlessly conveyed the pretentious vehicle, and the crunching wheels and jingling harnesses reverberated along the row of shops.

Laura wrapped her arm around Olivia's and leaned her head on her shoulder. "If you do not make this journey memorable enough for the both of us, I shall never forgive you."

The carriage swayed to a stop in front of the sisters, and the next several moments sped. Russell appeared in the receiving room doorway from the storeroom. Two liveried footmen descended from the carriage and lifted and secured her trunk and valise. One of the ebony horses whinnied, tossed its head, and stomped its hefty hoof against the cobbles.

Employing every ounce of tenacity she could muster, Olivia squeezed her sister's hand and kissed her cheek before she stepped toward the waiting vehicle. The footman turned the carriage's brass door handle and opened it, revealing a stern-faced Mrs. Milton inside.

"Oh good. You're ready." Mrs. Milton's snipped words were barely audible above the swirling activity. "And I'm glad for it, for I despise tardiness. Don't dawdle, then. Bid your farewells and we shall be off."

Olivia paused to glance back to where her trunk had been to ensure nothing was left behind, then she turned to wave a farewell to Laura and Russell before she accepted the footman's assistance. Once inside, she was enveloped by the opulent crimson velvet interior and overwhelming scent of lily of the valley and peppermint. She settled on the tufted seat across from Mrs. Milton, acutely aware of the older lady's sharp stare, the tiny black-eyed Pomeranian nestled on her lap, and the somber-faced maid sitting to Mrs. Milton's right.

Olivia spied her sister through the rain-streaked window, noting the sad arch of her brows and the way her teeth clamped over her lower lip.

Olivia was not an emotional creature, yet the moment's significance raged within her. This role she was playing—this glimpse into a different existence—started now. All the planning and contemplating of the past week was finally set into motion, and very soon the consequences of this decision would make themselves known.

The carriage lurched into motion, and her family's shop faded from view.

"This is my maid, Teague." Mrs. Milton's tone rang flat, as if discussing a mundane transaction. "Since you travel with no maid of your own, Teague will assist you as needed."

Olivia smiled at the wiry, dark-eyed woman, who merely nodded curtly in response. She gripped her fingers together in her lap. It would hardly be the time to mention that she'd never had a maid of her own, let alone a lady's maid. She and Laura always helped one another with any dressing needs, and if necessary, the chambermaid would aid her. The thought of a true lady's maid assisting her was as daunting as the assessment that was before her.

"And the modiste?" Mrs. Milton stroked the top of the dog's fur with her pudgy, ring-adorned fingers. "She provided you with five gowns and the necessary finishings, did she not?"

"Yes, ma'am."

"Excellent. She's by far the very best in London." Mrs. Milton's orotund voice echoed with authority.

The carriage hit a rut, and the entire conveyance tilted sideways before it righted itself.

"I do wish the driver would take care." Mrs. Milton clicked her tongue. "'Twill be a wretched journey if not. Have you traveled to Yorkshire before, Miss Brannon?"

"No, ma'am."

"A beautiful bit of earth. Different from London in every way conceivable. Cloverton Hall will be a fine introduction to the county for you. It is an impressive place—nearly two hundred years old."

A comfortable silence descended, for which Olivia was grateful. Mrs. Milton even managed to doze off, in spite of the uneven road with its jarring bumps and dips. By the time they left the busy streets of London behind and reached the open countryside, surrounded by verdant grass, ancient ash and oak trees, and open dirt road, a fresh wave of interest rushed over Olivia. This entire journey would be what she made of it, regardless of what she encountered at Cloverton Hall. And she would not allow a single opportunity to pass her by without exploring it to the fullest.

Chapter 6

"DON'T DAWDLE IN doorways, boy. It's impertinent. What's more, a man must never exhibit indecisiveness; otherwise others will never take him seriously."

Lucas could hear his father's voice as he hesitated at the door to the room that had been Timothy Avery's private office. He paused, allowing his hand to hover over the worn brass doorknob. Would he ever be able to pass through this door without thinking about the man who'd raised him? Each time he approached the threshold, a different emotion accosted him. Grief. Anger. Numbness. Determination. His father's death nine months prior, and the shock of it, had affected every aspect of Lucas's life.

He gripped the doorknob and pushed the door open. Inside, memories of an enterprising life lived in every crook and cranny. For years this cluttered chamber had been his father's domain, yet Lucas had spent nearly as much time here as he had in their house. He'd long since memorized the number of steps it took to reach his father's desk from the door, which floorboards squeaked, and at what hour the afternoon sun would slice through the window.

But most importantly, he'd learned all about the business—the buying and selling of antiquities and valuable rarities.

It had not been hard to get swept up into his father's view of the future. His contagious passion and enthusiasm influenced many. As a boy Lucas had hung on his father's every word. Relished the trips to Persia. Egypt. The Orient. All in pursuit of the unique. Lucas was passionate because his father had been passionate.

But now, everything felt different.

Everything *was* different, because not only was Father gone, but the scandal before his death cast a negative light on a legacy that should have been respectable. His father had always been a polarizing character, but the public accusation that he'd cheated multiple clients had cloaked his family in an unavoidable shadow that the business had not been able to shake.

Lucas didn't want to think that his father would be capable of deceptive actions, but sometimes the mere suggestion of dishonesty was enough to make it so. As things stood now, Avery & Sons faced ruin. Most of their long-standing clients and investors had left them, and as a result he'd been forced to dismiss the bulk of his staff.

Lucas stepped back toward the desk, where a framed drawing atop the teak inlay caught his eye. He lifted it. Charles, his older brother, had drawn it nearly two decades prior. The amateurish charcoal rendering of the two Avery boys had been their father's prized possession, and it had sat here, in this place of honor, every day since. But Charles had been killed in a battle in America six years ago, shortly after he joined the army. With both Charles and his father dead, Avery & Sons, as Lucas had known it, was no more. If he wanted any sort of future, he'd have to fight for it and make it his own.

Clarence Night, Lucas's clerk, knocked against the doorframe, stepped inside, and dropped a box atop a table just inside the door. "I've got those Milton records you wanted."

Lucas scowled at the ensuing plume of dust. "It's been a while since those have seen the light of day."

Night pushed his spectacles up on his narrow, hooked nose. "I don't think it's been opened since your father was partners with Brannon."

"Hmm." Lucas lifted a thin stack of yellowed papers and parchments from inside and held them to the fading light streaming in through the window. "There's not much in here."

"Mr. Milton always did prefer working with Brannon, as you know."

It had been one of his father's greatest frustrations—the inability to lure the business of Francis Milton, one of the most celebrated antiquities collectors in the country, from Brannon after their partnership ceased.

"Have any pieces from Milton's collection come to auction as of late?" Lucas inquired.

"Not that I've heard."

"Thanks for these. I'll take a closer look." Lucas dropped the papers back into the box and set the lid on top.

"Do you still intend to leave for Cloverton Hall in the morning?"

"I do. If all goes to plan, I'll return in a fortnight or so—definitely by Michaelmas. Send word if anything interesting happens, will you?"

After settling things with Night, Lucas quit his office with the box under his arm and headed to his mother's home—a large town house of red brick a few blocks from the shop.

The sun was already dipping down behind the uneven rooftops, shooting long yellow shafts of light through the smog and smoke rising from chimneys. He wound his way through the throngs of people and carts of vendors selling their wares.

Once he was at the town house door, there was no need to knock, but he still paused. He knew the conversation that awaited him on the other side of the door, and he was in no hurry for it.

Ever since his father died suddenly on that frigid winter night just after Christmas of the previous year, every visit to Lucas's mother was the same. Grief's devastating sorrow had seized her. What was more, the black marks against Father's reputation in the weeks preceding his death had enraged her, and she refused to release the blame she'd assigned to his accusers. Lucas had hoped that time would soothe the wounds, but if anything, it seemed to freeze her in an unceasing melancholy that pilfered any joy.

Determined to provide a distraction, he lifted his hand and knocked on the door. The spindly, white-haired housekeeper, Mrs. Smith, who'd been with the Avery family for as long as he could remember, answered. Her grin creased her weathered skin, and she fixed her rheumy brown eyes on him. "You're late today, Mr. Avery. I expected to see you earlier."

"I know." He stepped into the foyer and extended his black beaver hat toward her. "Is Mother at home?"

"She is, but she has a headache. She's taken to her bed. Again." She placed his hat on the side table. "That's not all, I'm afraid. A letter arrived earlier today that sent her into fits. I'm not sure what it's about, but it had quite an effect. I'll let her know you've arrived, though. She's always glad to see you."

Mrs. Smith gripped her skirt in her gnarled hand and turned to climb the entryway staircase, but then she stopped and pivoted. "I saw you pacing out there on the street from the window. Something on your mind?"

The question was a personal one, but there was no need for pretense with Mrs. Smith. How many times had her kind words eased his childhood anxieties and alleviated pressures when young life seemed insurmountable?

Yes, plenty of concerns weighed on his mind, such as how he was going to repair his business's reputation, and how he would afford to keep not only his own small apartment but his mother's home as well. But none of that could be discussed, regardless of the trust existing between them.

"All is well, Mrs. Smith."

As if satisfied with the answer, she smiled and then shuffled up the staircase with slow, aged movements.

Lucas showed himself to the front parlor to wait. Inside the long, narrow chamber, the strong, ever-present scent of tobacco tricked his mind into believing that his father might actually be in the same room. He glanced toward the two portraits flanking the mantelpiece—likenesses of his mother and father from their wedding trip to Greece. How young they both appeared—how full of happiness and hope. Perhaps one day he'd have a marriage like his parents had enjoyed, but at the moment such a thing seemed a far-off fantasy.

"Why did you not come to visit me yesterday?" His mother's airy tone interrupted his musings.

Margaret Avery stood in the arched doorway, clad in a high-necked mourning gown of somber ebony bombazet. Her pale, blotchy complexion and red-rimmed green eyes confirmed his suspicion—today her attitude and countenance would be no different than on his previous visits.

He skirted the question by closing the space between them, kissing her on her cheek, then offering her his arm to lead her back to the sofa. "Mrs. Smith tells me you have another headache."

"This malaise is my constant companion these days." She lowered to the sofa with a sigh and drew a woven blanket over her lap.

He sat next to her, noting the wan pallor of her cheeks and the dark circles looming beneath her eyes. "Perhaps a walk out of doors would help. We could walk to the park. It's not too hot, the sun is out, and—"

"No, no." She waved him off dismissively and retrieved a small stack of missives from the pocket of her gown. "I've no desire to be out of doors today."

He gestured to the letter in her hand. "Mrs. Smith told me you received a troubling letter."

"Hmm?" She lifted her chin, as if suddenly aware again of his presence. "Yes. From your aunt Frederica. She informed me that she intends to stay here again while she is in London before the Christmas season."

He frowned, unsure of the problem. His aunt, who'd never been married, often visited for a few months each year. "Good. Her presence will be a welcome diversion, will it not?"

"It certainly will not," Mother snipped. She stood and moved to the window, the thick folds of her gown rustling in the afternoon stillness. "I've no wish for company now. It's cruel to suggest otherwise. In fact, I'm surprised she would suggest such a thing. I'm in mourning, after all."

"Oh, I don't know. Aunt Frederica loved Father too. She was his sister. It's not good for you to spend so much time alone in the wake of all that's happened. She'll be a companion, and perhaps you—"

"I am not well enough for company. Anyone can see that."

Lucas snapped his mouth shut. It did not matter what he said; in her current state she was predisposed to find fault in any suggestion.

Silence once again fell on the opulent parlor, and he turned his attention to the familiar setting. Beyond the portraits, the feel of the chamber was so uniquely his family's. Blue-and-white Chinese vases flanked the three bay windows overlooking the street. A painted Indian screen stood in the corner, depicting life in Delhi. A collection of wooden and ivory carvings adorned the mantelpiece. It was the visual manifestation of the work his parents had so ardently adored.

His mother used to share his father's love of the exotic, but now she never inquired about the business. In the weeks following her husband's death, the mere reference to it would fling her into a state of despondency. Consequently, Lucas mentioned it only when absolutely necessary. And now it was absolutely necessary.

"I will be traveling to Yorkshire tomorrow."

"Yorkshire?" she cried with as much annoyance as he expected. "Whatever for?"

"Business dealings—hopefully—at Cloverton Hall. The new master has requested assistance in evaluating Mr. Milton's collection."

"What a shame for Mrs. Milton," she responded flatly before looking out over the street. "Life goes on for the living, does it not? What does he want to do with the collection?"

"He wants to sell."

She huffed. "It's truly a shame how quickly people wish to part with keepsakes of those no longer with us."

Lucas passed the next hour in his mother's melancholy company, endeavoring to lift her spirits and divert her attentions. But try as he might, his efforts were again in vain. He missed the mother who not even a year ago had welcomed him with smiles, comforted him with her positivity, and encouraged him with her optimism. He refused to believe those parts of her had vanished forever, but after a visit like today's, he felt heavy, as if he was carrying the weight of his father's loss all over again.

Chapter 7

"*TREAT EVERY CLIENT as if your entire business depends on them—as if their items, their hopes, are the only items that matter to your business.*"

Timothy Avery's words rambled in Lucas's mind as the Yorkshire countryside flashed by the mud-streaked window.

"*If you can do that, you'll have a customer for life.*"

Lucas could almost laugh at the irony of his father's advice, for in this instance, his entire business *did* depend on his ability to convince Wainbridge of how to proceed with the collection.

Lucas and Tate, along with Tate's valet, had departed London the previous day and, according to the driver, would arrive at Cloverton within the next quarter of an hour. The journey had been relatively uneventful, and every day, every hour, not spent in active pursuit of saving his business felt wasted.

"If you had to guess"—Tate's random musing once again broke the silence—"how much do you think that house is worth?"

Lucas pulled his gaze from the landscape. "Cloverton Hall?"

"Yes. Just think on it." Tate leaned forward and rested his elbows on his knees. "I've heard the name Francis Milton all my life. Father was always envious and said Milton's collection put his own to shame. We both know Father's collection is impressive. Milton's must be absolutely massive."

Vincent Tate, William's father, had been one of their more extravagant clients for as long as Lucas could remember, but when news of his father's scandal came to light, the elder Tate severed ties with Avery & Sons. The younger Tate much preferred gambling and women, and as the oldest son of a very wealthy landowner, he could afford to bet on a young but promising antiquarian.

"I couldn't begin to guess," Lucas responded with a shrug. "I'm surprised you've not visited Cloverton before. You and Wainbridge seem thick."

Tate scoffed. "Believe me, I've dropped plenty of hints that I expected an invitation, but Wainbridge ignored them completely. But you heard him at Brooks's. Poor chap. He'll be forced to contend with reality sooner or later, and the fastest way out of his current dilemma is to marry well. Mark my words: I'm sure a lovely selection of eligible ladies will be present."

"And, of course, you need not marry," gibed Lucas.

"No, of course not. Only for love, should I choose. Speaking of that, I'm told Miss Haven will be in attendance, and she's always a good sport."

"I seem to recall that she didn't recognize you when we encountered her at the opera last year."

"Ah well, never mind that. We're both a little older, a little wiser. All that aside, my sole objective is to support you. And my investment, of course."

"Very selfless."

Tate snickered at his own jest and smoothed his decidedly blond hair from his broad forehead. "But I do hope you intend to have a little fun at Cloverton and not completely bury your nose in those dusty relics. Besides, you've yet to meet Wainbridge's sister. She'd be the perfect match for you. I'm sure Wainbridge would include some artifacts in her dowry if you two were to hit it off."

"Tempting, but if the Wainbridges are in need of funds, I doubt Miss Wainbridge will look my way."

"Don't sell yourself short, Avery. You've qualities besides money," Tate heckled good-naturedly. "Surely there is something about you that women would find attractive."

"I can always count on you for a boost of confidence."

Lucas had long since given up trying to imagine what it would have been like to be carefree and affluent, like Tate and so many of his other clients. His business required him to interact with this social class regularly, but he'd never truly been one of them. The women might flirt with him, but he was hardly wealthy enough to entice one of them toward matrimony. Invitations to events like this had been driven by business, not pleasure, and every resulting relationship was a bargain to be struck.

"At last!" Tate leaned forward to look out the window. "The infamous Cloverton Hall."

Lucas angled his head. Brilliant afternoon sunlight filtered through the ancient ash trees, which largely obscured the view of the opulent building of gray stone, but he waited patiently until they cleared the forest and the majestic structure fully appeared over the hill. Like glittering mirrors, dozens of symmetrically aligned windows reflected the sunlight, and several chimneys jutted up from the slate roof into the clear azure sky. Most would see an impressive country home, but he saw nothing but opportunity.

When their carriage pulled to a stop on the circular drive before Cloverton's main entrance, Wainbridge was there to meet them, along with an attractive, willowy woman and an impressive bevy of servants.

"That's her," whispered Tate. "Miss Isabella Wainbridge. A delight, is she not?"

George Wainbridge stepped forward to greet them, hands outstretched, a broad, easy smile on his face. "You've made it! And in one piece, I'll note. Avery, you must be a saint to survive being trapped with Tate in a carriage for such a duration."

Lucas laughed and shook hands with the man. "I consider it a great test of my patience."

Tate's grin creased his full, round cheeks. "I'd be offended if I were not so elated to see Miss Wainbridge again." He extended his hand toward her to draw her into their conversation.

A demure smile curved Miss Wainbridge's bow-shaped lips. Sunlight fell on her graceful features and played on the honey-hued curls piled atop her head.

"Ah, Isabella." Wainbridge took his sister's arm. "You've not met Mr. Avery yet, have you?"

"I don't believe I've had the pleasure." She fixed entrancingly dark eyes on him with astounding confidence. "Welcome to Cloverton Hall, Mr. Avery."

He bowed. "Thank you."

"And me?" Tate blurted. "Do I not warrant a welcome?"

Miss Wainbridge rewarded Tate's attempt at humor and laughed prettily, placing a dainty hand familiarly on the sleeve of his coat. "Oh, Mr. Tate. I thought that went without saying. How could you not be most welcome?"

Tate lowered his voice, as if taking both the Wainbridges into his confidence. "And Mrs. Milton? Is she here? I confess, I cannot wait to meet the woman who has caused such a commotion for the two of you."

Miss Wainbridge shook her head. "She's not yet arrived, I fear. We expected her yesterday to help greet the first of the guests, but this morning we received a missive that a broken carriage wheel caused a delay."

Tate rubbed his hands before him. "At least we're not the last to arrive."

"No, no. You've not missed a thing," Wainbridge assured. "But then again, we'd not even consider beginning the festivities before your arrival. As it is, the other guests have already settled in their chambers. Dinner will be served soon, and if you do not wish to eat in your traveling attire, you'd best get to your room and set about making yourself presentable. Come, I'll take you up myself."

After instructing a footman to assist Tate's valet, the men stepped inside a large vestibule at the entrance. Lucas had been prepared for opulence and extravagance, but not even his imagination had done Cloverton Hall justice. Intricately carved arches rose to meet the high plaster ceiling, which boasted vibrant murals of angels and cherubs, painted meticulously in the style of the Italian masters. The soles of his traveling boots tapped on the Purbeck marble floor, and even at this early hour, candles blazed in suspended candelabras from every corner of the hall, shedding even more light on two early-sixteenth-century oil paintings in gilded frames.

There would be time to explore later, and Lucas peeled his attention away from the artifacts. He followed their host from the foyer to a corridor leading to the main staircase. Wainbridge and Tate continued chatting, but try as he might to ignore it, all that surrounded Lucas robbed him of speech. Such extreme attention to order and detail—a colorful Turkish pile carpet hung from a golden rod, and a series of Dutch landscape paintings graced the wall of the lower part of the staircase. Two pear-shaped Japanese vases sat atop a lacquered table on the landing between two windows.

Modern tastes would dictate that this space was cluttered, but to Lucas this was the domain of a skilled collector. All talk of buying and selling would have to wait for a more appropriate time. For now his focus must be on developing a rapport with Wainbridge.

"Miss Haven is here, I trust," Tate remarked as they ascended the stairs and traversed the landing.

"She's here, along with her determined chaperone." Wainbridge pivoted to climb the second half of the staircase. "You may have to take your place behind the other men waiting for her attention."

"Chaperone?" Tate grimaced. "That's disappointing."

"Come now, you know how these things go. All the ladies have one, I'm afraid." Wainbridge motioned for them to continue up the stairs. "A guardian, a sister, a lady's maid—someone along those lines to guard their virtue. But don't despair. This house is large but filled to the brim with guests. Speaking of that, I hope you'll not be offended with your arrangements. Even in a house this size, space is not limitless."

Tate's forehead furrowed. "What does that mean?"

"You'll see."

They landed on the first floor, and then Wainbridge directed them up another narrower, steeper staircase to a far less opulent second floor. The noticeably lower ceilings were mere inches from the top of Lucas's head, and the windows were smaller and set deep in the wall.

"You two will share a chamber," Wainbridge said without looking back at them. "Here, on this floor."

"Is this not the attic floor?" Tate sniffed.

"Don't be foppish." Wainbridge's heels clicked on the polished planked floors until he stopped before a closed door. "Fielding and Whitaker are up here as well. Although they did not complain as much as you."

Tate harrumphed.

"Truth be told, you're not the only late additions we had to the gathering. My aunt also invited a mystery woman. We've all yet to meet her."

"How curious." Tate ducked to miss a low crossbeam. "Anyone we know?"

"Heavens, no." Wainbridge shook his head. "I don't even recall her name. A *friend* from London, so my aunt claims, and yet neither Isabella nor I had ever heard of her." The door squeaked on ancient hinges as Wainbridge opened it, and light from the chamber's two windows spilled to the corridor. "Here's where you'll stay."

Tate entered first, bending to fit under the low threshold, and Lucas followed. The chamber's simplicity struck him—a slanted ceiling, two small beds, a plainly woven rug over a wood-planked floor, two straight-backed wooden chairs, and a washbasin—absolutely none of the extravagance present on the lower floors.

Tate snorted in disdain.

"Oh, come, man, it's not that bad," quipped Wainbridge. "Next time you're at Cloverton, you can have your pick of the house. For now, this will have to suit." He extended the key to Lucas. "You'd best not tarry. Dinner will be served within the hour, and unless you two want to appear like ruffian highwaymen, you'd best be about it."

With a wink Wainbridge left and closed the door behind him.

Tate dropped to a bed, tossed his discarded hat next to him, and scratched his head. "There's barely room for my trunk."

"You'll survive." Lucas popped open his satchel and prepared to clean up. "Besides, you've talked of naught but Miss Haven for days. If you don't want to meet her with mud splattered on your breeches, you'd best stop complaining and wash up."

Lucas could appeal to Tate's vanity, because to his friend, that was all that mattered—flirting, impressing ladies, and improving his standing amongst all the guests.

Lucas needed to impress as well, but his goal was far different than Tate's. Tate possessed fortune enough to last him two lifetimes. Lucas did not—he had only his knowledge, his skill as a purveyor, and the ability to make people feel comfortable. He would need all three if he was to make a success of this event.

Chapter 8

NEVER WOULD OLIVIA have believed that such a beautiful structure could exist. She'd seen sketches of such stately homes, and the occasional pastoral painting featuring such a scene would come across the shop from time to time. But the charcoal drawings and faded renderings could not prepare her for the magnificence before her.

She spied it from the carriage in fleeting glimpses between the ashes and oaks. The late-afternoon sun highlighted Cloverton Hall's warm gray stones and glinted from the myriad intricate multipaned windows, the effect of which bathed the surroundings in a golden glow.

The moment the carriage rocked to a full halt, the door was opened and a footman dressed in deep emerald livery took great care in assisting Mrs. Milton from the carriage. Olivia and Teague alighted from the conveyance after her.

How Olivia's muscles relished the change of position, and as the cool breeze brushed against her flushed cheeks and forehead, her optimism and eagerness flamed anew as she soaked in the details around her.

A throng of servants stood at the ready, and they curtsied and bowed toward her as she passed them. Intimidation rushed her. Would they treat her as such if they knew where she came from and who she really was? Even with her doubts, she'd not allow herself to feel awkward or out of place. She *could* not, for if she entertained such thoughts, they might lodge in her mind and refuse to leave.

She followed Mrs. Milton up the stone stairs, through the intricately carved oak doors nearly twice her height. Each step expanded her glimpse of what awaited her behind the door. And then her breath caught.

Once inside the glistening vestibule, she lifted her gaze to take in the painted ceiling, more than two stories above her head. Extravagance surrounded her: elegant carvings of stone and Italian marble busts perched upon their pedestals. Fresh magenta dahlias and fuchsia chrysanthemums overflowed a footed silver bowl. Every surface gleamed in the radiant sunlight streaming through the symmetrical banks of tall, north-facing paned windows. It was as if she'd entered another world—one of lavish splendor, of the sort of life she had only dreamed existed.

Olivia gathered her wits about her and untied her poke bonnet's satin bow, self-conscious of her trembling hands.

As she lifted the hat from her head, a young blonde woman, clad in a long-sleeved empire-waist organza gown in the palest shade of goldenrod, hurried into the vestibule with her arms outstretched toward Mrs. Milton. Her glossy, honey-hued hair was gathered atop her head, and her genuine smile drew Olivia to her.

The attractive lady reached for Mrs. Milton's hand, pressed a kiss to her withered cheek, and stepped back. "Aunt, we expected you hours ago! How worried we were when we received the news of the carriage's wheel. I hope you did not encounter any additional trouble."

Mrs. Milton barely turned her attention from her gloves. "No more trouble than normal."

The woman turned her mahogany eyes toward Olivia, her cheeks rosy, her enthusiastic expression bright. "And you must be Miss Brannon. I've been so eager to make your acquaintance ever since we learned you would be joining us. Welcome to Cloverton Hall!"

Olivia smiled, determined to match the kind energy. She returned a curtsey. "Thank you. I'm so happy for the invitation."

Mrs. Milton removed her kid gloves finger by finger. "This is my niece, Miss Isabella Wainbridge."

Olivia refused to allow surprise to write itself on her features. Mrs. Milton had not mentioned a niece, not even once through the entire three-day journey, and yet Olivia found it a gratifying revelation. "I'm pleased to meet you."

"You must be exhausted," Miss Wainbridge continued amiably, as if oblivious to her aunt's brusqueness. "I will call for some tea, and you can—"

"Have tea sent to our chambers," Mrs. Milton interrupted and fixed her sharp eyes on her niece. "I trust the Blue Room has been prepared for Miss Brannon?"

Miss Wainbridge's brow furrowed. "The Gold Room has been prepared for Miss Brannon, on the east end of the first floor with the other ladies. It is so lovely, and it—"

"No. She's to be in the Blue Room. I was quite explicit in my letter."

Miss Wainbridge's delicate jaw twitched. "I hate to disappoint, Aunt, but Miss Kline is in the Blue Room at present."

"She must be moved, then."

Olivia should protest—she should declare the Gold Room more than adequate. The last thing she wanted to do was cause a stir while a guest under this roof, but before she could speak, approaching footsteps, confident and full of purpose, echoed from the adjoining corridor.

She could surmise the owner of the footsteps before she even saw him.

Mr. Wainbridge.

He was uncommonly handsome, with jet-black hair and a broad smile. He shared the color of his sister's enchanting dark eyes. His intricately tied linen cravat was brilliant against his tanned skin, and the precise cut of his pewter broadcloth tailcoat emphasized a tall, athletic figure.

"Aunt!" His rich baritone voice echoed in the cavernous space. "We'd almost given up hope of you arriving today."

"Had I a choice?" she snipped. "The guests began arriving yesterday, did they not? You simply cannot host guests without a hostess. You'd be a laughingstock."

Seemingly unaffected, or perhaps amused, Mr. Wainbridge grinned, reached forward in a familiar act, took the older woman's hand in his, and pressed it to his lips. "You're right. How good you are to save us from utter humiliation." He lifted his gaze to Olivia. "And you must be Miss Brannon."

Olivia opened her mouth to respond, but Mrs. Milton took her arm and, by doing so, silenced her. "It is. Miss Brannon, this is my nephew, Mr. George Wainbridge. Has a dinner hour been set?"

"Y-yes," he stammered in a shocked response. "We will dine in about an hour. But I—"

"That will not do. Instruct Mrs. Dareton to delay it by one hour."

Miss Wainbridge frowned and cast a worried glance toward her brother. "But, Aunt, the guests have already begun to gather in the drawing room. Another hour would be—"

"Miss Brannon and I must have time to prepare, especially now that we must wait for Miss Kline to vacate the Blue Room. No, no. This is the way it will be done. Miss Brannon, come along."

Olivia hesitated. She was drawn to the siblings' warmth and friendliness, but she had to remember why she was here. She was at Cloverton Hall as a guest of Mrs. Milton for a very specific reason, not to feel welcomed or comfortable.

Olivia curtsied and turned to follow Mrs. Milton, but Miss Wainbridge placed a soft hand on her arm to halt her. "My brother and I are very happy to meet you, Miss Brannon. I hope we can get better acquainted during your time here."

In the wake of the kind sentiment, Olivia realized exactly how much of a physical toll the journey had taken on her. She was tired. On edge. And even homesick. But she straightened her shoulders. Every bit of discomfort would be worth it if she met the goal ahead of her. With renewed determination, Olivia smiled in response.

She fixed her gaze on the back of Mrs. Milton's retreating form as she followed her toward the great staircase. Now was not the time to become distracted by the numerous artifacts all around her and the voices of other guests wafting through the open doorways.

She lifted the hem of her traveling gown to ascend the great staircase when two gentlemen turned the corner at the landing above her and caught her attention. Olivia's eyes met another's so familiar that she nearly stopped in her tracks.

Lucas Avery.

It could be no other.

His olive-green eyes widened in recognition. His pace slowed.

Fearing he might address her, Olivia flicked her gaze forward and refused to look in his direction. From the corner of her eye, she spied him bow toward Mrs. Milton and then toward her.

Still, she did not look toward the two men. Even after she turned the corner at the landing and ascended the second flight of stairs, she declined to glance back.

In that single, unexpected moment, her optimism and eagerness fled, making her steps feel sluggish and her head abnormally light.

Mr. Avery *knew* her.

What was more, he could very well be here for the same reason she was. Would she be in some sort of competition with him? Or worse, would she have to work with him?

It would do no good to speculate, not until she was able to gather more information. But she knew one thing: the Averys were not to be trusted.

Chapter 9

VERY LITTLE CAUGHT Lucas off guard. He'd witnessed enough transactions, traveled in enough unfamiliar cities, and attended far too many society events to be truly dumbfounded by much.

The presence of none other than the incomparable Miss Olivia Brannon, however, stunned him so much that he'd had to look her direction twice as he turned on the landing—once to identify her and again to confirm it.

There was no denying who she was, but why she was here remained to be seen.

She had to have recognized him. But she said nothing.

Tate took notice of her as well, and once they reached the ground floor and she was out of earshot, he whistled low. "Wainbridge is certainly delivering on his promise to host as many beautiful young ladies as he could invite. Lovely. Just lovely. If she is the sort we are to spend the next week and a half with, we are fortunate men indeed, Avery."

Lucas smoothed his hair back from his forehead. If Tate knew the truth about Olivia's fiery and determined personality, he'd probably think twice about such a statement. But Lucas would say nothing about her—not until he'd had the chance to speak with her. "Calm yourself. That's but the first young woman to cross our path besides Miss Wainbridge, and already you're making assumptions."

"Assumptions?"

"Yes, *assumptions*. Assumptions that the woman on the stairs would find you the least bit attractive. Besides, I thought your sights were set firmly on Miss Haven."

"That is true, but 'twould hardly be fair, or even sporting, to completely disqualify the lady before we even know her name. Am I not, after all, in my heart of hearts a true romantic? One never knows what unspoken charm will draw one soul to another."

Lucas huffed at the ridiculous—yet characteristic—arrogance of the statement. What must it be like to have such a simplistic, singular outlook on life? "Come, Romeo. If you're determined that all the ladies present should fall for your charms, you'd best be about it. After all, you've less than a fortnight."

Tate playfully slapped the back of his hand against Lucas's shoulder. "More than enough time."

They arrived in the drawing room, and the opulent chamber scintillated with promise. Well-dressed gentlemen in starched cravats and tailored coats and women in shimmery fabrics and dripping in jewels were gathered—laughing, talking. A voltaic spark of energy surged in Lucas's chest.

He was more than capable of handling George Wainbridge, the Cloverton collection, and any other undertaking that might cross his path. Miss Brannon was a surprise, yes, but it was just that—a fleeting surprise. It didn't matter why she was here; it would not affect him. Not for a single moment. For now he had to put the odd encounter behind him, for he could not forget his purpose.

———————————

Olivia waited for the chamber's heavy paneled oak door to latch closed behind her before she released a long, steady breath.

Finally, alone.

The silence and solitude that the Blue Room afforded showered down on her—a welcome balm to her harried nerves. Her mind raced with all she'd just learned about the Miltons and the Wainbridges . . . and with the man she'd just seen.

She groaned at the recollection. Lucas Avery's eyes had widened. He'd looked her way twice. He'd recognized her. She hadn't expected to be acquainted with anyone at Cloverton Hall, and yet Lucas Avery, more than almost anyone, had the capacity to completely ruin her entire plan.

She loosened the front buttons of her rumpled traveling pelisse and shrugged it from her shoulders. She'd simply have to speak with him frankly, professional to professional, and ask for his discretion. The idea of asking Lucas Avery for a favor, be it great or small, aggrieved her, but what could be done?

With a cleansing sigh she propped her hands on her hips and turned her attention to the chamber that would belong to her for roughly the next week and a half. She did not fully understand why Mrs. Milton had been so insistent that she stay in this particular room, but its sheer grandeur squelched the nagging thoughts of Mr. Avery. Two large mullioned windows overlooked Cloverton Hall's main drive, and the afternoon light sliding through the paned glass highlighted Saxon-blue Chinese wallpaper that boasted birds and flowers, leaves and rivers. A giant carved mahogany canopied bed with indigo damask curtains stood perpendicular to the windows, and the wall opposite it boasted a grand chimney-piece with a ceramic sculpture of two dogs atop it.

Every tabletop and every bit of wall space of the chamber was adorned with artifacts begging for further study, but it was the windows and the landscape they framed that lured her.

She moved to stand before a window and traced her finger along the azure brocade curtain's golden fringe, soaking in the sight of the lush grounds in colors of jade, sage, and chartreuse, stretching as far as she could see. The leaves of ancient elm trees danced and swayed in the early September breeze, projecting lacy patterns onto the manicured lawn beneath. How elegant it all was—how gorgeous and deliberate. Not a leaf or twig was out of place. Fluffy clouds hung over the distant woods, almost painfully bright in their wispy pureness.

Such a stark contrast from London, where even on days when the sky was blue, the ever-present film of soot and smoke dimmed its vibrancy. What would it be like to live such a life surrounded by this sheer beauty?

A distant soft knock sounded, and Olivia whirled.

But no one was there.

The knock sounded again, coming from behind the paneled wall. Then the entire panel of the wall swung open.

Olivia jumped.

A young servant woman with coppery curls poking from beneath a white mobcap leaned her head through the unexpected doorway. "I don't mean to interrupt. Miss Teague is helping Mrs. Milton prepare for dinner, so she asked me to assist you."

Olivia gave a little laugh to mask her shock. "I had no idea there was a door there."

"There's doors like this all over Cloverton, but most don't know of 'em." The maid pushed the door open wider and entered the chamber with a large bucket in her arms.

"Where does it lead?"

"There be two dressin' rooms through t' door, and they both connect to t' mistress's chambers."

The young woman balanced the basin of water she was carrying against her hip and closed the door behind her. She then placed the basin atop a table between the two windows.

"What's your name?" asked Olivia.

"Tabitha, miss. Tabitha Martin." She wiped her hands on the linen apron tied around her waist. "Mrs. Milton said yer t' dress in t' yellow lutestring tonight."

Olivia looked back to her trunks, which had yet to be unpacked. How odd it seemed that someone—anyone—would dictate to another adult what gown to wear. Perhaps this was how it was done, and she'd not risk angering Mrs. Milton for such a trivial request.

Olivia knelt in front of her trunk, unlocked it, pulled the shimmery gown away from the others, and shook out the folds. "I fear it's quite wrinkled."

"I thought it'd be when she said it was o' lutestring, so that's why I brought this." Tabitha motioned toward the bucket of water. "Steamin' hot water will get t' wrinkles out. We'll have to work quickly a'fore it cools."

The woman hastened to position the gown above the steam, and then, at Tabitha's direction, Olivia settled at her chamber's small dressing table. The maid took down Olivia's hair, brushed the chestnut locks, and then twisted it loosely high atop the crown of her head. She secured it with small pearly pins and then wove a length of delicate lace ribbon among the pins. She pulled a few carefully placed long, curly locks free from the style to frame her face.

Tabitha then assisted Olivia in doffing her heavy wool traveling gown and donning the much lighter primrose gown. After slipping her stockinged feet into a new pair of dainty slippers fashioned from soft kidskin, Olivia turned to assess her reflection in the narrow looking glass opposite the windows.

Surely a stranger was staring back at her.

Normally, her wavy hair was loosely bound and pinned at the nape of her neck, but having the hair higher on her head added height. The squared neckline was much lower than she was used to, but the dainty lace trim adorning the bodice added elegance. The gown's shape, luster, and flounced hem transformed her from a mere antiquities purveyor's daughter to someone much more refined.

A smile tweaked the corner of her mouth. Olivia *felt* beautiful. A sentiment that she had neither time, space, nor inclination for at home.

Another soft knock on her door interrupted her musings, and Tabitha answered it, revealing Miss Wainbridge. Without invitation she walked into the chamber in a billowy cloud of striking lavender taffeta. "I do hope I'm not interrupting."

"N-no, no, not at all," stammered Olivia. "We were just finishing."

"Oh good. I was hoping to have a moment to speak with you, alone, if you're agreeable."

Tabitha dismissed herself, and a dainty smile softened Miss Wainbridge's oval face once they were alone. "I only wanted to apologize for the manner in which you were greeted. My aunt's manner was quite abrupt. I hope you weren't offended."

"I'm not offended in the least." Olivia stood from the dressing table and turned to face her. "I think the journey was quite taxing for her."

"That's no reason why the conversation should have been so terse." Miss Wainbridge stepped to the window, touched the curtains to peer down to the front drive, and then turned and trailed her gaze from the elaborate plaster molding, down the papered walls, to the polished floor. "I have loved this room from the moment I laid eyes on it. I do hope you find it satisfactory."

Still gauging Miss Wainbridge's trustworthiness, Olivia measured her response. "It is lovely. I feel quite at home."

"Good. As you may know, my brother and I are fairly new to Cloverton Hall, and we are still becoming acquainted with it ourselves." She joined Olivia near the dressing table, lifted a discarded length of ribbon, and wove it absently through her long fingers. "I confess, I'm curious. My aunt told us you're a friend of the family. How is it that you are acquainted?"

The sense that her hostess was prodding for information resonated. Intent upon not divulging too much information, Olivia said, "My parents and your aunt and late uncle were friends."

"They must be very great friends for her to invite you to accompany her. And you must be a saint." Miss Wainbridge's airy laugh sounded like tinkling bells, and she shook her head, causing her clinquant earbobs to sway. "I'm sure you've gathered that my aunt is not fond of many people—myself and my brother included."

Olivia pressed her lips together.

"My aunt is very well respected," Miss Wainbridge continued matter-of-factly. "And it is most kind of her to preside over our party as hostess. I'm certain that her presence here has eased the minds of many mothers permitting their daughters to attend. I don't mind sharing that it's very important to my brother that this party be a success."

Miss Wainbridge leaned to assess her own reflection in the looking glass and smoothed a perfectly shaped curl at the side of her face before returning her attention to Olivia. "Have you been to Yorkshire before?"

"No, I have not."

"We are quite isolated here, I find. You reside in London, if I'm not mistaken."

"I do."

"I was in London for the entire Season. My brother took a house there, in Mayfair. I wonder that I never saw you there, at gatherings or shops or outings."

It was only natural that the young woman would assume they would be in the same social circles, given the circumstance. How would Miss Wainbridge react to the knowledge that Olivia had spent her summer days at her uncle's shop and not at concerts and cotillions?

"Perhaps we have and didn't know it. London can be so crowded."

"True. But we are here now, and I am eager to know you better. Are you acquainted with any of the other guests in attendance?"

Olivia would not reveal she was acquainted with Lucas Avery—not until she absolutely had to. "I don't believe so."

"Well, I will personally see that you are introduced to each one." The brightness Miss Wainbridge had displayed when first entering the chamber returned, and she squeezed Olivia's hands in her own. "I will leave you to finish your preparations. The others have gathered in the drawing room, but I'm sure you are waiting for Aunt to come down. I must get back to them, but I shall see you soon?"

Olivia agreed, and then the young lady, in a flurry of lustrous fabric and a wafting rose scent, exited the chamber.

Once all was silent again, Olivia sighed and turned once more to assess the new version of herself that peered back at her from the mirror.

Miss Wainbridge did seem genuine, kind, affable—the sort of person whom Olivia would, under normal circumstances, warm to and count as a friend. But time had also taught her to be cautious. If all the years of working with the wealthy had taught her anything, it was that the affluent operated under a different set of rules and ethics. She'd developed a keen sense of judgment when it came to character, and she needed to rely on her experience, especially now that she was blurring the lines of what it meant to be one of them. Yet as she sat in the stillness, the heavy weight of guilt dampened her. She did not believe in telling falsehoods. She abhorred deception, and yet the path she was on dictated both.

True, she might never see these people again, and if she were to be successful in this one opportunity, she would have to take greater control of her emotions. Otherwise, this entire endeavor could prove more harmful than helpful. And that simply could not be.

Chapter 10

OLIVIA'S FATHER HAD told her the story behind the Vinci necklaces dozens of times. Andrea Vinci was one of the most sought-after jewelry makers in all of Italy at the turn of the previous century. At the height of his fame he became greedy. He employed his artistic skill and created jewelry out of glass and metal. The pieces appeared luxurious and his reputation was sterling, so no one questioned him when he sold them for the same price as his authentic pieces. His clients paid whatever price he asked because they *believed* them to be valuable—not because they were.

She secured the Vinci necklace around her neck and pivoted. The fire's light caught the expertly cut glass stone and refracted glimmering slivers of light against the papered wall. She smoothed her fingers across the piece and rested her fingertips on the sleek pendant.

What would her father think of this scenario?

She returned to the mirror to assess her reflection, uncomfortably aware that she was assuming a role she'd never played before. Donned in this gown she now looked the part, but would she act the part?

She straightened the necklace and patted a curl into place. She had no choice but to fight those feelings of nervousness and inadequacy as they rushed her.

Because that was all they were—*feelings*.

They were not a reflection of reality. She was at Cloverton Hall by invitation, after all. She possessed a unique skill—a skill she was proud of. She could not—would not—allow herself to feel any less than the other women simply because of money.

When Mrs. Milton was ready to join the others for dinner, they made their way through the long first-floor corridor, which was shadowed with the evening's gathering darkness. Candles wavered in their sconces on the paneled walls, casting flickering amber light on every manner of painting and bauble that lined the broad walkway. As they approached the great staircase, Olivia decided to use this time to her advantage. "You mentioned you are the hostess for the gathering. Does that mean you know all the guests?"

Mrs. Milton took Olivia's arm and leaned heavily on her for support as they descended the stairs. "I'm familiar with some of the ladies and their families, but the men are from George's set. I'm sure these gentlemen and ladies will be agreeable, but every person is here for a purpose. Ladies seeking an advantageous match. Gentlemen on the prowl for their own self-indulgent pursuits. Consider yourself warned, my dear, not only against the men but the women as well."

"The women?"

"They know nothing of you. Therefore, you are competition for attention from the men. Marriage, my dear. I daresay marriage is on the mind of many in attendance."

Olivia stiffened at the suggestion. There was far too much she hoped to accomplish before she would succumb to that fate. Eager to put her client's mind at ease, she placed her hand atop Mrs. Milton's. "My business here at Cloverton Hall is purely professional."

"Is it?" Mrs. Milton raised a sparse sable brow. "I've yet to meet a woman who'd overlook an opportunity to further her station. No doubt someone will endeavor to tempt you, but keep your business to yourself. Should anyone inquire as to the nature of our relationship, all you need tell them is that you are a friend. Reveal nothing of significance of yourself, not only for the sake of our little project but for yourself. No one is ever as they seem."

Mrs. Milton fell silent, and with each step down the great staircase, the volume of the voices emanating from the drawing room increased. At the stair's foot they turned into the drawing room, and the magnificence that met Olivia stole her very breath.

Thick painted oak panels covering the tall walls were broken by four separate windows and two veranda doors on the chamber's far side, all of which were open to allow the breeze in from the south garden. Small clusters of chairs and sofas were spread throughout the space. Portraits in heavily gilded frames depicting various generations of Milton family members adorned nearly every spare bit of wall, and heavy wine-hued tapestry curtains hung from the ceiling to the floor.

No fire lit the broad marble grate, but dozens of beeswax candles flickered around the room, adding a warmth and glow that infused magic into every detail. Happy chatter and spirited laughter from genteel women in smart gowns and from sporting men in high-collared wool tailcoats echoed from every surface.

Olivia did not have time to consider where she would stand or whom she would speak with, for Miss Wainbridge was at her side.

"Aunt! Miss Brannon. You've joined us at last."

"Isabella." Mrs. Milton sniffed her greeting. "It is a wonder we made it at all, being in such a rush."

"Well, you're here now, the both of you, and I'm glad for it. It would have been such a shame for you to miss the first gathering."

Mrs. Milton's imperious expression remained stoic. "I must speak with Mrs. Dareton on the seating arrangements. I trust I can rely on you with the task of introducing Miss Brannon to your guests?"

Without waiting for the young woman's response, Mrs. Milton disappeared.

Miss Wainbridge's eyes narrowed as she watched her aunt's retreating form. "She's been here just above an hour and already she is displeased."

Olivia tried to read the meaning behind the words. Was it judgment? Annoyance? Insecurity? "Who is Mrs. Dareton?"

Miss Wainbridge refocused her attention on Olivia. "Mrs. Dareton is the housekeeper. I can only imagine what tasks she is going to send that poor woman on." Miss Wainbridge looped her arm through Olivia's as familiarly as sisters. "But on a more pleasant note, I'm quite elated to be the one who gets to introduce the newcomer to the guests. Everyone is curious to learn the identity of Mrs. Milton's mystery guest."

Olivia tensed at the thought of being the topic of conversation. "There's no mystery, I assure you."

"Do not underestimate the intrigue you bring to our little party!" Miss Wainbridge cast a coy glance at two of the men in the far corner, one of whom wore a crimson soldier's coat and was staring in their direction. "The men are already taking notice. Who could blame them? You've captured their fancy."

"I think that assessment may be a bit excessive."

Miss Wainbridge tittered charmingly. "Are you really as modest as you seem? My uncle might be dead, and the fortune might have passed to my brother, but Agnes Milton is still as influential as ever. Her tastes and opinions once set the tone for the entire ton, and such esteem does not vanish overnight."

The paradox was too unbelievable. Just last week Olivia was wearing an apron, covered in the dirt of decades-old, discarded items. But she straightened her shoulders and lifted her chin to look out over the guests again. Tonight, however, she was a *mystery*.

"Oh look, there's George at last!" Miss Wainbridge exclaimed, and Olivia turned to see the gentleman entering from a door on the far wall.

Miss Wainbridge motioned to her brother, and he lifted his head in response.

Olivia had noticed that Mr. Wainbridge was a striking man upon first arrival, but now that she was calmer and rested, she took fresh notice of his appearance. His uncommonly dark eyes were wide and alert, framed by strong brows, dark lashes, and high cheekbones, and his height commanded attention. His cleft chin, while far more pronounced than his sister's, left no question that these two were related. His manner was so easy, his smile so effortless, that it was impossible not to feel at ease, not to mention welcomed, in his presence.

He wove his way through the guests until he was within speaking distance.

"George, see who has managed to join us." Miss Wainbridge angled her body to include Olivia in the conversation.

His white smile flashed and he bowed. "Miss Brannon! I'm glad to speak with you again, for I was uncomfortable with our earlier greeting. I do hope you were not made uneasy by it."

"Not at all. And I must thank you for your hospitality, Mr. Wainbridge. I know I was not on your original list of invites. It must have been quite inconvenient to have a last-minute addition."

"Quite the contrary. My aunt and I do not see eye to eye on many things, but I think we both agree that you are a pleasant addition. But I fear I'm at a disadvantage."

Mr. Wainbridge inclined his head toward Olivia and lowered his voice. "You see, you know more about me than I know about you. My aunt does not care for me. It's not much of a secret, yet I fear it is necessary for me to plead my case to you. She does not know me or Isabella, not really. I can only hope her predisposition does not cast a shadow on your impression of us."

Olivia noted his hopeful expression. His ingenuous eyes. He looked at her in a way that made her feel like he really saw her—in a way most people did not. It was . . . nice.

Mrs. Milton's warning of not revealing too much flared, yet Olivia was still mistress of her own mind and actions. "I may be your aunt's guest, Mr. Wainbridge, but I possess my own opinions."

"Well then, such a relationship speaks to your credit. My aunt finds fault with most people. The fact that she found such goodness in you is quite a feat."

How simple it would be to warm to the siblings and their inviting temperaments and to immediately count them as friends. Their cordial welcome had certainly stood in stark contrast to Mrs. Milton's cooler, more distanced treatment, but ultimately Olivia had to remember *why* she was here. Her top priority, above all else, was to assess a collection she had yet to see.

Chapter 11

WHAT ON EARTH was Olivia Brannon doing at Cloverton Hall?

The question vexed Lucas as he settled himself in the formal dining room. All around him polite chatter and reserved laughter echoed from the nearly twenty participants seated at the long table. Each person employed their finest manners and best behavior for the opening dinner. Glass and porcelain clinked. Silver sparkled, and an aura of expectant anticipation hovered over all. Lucas knew most of the guests. Many were friends of Tate and often present at his social gatherings. But never had he seen Miss Brannon among them.

Lucas took a sip of his wine and cast another glance in the young woman's direction. At one time he considered Olivia Brannon a friend, but after their fathers dissolved their business partnership, that friendship faded rapidly. When Mr. Brannon was still alive, Lucas would often encounter Olivia at auctions and the sort, but since his death, Lucas had seen less and less of her.

It was no secret that Brannon had taught his eldest daughter everything he knew, and every agent and purveyor in the antiquities business knew who she was. Even now that Thomas Brannon was at the helm of Brannon Antiquities, it was generally understood that she was the driving force behind most of their transactions.

By all accounts she was intelligent. Astute. And doggedly determined.

"I am growing concerned."

The coy feminine voice to Lucas's right claimed his attention.

Miss Caroline Stanley's wide-set, soft russet eyes were fixed on him, and her delicate pink lips were drawn in a distressed, albeit flirtatious, pout.

Lucas angled his body to focus on his charming dinner partner. "We can't have that. What's troubling you?"

"You and I have been acquainted for at least a decade, have we not? In all that time I've never known you to be so solemn. It's quite distracting, and I don't like it."

An easy smile formed. He'd always liked Miss Stanley and her gift for witty banter. "Am I to understand that *I* am the source of your concern?"

"Of course!" Her titian brows drew together, resulting in a prettily furrowed brow. "This is our first evening at the lovely Cloverton party, and you already seem bored and distracted. We've not seen one another in months and have so much to catch up on. One would think you did not want to be here at all."

Lucas sobered at the censure. He had to remember that he was here to save his business. That meant being friendly. Building a reputation. Every choice—every action and conversation—was a gamble that he was focusing his time and effort on the right project at the right time. "I can assure you, Miss Stanley, that nothing is further from the truth. I am merely observing."

She lowered her voice, as if taking him into her confidence. "Do you mean you are observing Mrs. Milton?"

"Mrs. Milton?" He chuckled, casting a glance at their hostess. "What makes you say that?"

"I saw you watching her. I can't say I blame you. I've never met her in person before, although I have seen her at gatherings and balls from time to time."

Lucas shrugged. "I'm curious about her, 'tis all. She has quite the reputation."

"She is an intimidating creature, to be sure. I once saw a young woman crying because Mrs. Milton told her mother that she thought her dress inappropriate for the weather. The weather! Her opinion has the power to either make a person the talk of the Season or ruin them forever." Miss Stanley shook her head, causing the curls on either side of her face to dance. "How different she is from the Wainbridges. Imagine what it must be like to have her as an aunt. But how fortunate that Mr. Wainbridge was able to convince her to preside over the party as hostess. I have it on good authority that she has not personally hosted a single event since Mr. Milton's death. I'm quite certain my mother never would have consented for me to attend otherwise. And I was also glad to learn that you are among the guests. You were greatly missed over the summer. But Mr. Tate told me you have been traveling?"

"I returned from Italy two weeks ago."

"A trip for pleasure, I hope?"

"Business, I'm afraid. I was finalizing some of my father's dealings there."

"Yes, I heard about your father." Her tone lowered in solidarity. "I was very sorry to hear it."

He took another drink to hide any emotion that might reveal itself in his expression. How could nine months have already elapsed since his father's death?

"Well then," she exclaimed, her polished tone brightening, "we must do our very best to make sure you are happy and have no reason to be melancholy while you're here. Diversion is always the best remedy when plagued with grief, I've found."

Lucas wished he could see the world so simply—to merely demand a distraction and find respite from a wound he doubted would ever really heal. But to him, relief would come through working hard and securing a future for his business.

"Now, tell me . . ." She leaned over and glanced around the table, a sparkle twinkling in her eyes. "You always seem to know the most unique details. Do you know anything about the young lady sitting next to Mrs. Milton?"

He looked toward Miss Brannon. She was bound to be a topic of conversation sooner or later.

Miss Stanley continued, "No one seems to know anything about her—where she lives or who her people are. Not even the Wainbridges. Miss Wainbridge told me she was a particular friend of Mrs. Milton, and that Mrs. Milton insisted Miss Kline actually be moved from her bedchamber so that this new guest might stay there. Miss Kline was quite put out. Isn't that curious?"

He leaned back in his chair, feigning nonchalance. "Well, whatever her story, I'm sure we'll all know it soon enough. No one can keep a secret for long."

Miss Stanley giggled. "How right you are, Mr. Avery."

The soft hum of polite conversation floated around him in hushed tones and restrained laughter. He knew how these parties would go . . . he would speak with Miss Brannon yet tonight. There would be no way around it.

He studied her more closely, as discreetly as he was able. The gentle—and attractive—slope of her nose. The fullness of her florid lips. It was coloring that tied her to the Edward Brannon he recalled—chestnut hair, hazel eyes that were more gold than green, a clear, fair complexion. She was not dressed as a plain shopgirl, as she had been in most of their other encounters. She was elegant, refined. Always before he'd seen her as Mr. Brannon's impetuous daughter. Now she seemed every bit a lady in her own right.

The relaxed state he'd just enjoyed was beginning to dissipate as the possible motives for her attendance continued to develop in his mind.

Lucas had assumed that the business relationship between the Brannons and Cloverton Hall died with Francis Milton. Furthermore, George Wainbridge had definite plans for how to handle the collection moving forward.

And yet, *she* was here. And she seemed so friendly with the Wainbridge siblings.

It was too coincidental. Wasn't it?

Lucas endeavored to pay attention to the ebullient Miss Stanley's recounting of her sister's recent nuptials and the list of those in attendance. Yet his thoughts raced.

At one point Miss Brannon glanced his way across the broad dining table. In the midst of lively chatter and laughter, the spark of recognition flared between them.

Then the guest to her left said something to her, and the thread that connected them for that brief, magnetizing second snapped.

In that singular moment his entire purpose for being at the house party intensified.

She was competition.

There could be no way around it.

Every aspect of the first dinner at the Cloverton house party competed for Olivia's attention. The matching pewter octagonal bowls on either side of the carved marble fireplace—decidedly Persian. The ancient painted Chinese screen depicting cranes and exotic fish adorning the opposite wall. The very table she was sitting at, with its teak inlay and intricate carvings along the edges. The elegant women clad in shimmering gossamer and Brussels lace, with jewels strung about their necks, strands of gold thread sewn into the very fabric of their gowns, and fresh flowers tucked into their hair.

Never had her senses experienced such an onslaught of so many new and interesting things. And yet she was equally aware of the inquisitive glances toward her. Miss Wainbridge had been right;

Olivia's very presence was a novelty to this group—a newcomer who may or may not have the power to disrupt the social balance.

Olivia straightened her shoulders and lifted her chin, assessing the other guests with a fresh eye. Every single one of them possessed a self-assuredness and confidence that both struck her and reminded her of visiting clients with her father.

Now, although it was a mere charade, she was on the other side of the interaction.

New rules. New etiquette. New everything. She would do the only thing she really could do at the moment, and that was to appear completely in control and entirely at ease. Wasn't that what offering opinions and advice in a man's business had taught her? For her whole life people had made assumptions about her and her abilities, and each time it made her want to prove herself even more.

Yet one thing was preventing her from giving in to her new role completely.

Lucas Avery.

She'd noticed him watching her.

Olivia glanced to her left at Mrs. Milton. This situation would perhaps be easier if the woman acting as her chaperone would at least communicate with her or show some form of solidarity, but the older woman had said very little since being seated in the dining room. Olivia had assumed, even hoped, that Mrs. Milton would warm to her once they'd arrived at Cloverton Hall, but the opposite seemed to be true.

Olivia recalled how her father's disposition had changed after her mother had died. His once jovial demeanor morphed into a much more somber, more cynical one, and with each year that followed, his pessimism intensified.

It couldn't be easy for Mrs. Milton, coming into a home that had once belonged to her and seeing that changes were being made. Olivia had to remember that Mrs. Milton did not invite her on a holiday. She'd asked her to perform a task with very specific parameters. It was up to Olivia to manage her own emotions and fulfill the expectations that had been set before her.

As Olivia pushed the roasted partridge around her plate with her fork, she sensed the uncomfortable weight of someone's attention on her. She glanced to her right to see Mr. Fielding's red-rimmed eyes fixed on her. A smirk curved his thin lips into an expression that made her shift uncomfortably in her chair.

He had an uncommonly narrow face, a pointed nose, and a small mouth that seemed very much like a weasel's. She'd been introduced to him only minutes before they entered the dining room, and now she'd have to endure the entire dinner by his side.

"Lost in thought, are you, Miss Brannon?"

"No, no." She smiled, masking her reaction to the strong scent of wine lacing his breath. "Just admiring the decor."

"Ah yes, it is interesting, is it not?" He did little to hide his assessment as he looked around the dining room. "A bit eccentric for my taste, but I'm told the former master was quite extreme in his passions."

Olivia stiffened at the words, refusing to look in Mrs. Milton's direction and hoping she'd not overheard the comment. "Are you from London, Mr. Fielding?"

"No, heavens, no. I'm from Derbyshire, but I do spend a great deal of time in London. Did I not hear Wainbridge say that is where you call home?"

"It is."

"I adore London," he exclaimed before indulging in a noisy swig of claret. "I was there not three weeks ago. A fabulous outing. I don't recall seeing you at any events, though. I'm sure I'd have remembered."

The unmasked flirtation in his tone unsettled her. She lowered her fork and tapped her napkin against her lip, attempting to ignore the tone behind the words. "No, indeed you would not have seen me. I may live in London but fear I'm not in society much."

He emphatically clicked his tongue. "A true pity. At least for the next couple of days, however, we shall have to make up for lost time."

Heat crept up her neck as the innuendo hit home. Russell's words came to her. *They are not like us. They operate under a different set of rules. Nothing will be as you know it.*

She glanced toward Mr. Avery, who was looking in her direction.

For a moment, they locked eyes.

Did he know and understand these rules? Or was he like her— playing a role?

She snapped her attention back to Mr. Fielding. Determined to take control of the conversation, she asked, "Have you visited Cloverton Hall before?"

Mr. Fielding shook his head, disheveling his thinning, auburn-tinged hair even further. "Never, although I must say that it far exceeds my expectations. I've heard Wainbridge speak of it often over the last several months, and in nearly each instance I accused him of exaggeration. But now that I'm here, I must say his descriptions of it hardly did it justice. And you? Have you ever been here?"

"No."

"I only wondered because Wainbridge said you are closely acquainted with Mrs. Milton, who, if I am not mistaken, is the widow of Cloverton Hall's former master." He lowered his voice to a rough whisper and leaned uncomfortably close to her ear. "I know her reputation as a leader in society, but I hear she's quite a beastly woman to be around."

Olivia retracted from his nearness and scooted her chair back as discreetly as she could manage, unsure of how to respond to his blunt statement. She knew one thing for certain: she would not be drawn in. Goodness, she didn't even know Mrs. Milton; she would not engage in a conversation about her, especially a negative one. She tossed her head, giving an attempt at an air of confidence, and shrugged one shoulder. "I'm afraid I don't understand your meaning, sir."

"Don't you?" He dragged his napkin over his thin lips. "Well then. You must be privy to knowing something about Mrs. Milton that the rest of us do not."

She hesitated and stared down at her plate.

"There now, I caught you!" he exclaimed heartily. "Very well, you can keep your secret, for I'll find it out by the end of the party. In the meantime, I'm endeavoring to stay in her good graces."

Olivia decided in that moment that she did not care for Mr. Fielding. There was no need to be quiet or shy with her response. After all, he would never see her again after this. She could, for the night, be his equal until such a point that she was not. "Endeavoring? Am I to take it, then, that your normal behavior would inherently cause her to think ill of you?"

His exuberant laughter rose above the other conversations, and he wagged a finger at her. "You are quite a perceptive little bird. Quite perceptive indeed. But you're attempting to change the subject, and that I simply will not allow."

His voice was barely above a whisper now. "Wainbridge told me everything. How the old woman despises him—indeed, how she despises the entire group gathered—but she has no other choice but to play hostess because she has nowhere else to live."

Olivia couldn't hold back the rise of her brows.

"See? That did get a reaction."

"Of course it did. I think it very uncouth of you to say such cruel things."

"I am only repeating what was said to me." Mr. Fielding raised his hands to proclaim innocence. "But you're right. It was *uncouth*, as you put it. Forgive me. Besides, we should be grateful, shouldn't we? She is, after all, our hostess. If not for her, so many anxious mamas and overbearing guardians might not have consented to allow their daughters to join in the party. And then where would the fun be? And at the end of the day, we're all rogues. But at least I am not the worst."

When Olivia did not immediately respond, Mr. Fielding pushed back in his chair and heaved a dramatic sigh. "Oh dear. I've offended."

Olivia met his gaze. "You've not offended me, Mr. Fielding, but I'd caution you to remember that people are not always what they appear to be."

"Isn't that the beauty of it?" His gray eyes twinkled. "I'd dare anyone here to really show their true selves."

A sharp rebuttal simmered on the tip of her tongue—but she did not allow it to pass. It was no use—the man was intoxicated.

As if suddenly bored with her, Mr. Fielding turned and began speaking to the lady on his other side.

Grateful for the reprieve, Olivia took a sip of the claret in front of her. *I am not really a part of this. These people are not my friends.*

She cast a glance over to Mrs. Milton, who was no longer speaking to the gentleman on the other side of her. She was, instead, staring at a painting on the far wall. Silently. Solemnly. The nearby candlelight flickered and cast light on her withered, wan cheek, emphasizing the lines and the wrinkles there.

In that moment Olivia's empathy ached for Mrs. Milton. The dynamic between the older and younger generations was tense, and Mrs. Milton was facing it alone.

In a welcome distraction Mr. Wainbridge stood from his chair at the table's end and lifted his hands, and the group fell silent. All eyes turned to their affable host, whose genuine enthusiasm and unmistakable charisma lit the space.

"My dear friends, let me take this opportunity to welcome you to Cloverton Hall. I know it's not always easy to travel all this way and be away from your lives for so long, but I have been so eager to share Cloverton with you. While you are here, please enjoy yourselves. Tomorrow the gentlemen will take to the outdoors, and my sister and aunt have been busy planning activities for the ladies. A special guest will be arriving tomorrow, and we'll all attend the Whitmores' ball later this week. Before our first dinner together comes to an end, I also want to thank my aunt, Mrs. Milton, for agreeing to act as our hostess for the week. Her knowledge and reputation are beyond compare."

Olivia shifted and looked to the older woman, whose expression remained dour. At length, she stood. "Now, ladies, let us take that as our cue to withdraw and leave the gentlemen to their port. Miss Brannon, take my arm."

Olivia, surprised by the invitation, rose to her feet, and Mrs. Milton placed her hand on Olivia's arm. It was odd after being ignored that Mrs. Milton would point her out, but in truth, Olivia was grateful to feel as if there was a place for her.

Chapter 12

"WHO KNOWS?" TATE sank to the chair next to Lucas, ignorant of how his port swirled and splashed in his glass. "Miss Haven seemed quite smitten with me when we spoke prior to dinner. This might finally be the night that she realizes she is in love with me."

Lucas groaned. Tate thrived on romantic spectacles and dramatic displays, and as with any truly memorable house party, everything about this gathering contributed to an environment ripe for dramatics. He moved his foot to give Tate more room. "I seem to recall you saying something very similar at the Hammonds' Lady Day Ball earlier this spring. Except the lady in question was Miss Ernest, if memory serves."

"No, no. You're mistaken. That was mere flirtation. This . . . this is altogether different. But before I get ahead of myself, I must be practical, for I have a rival. Wainbridge has declared his intentions. A part of me fears I've met my match."

"Come now, Tate. That defeatist attitude doesn't sound like you," Lucas bolstered. "Besides, his fortune is compromised, at least for the time being. Miss Haven, lovely as she is, strikes me as one swayed by that particular attribute."

"Look around, Avery! Does our host not *appear* to possess a fortune?" Tate swung his arm out wide, once again disturbing the amber liquid in his glass. He lowered his voice and leaned closer. "No one else is aware of his situation. What's more, Miss Haven's family estate is not even an hour from here by carriage. And unless the gossipmongers are about, she undoubtedly considers him a catch. I daresay he'll swoop in, woo her, and secure an agreement before any truths can be revealed."

"Well then. You'll have to rely on charm alone," Lucas bantered. "But I'd not commit myself, were I you, for what of Miss Wainbridge? She was pleased to see you."

"Now she's a pretty girl." Tate rubbed his chin in contemplation. "And I considered her. I even broached the idea with Wainbridge, out of respect. He is her guardian, you know. But he opposed it."

"On what grounds?"

"I haven't enough money."

Lucas coughed as he nearly choked on his drink. "You? Not enough money?"

"Ridiculous, I know. The issue is that I have wealth but no title, but Whitaker, on the other hand, will inherit both one day, so he is infinitely preferable."

Lucas looked over to Robert Whitaker, a robust, squat, florid-faced man clad in a crimson officer's coat and engaged in a bout of raucous laughter with Mr. Fielding. He was likely a decade the lady's senior. "They don't seem to suit."

"Ah, ah, ah." Tate chuckled, tugging at his cravat until it loosened about his neck. "Need I remind you how attractive money is?

It's the most enticing trait one can possess, and it blurs a multitude of sins. But enough of me and my woes, eh? Did you enjoy your conversation with Miss Stanley at dinner? She certainly seemed to."

"I did. I've always liked Miss Stanley. She's a good sort."

"And she gets more handsome every year, does she not? Those entrancing doe eyes of hers?" Tate whistled low. "Stunning. But you heard about her father, I'm sure."

"I heard he suffered a banking loss."

"Not just any loss, but essentially his entire fortune! It's all rather recent. I just heard of it myself last week. I'm sure Wainbridge knew nothing about it when the invitations went out. And yet, see how she's conducted herself? As if nothing has changed. No doubt she's hoping to contain the news as long as possible, but things like that never stay secret for long. And speaking of secrets, we've yet to comment on that lady next to Fielding at dinner. She was intriguing, no?"

Lucas stiffened at the reference. He supposed it might have been possible that Tate and Miss Brannon had encountered each other at some point, but if they had, Tate clearly didn't remember.

Tate continued, "I'm told she hails from London, but I've never seen her before. If this young woman is with Mrs. Milton, there must be something compelling about her. Perhaps she's a relative. Maybe an heiress? Merely a companion? Every party needs a conspiracy of sorts. She must be here to stir curiosity, because otherwise it is just the same people staring at each other all day."

Lucas raised his brows. "Did you say conspiracy?"

"Yes. But don't you get caught up in it." Tate pointed his forefinger at Lucas. "We need you to be in full concentration. The better you can do your job, the more money Wainbridge will make, and then the more money we *all* can make."

Lucas clapped his hand on his friend's shoulder. "That's what I appreciate most about you, Tate. Your concern for my future and well-being."

"I'll make you a bargain." Tate ignored the sarcasm and settled back against his chair. "You do this task, and then we'll throw all our efforts into finding you a wealthy wife. Then you'd not have to rely on me for your business dealings."

"What would you do then?" Lucas gibed.

"I'd manage."

"What's the laughter about here?" Wainbridge approached, his face flushed and his eyes red, a decanter in his hand. "Am I missing the jest?"

"Hardly." Tate tilted his head, as if about to reveal a great secret. "We are merely attempting to make sense of the fairer sex. Have you any advice for us?"

Wainbridge extended the decanter toward Tate and refilled his glass. "Advice? No. But I wish you the very best of luck. When you solve the puzzle, I expect you to share your secrets with me."

"This is quite a gathering." Lucas lifted his glass, shifting the conversation. "You must be proud to show off Cloverton Hall at last."

Wainbridge's expression darkened. "It's magnificent. But you know the truth of it. It is hard to celebrate it when it feels more like a noose than a distinction."

"Well, that's why we're here. In fact, I've already seen many pieces that'll do well for you. Take that decanter in your hand. It's at least a century old. I'd very much prefer it if you set it down instead of waving it around like you are."

Wainbridge snorted. "You can have it and every other dusty relic around here if it will bring in money. Tomorrow I'll show you the study and the library, and you have my permission to go anywhere in the house you like. Just be discreet. My aunt would be furious if she knew what we were up to. That woman is destined to be a thorn in my side, but let's not talk of her anymore. She already influences too many of my thoughts. But for tonight, we make merry."

It would be nice to relax, to truly partake in the festivities, but his father's words echoed in his mind. *"No one will trust a man who loses controls of his senses. It takes but one mishap to abolish trust, and once gone, it's nearly impossible to restore."*

Lucas was not here to be pampered and entertained. His responsibilities were very specific and finite, and as such his behavior had to be different. He'd need to be master of every skill he possessed, for his entire financial future was riding on his ability to truly earn Wainbridge's trust and oversee any transactions related to the Cloverton estate.

Miss Brannon flashed in his mind . . . again. Her presence here was the one potential stumbling block. He needed to know what he was up against—the sooner, the better.

Chapter 13

OLIVIA HAD NEVER learned to play whist. She'd heard of the card game but never had the time or the inclination to learn.

Until now.

She sat in a straight-backed chair along the drawing room's west wall, cup of tea in hand, alone. More than two hours had elapsed since the ladies left the men in the dining room. Two card tables were positioned in the chamber's center with four women seated at each. Olivia had not been invited to play, but she did not mind, for now she could observe the other female guests without drawing attention.

The four other young ladies were at the table nearest to Olivia, partnered in groups of two. Miss Esther Haven, a stunning, statuesque woman with flaxen hair, was partnered with Miss Caroline Stanley, who possessed coppery curls, soft brown eyes, and an airy, contagious laugh. Miss Rebecca Kline, a petite, buxom lady with full rosy cheeks and observant obsidian eyes, was partnered with Miss Wainbridge.

At the other table sat Mrs. Milton and three of the chaperones.

By the time the men reunited with the ladies in the drawing room, the hour had grown quite late. Mr. Wainbridge and Captain Whitaker were the first to join them, followed shortly by Mr. Fielding,

Mr. Tate, and Mr. Avery. They brought with them an informal air laced with laughter and good humor, and in the blink of an eye the stuffy, somewhat sedate room had become a flurry of activity.

Mr. Wainbridge opened the veranda doors, and cooler, restorative air streamed in. The ladies abandoned their games and tables, and a fresh wave of footmen arrived with trays of cakes and beverages.

In the midst of the activity, Mrs. Milton found Olivia and took her arm. "Stay by me, Miss Brannon. Besides my nephew you've only been introduced to Mr. Fielding, correct? A reminder—speak with none of the other men until you've been formally introduced by George, Isabella, or myself. In fact, the fewer people you speak with, the better."

A slight flush warmed Olivia's cheeks and neck. What would Mrs. Milton think if she knew the existing connection that Olivia had with Mr. Avery?

At length Captain Whitaker, a round, short man whose flushed cheeks nearly matched the shade of his officer's uniform, approached Mrs. Milton, and after a polite introduction, Olivia found herself engaged in a cordial, albeit dull, conversation. Try as she might, she could not concentrate, for all the while she was acutely aware of Mr. Avery—where he was standing, with whom he was speaking, when he laughed, and, most notably, when he looked in her direction.

Despite her poor opinion of his family, Olivia could admit that Lucas Avery was a handsome man. She'd always thought so, but she'd been loath to admit it. His umber-hued brown hair was a little darker than her own and just long enough to be fashionable. His eyes, even from a distance, were an unusual shade of pale green, enhanced by the deep moss shade of his worsted wool tailcoat.

She did try to focus on Captain Whitaker's recounting of his most recent visit to Covent Garden, but as time and the story plodded on, her concern that she might not be able to speak with Mr. Avery that evening grew. And even as she smiled and spoke as circumspectly as possible, she could feel eyes assessing her, adding to her uneasiness.

Olivia stayed close to Mrs. Milton's side, as instructed, but when one of the chaperones asked to speak with her privately regarding Miss Haven, Olivia saw her chance.

The moment Mrs. Milton was out of sight, Olivia excused herself from Captain Whitaker, but when she looked around the crowded chamber, Mr. Avery seemed to be gone. What was worse, she spied Mr. Fielding approaching her. Fearing she might become embroiled in another unpleasant conversation, she whirled around and, in doing so, nearly collided with Mr. Wainbridge's shoulder and disrupted the drink in his hand.

And then she saw Mr. Avery, standing just behind him.

He was looking at her. And . . . smiling?

She forced her flustered attention to their host and the liquid that had splashed onto his sleeve. "How careless of me! Please forgive me, Mr. Wainbridge. I did not see you there."

"Not at all. In fact, it's a small price to pay to see that you've escaped my aunt's clutches," he japed, procuring a handkerchief from his coat and swiping at his dampened sleeve. "She seems intent upon keeping you to herself."

Olivia recognized the inebriated tint of his eyes and cheeks. "She just introduced me to Captain Whitaker."

"Whitaker's a great friend of mine." Wainbridge's casual demeanor and relaxed posture were a sharp contrast to the polished man she'd met earlier in the day. "What do you think of him?"

"I've only just met him, but he seems friendly enough."

Mr. Wainbridge chortled. "Friendly indeed. Well then, you must permit me to introduce you to another one of my friends. Mr. Lucas Avery."

Her eyes met his. This was the moment. He might expose her. He might not.

She smiled, just as she would with any introduction. "A pleasure."

He bowed.

"You may not know it, but you and Avery here have something in common."

Olivia's heart thudded in her chest. "And what is that?"

"London. You both reside there. Such a small world, is it not?"

Relief trickled through her. "It is indeed, Mr. Wainbridge."

He grinned. "Good. I will leave the two of you to get acquainted while I go find another coat." Mr. Wainbridge clapped his hand against Mr. Avery's broad shoulder as he left them.

And then she and her adversary were alone.

Years had passed since the last time Olivia had actually spoken to Lucas Avery. She'd heard about his successes and transactions, about his travels and his father's death, but never had she expected to speak with him. Yet this conversation was inevitable. In the short time since she first saw him on the staircase, she'd been imagining what she'd say to him when they finally did speak, but now that he stood in front of her, her mind was devoid of thought.

The confidence in his voice, the familiarity of it, combined with the unwavering directness of his gaze, bemused her. "I'm surprised but pleased to see you here, Miss Brannon."

She'd show no discomfort—a skill she'd honed over years of working with men who did not take her seriously. "Not nearly as surprised as I am to see you."

He chuckled but did not break their eye contact. "It's only that I've never seen you at these gatherings before."

These gatherings? She knew his clients were well-connected members of society, but the thought that he might interact with them socially hadn't crossed her mind. "Mrs. Milton was kind enough to extend an invitation, and I was grateful to receive it."

He lifted his brows as if to signal a change in topic. "A Vinci, if I'm not mistaken."

Her fingers flew to the bauble. Of course he'd recognize the setting, the filigree of the notable impostor piece. "Very astute, Mr. Avery."

"The metalwork is unparalleled. I've always been partial to his work."

She fought her anxiety and kept her tone light. "You're aware of its secret, then?"

He lowered his voice, as if taking her into his confidence. "Every antiquarian item has a secret, but I'd wager you know that better than anyone."

His words were so calm, so amicable, as if coming upon an old family rival was mundane business. But then again, he likely had nothing to hide.

A bout of laughter from across the room drew her attention. She looked over her shoulder and spied Mrs. Milton reentering the drawing room.

If Olivia wanted to speak with Mr. Avery, she needed to do it now.

She turned around with renewed determination. "This will seem an odd question, but have you informed Mr. Wainbridge that you and I were already acquainted?"

"I have not." His brows drew together, a twinkle brightening his eyes. "I was concerned that you might not want everyone to know you were associated with a lowly merchant."

The easy nature of his tone would ease most, but she remained wary. The Averys were famously skilled in the art of conversation—and manipulation.

She glanced up to see Mrs. Milton approaching. "I was hoping to ask you a favor."

"Anything."

"Whatever you know of me, of my family, I would appreciate it if you could, at least for the time being, keep it to yourself. You see, I—"

Olivia snapped her mouth closed as Mrs. Milton came within earshot and pivoted to face her hostess. "I do hope Miss Haven is all right. Her chaperone seemed quite concerned."

"A headache." Mrs. Milton stopped by Olivia's side. "Brought on, no doubt, by travel and a change of the weather. I'd wager tomorrow she will feel well enough." She fixed her eyes, hard and heavy, on Mr. Avery, as if finally taking notice of him.

He bowed, but Mrs. Milton did not address him. Instead, she reached her hand out toward Olivia. "Come, Miss Brannon. The hour has struck eleven. I'm certain the ladies are ready to retire for the evening."

Olivia curtsied toward Mr. Avery in parting before allowing Mrs. Milton to take her arm. As they joined the group of ladies in the center of the room, Olivia observed Mr. Avery's retreating form.

She'd done it. She'd made the request of him. Mr. Avery had not had time to respond before they were interrupted, but at least she'd made her request known. Either he'd honor it, or he would not.

It was as simple—and as complicated—as that.

Chapter 14

WHEN OLIVIA RETURNED to the Blue Room, a cheery fire roared in the grate and beeswax candles in chambersticks and candelabras illuminated every corner and tabletop. The finely woven wool blankets atop her mattress tick had been turned down, the velvet curtains had been loosed from their holdings, and her nightclothes had been pressed and draped over the chaise lounge.

She dropped her shawl on the high-backed chair next to her bed and stood for a moment, allowing the silence and soothing glow of saffron light to soothe her frayed senses. Somehow she'd managed to successfully navigate her first dinner at a house party without any glaring mishaps. What was more, she'd been able to talk with Mr. Avery.

With a satisfied yawn she unclasped the Vinci necklace and held it, admiring yet again the way the fire's light sparkled against the intricately cut angles. The more she considered her conversation with Mr. Avery, the more it was oddly gratifying that he noticed it and appreciated it in the same way she did. In fact, speaking with him was not nearly as uncomfortable as she'd anticipated. He'd been cordial. Personable. But wasn't that the Averys' gift? To make others feel comfortable and then take advantage?

Mrs. Milton interrupted her musings by appearing in the doorway to the dressing room, shattering the thought that she was finally able to be alone for the night.

Teague followed her, still fully dressed in her daytime attire.

"You were speaking quite familiarly with that young man," Mrs. Milton proclaimed as she crossed the threshold. "Mr. Avery, was it? I wasn't aware you'd been introduced."

Olivia carefully chose her words. "I am acquainted with his family."

Mrs. Milton's wrinkly cheeks colored, and she huffed in disgust, if not anger. "How exactly are you acquainted?"

Olivia flicked her eyes toward Teague in search of some sort of assistance or explanation, but found none. "His father and my father were business associates many years ago."

"So he knows of your expertise," Mrs. Milton surmised sharply. Olivia could only nod.

"Will he deduce why you're here?"

"I—I don't know."

"You said a business associate," she blurted. "What exactly do you mean by that?"

Olivia selected her words with care. "Our fathers were once business partners, but they separated more than a decade ago. His father, Timothy Avery, died earlier this year, but Mr. Lucas Avery now operates Avery & Sons."

"I knew I recognized that name!" She flung the words almost like an accusation. An enraged expression darkened her eyes, and

Mrs. Milton began to pace. "The insolence! I know what he's doing. *I know.*"

Confused at the odd reaction, Olivia attempted to follow her meaning. "Mr. Avery?"

"No. My nephew. He clearly has invited Mr. Avery to sell my husband's collection."

Hoping to calm the agitated woman, Olivia lowered her voice. "It is possible that Mr. Avery is simply an acquaintance? From what I observed he seemed to be quite friendly with everyone, and I—"

"No, no," Mrs. Milton snapped. "George sees only money, not the time, the effort that has gone into making Cloverton Hall what it now is."

Olivia wanted to offer comfort, but what could she do? Or say?

In truth, she had no doubt that was exactly what Mr. Avery was doing. The relationship between Brannon Antiquities and Cloverton Hall died with her father, and since then every antiquities dealer had been vying for a foothold to the infamous collection. Clearly Mr. Avery was building a rapport with Mr. Wainbridge.

The older woman pointed a podgy finger in Olivia's direction. "You must find out what he is doing here."

"Me?" Olivia's hand flew to her chest. "Oh, I couldn't. I'm certain he's—"

Mrs. Milton's aggressive visage silenced her.

It seemed an impossible request. Making such inquiries of Mr. Avery would result in disaster, but whether she liked it or not, she had no choice but to appease Mrs. Milton. She needed to stay in the lady's good graces to ultimately be successful and reach her goal of being self-sufficient. "I'll find out what I can."

Commotion sounded, and as Tabitha entered the chamber, the tension eased.

Mrs. Milton's countenance softened. "Tomorrow morning I'll introduce you to my collection, and tomorrow afternoon and evening there will be activities that, unfortunately, require both our attendance. Consider what I've said, and don't forget it. I'll bid you good night, then." Mrs. Milton, followed by Teague, retreated through the paneled door, leaving Olivia and Tabitha alone in the Blue Room.

Olivia was in no mood for conversation as Tabitha helped her doff her gown, let down her hair, and wash her face. Once Tabitha had departed, Olivia extinguished the candles, and the only light that remained was the simmering fire in the grate and the slivers of white moonlight that filtered through the gaps around the curtains. Otherwise, all was silent and dark and still, save for the occasional burst of masculine laughter emanating from the floor beneath her chamber.

She crawled atop the soft mattress tick. Her body called for rest, but her mind was alive with all she'd witnessed.

The evening had spun by at such an alarming pace. Dazzling beauty and magnificent manners. Intriguing chatter and intoxicating elegance. She'd tasted champagne. A gentleman had flirted with her. She'd been treated as an honored guest.

Yet homesickness crept in.

The Blue Room seemed extravagant. The voices from below were disquieting. Furthermore, her encounter with Mr. Avery had revived memories that had long lain dormant—memories of her father, of her family. Of how events had converged to get them all to the point where they were today.

Her greatest childhood desire had been to travel with her father to all of the exotic places he had visited, like her mother had done when Olivia was young. China. India. Egypt. Her mother's stories had fueled Olivia's imagination, and she had determined that she would be exactly like her mother.

But then Olivia's mother had died.

And then her father had died too.

With each loss, her world shifted, and the luminous dreams that once had blazed before her faded to lackluster hopes. Now she'd likely never travel to Egypt or India. Her father's business was barely surviving, and if it weren't for Mr. Milton's strong relationship with Father years ago, she might never have even been offered this opportunity.

But she'd made it to Cloverton Hall and survived her first day. And the fact that she was here to assess antiquities in some way made her feel closer to her parents than she had in a very long time. It was a chance to prove herself.

Chapter 15

LUCAS NEVER SLEPT past dawn. It was yet another trait his father had drilled into him—lounging in bed and wasting daylight was an unforgivable offense.

Now, the first light of day was inching through the attic chamber's two deep-set, narrow leaded windows. Tate slumbered across his narrow bed, still fully clothed in the previous evening's dinner attire, but Lucas had kept his senses about him and was ready for their first full day at Cloverton Hall.

The day's agenda was straightforward. The men were to spend the morning hunting pheasants, and then they'd dine with the ladies upon their return in the evening. But before that, Wainbridge had indicated that he wanted to meet with him privately prior to the hunt to discuss Mr. Milton's collection.

Lucas poured cold water from the jug into the basin near the far wall, washed his face, cleaned his teeth, wet his comb and attempted to tame his unruly hair, and dressed quickly in attire appropriate for the morning's hunt. Normally, he'd be excited for such an impending conversation, but as he saw to his ablutions, one nagging question continued to pester him: Why was Olivia Brannon here?

Her parting words to him roiled in his mind: *"Whatever you know of me, of my family, I would appreciate it if you could, at least for the time being, keep it to yourself."*

On the surface it seemed a reasonable request, but the more he considered it, the deeper the question developed. What was more, the entrancing expression in her hazel eyes and her intriguing smile allowed him to think of little else..

Once he was ready, Lucas made his way down to Wainbridge's study on the ground floor. He rapped his knuckles against the doorframe.

"Ah, you remembered." Wainbridge motioned for Lucas to enter.

Like Tate, Wainbridge was still clad in the previous evening's attire. The start of a dark beard hugged his pronounced jawline, and his discarded coat had been tossed over his desk. All around the untidy study, candles sputtered in pools of their own wax, and several blankets were piled on the lounging chair under the window. Stale dust and lingering smoke incensed the entire room, and haphazard piles of papers cluttered the desktop. Crates stood several deep along the far wall, and a half-eaten tray of food and drink littered the table at the chamber's center.

Lucas stepped in farther and paused to straighten an empty glass that had been set on its side. "Did you spend all night in here?"

Wainbridge waved a dismissive hand and responded with a lopsided smile. "Ah, you know how these things go. No one sleeps at a house party."

Lucas would not argue.

"What's that you've brought with you?" Wainbridge gestured to the packet in Lucas's hand.

Lucas held up the portfolio. "Transaction records. My father and your uncle had a handful of dealings well over a decade ago. Since I was unsure about what sort of records Milton had maintained, I brought the little information I had, just in case."

He handed the bound package to Wainbridge, who opened it and flipped through a few pages. "This is a preposterous amount of money. And spent on what? Pots and statues and the sort?"

The shock in the man's expression was a clue about his host. Clearly Wainbridge did not come from money himself. Most of the wealthy elite would not bat an eye at such figures.

Wainbridge massaged his forehead before he handed the packet back. "All I know is that I want to sell all of it. Quickly."

Lucas assessed the chaotic room, already taking a mental inventory of the paintings. The ceramics. The furniture. "Have you spoken with any other brokers?"

"Most certainly. I've been contacted by several. One all the way from Spain, if you can believe it. Come with me. I want to show you something."

Lucas followed Wainbridge as he opened a wide paneled door on the far wall to a connecting chamber.

"This is the library." Wainbridge swept his arm dramatically about the space.

Lucas's gaze darted from the cluttered shelves on the far wall, to the high corner shelves of chinoiserie, to a full-size marble statue in the room's center. Busts, vases, paintings, figurines, and books filled every corner and empty space.

"What do I even do with all of this?" Wainbridge lamented, kicking at a crate with the toe of his boot.

Lucas inhaled. Deeply. The history and culture surrounding him engaged every corner of his mind. Whereas Wainbridge saw a mess, Lucas saw opportunity. It energized him.

He dragged his finger through the dust atop a small wooden box. "I know this all seems like worthless fodder to you, but some people would sell their soul for the opportunity to walk through here."

"And you know those people?" Wainbridge scoffed as he lifted a figurine, glanced at it, then dropped it back on the table. "I can't imagine anyone paying a farthing for this, let alone a sum of significance."

"As I alluded when we met at Brooks's, there are two ways to proceed. The fastest method does not guarantee the largest income, but it would get you money quickly. The second method could take months, even years, but it would yield the highest income."

Wainbridge folded his arms across his chest. "I'm listening."

"For the most profitable option, we'd begin by cataloging everything you want to sell. I'd record it, inspect it, research it as necessary, and then assign a value to it. I'd then notify my colleagues and clients that the items are available, and then I'd solicit responses and sell each item to the highest bidder. But like I said, it could take months, even years, seeing that many of those clients reside overseas. My fee would be based on a percentage of the final sale price."

"And the faster option?"

"The faster option would be that my business would purchase items. They then become my inventory to dispose of as I see fit. I could either turn a larger profit with them or suffer a loss. I would assume all the risk, and that is the reason for the lower purchase price. This is how Tate is involved with my business. He helps assume the financial risk but also accepts the financial rewards on the sales of the pieces."

"I see," Wainbridge muttered.

"Most collectors keep their items cataloged. I've no doubt that your uncle left behind a ledger, or ledgers, detailing the items he owned."

"That's just the thing. There's very little. I'm sure if he had them, they're somewhere in here, but I've scoured this study and the storage rooms. I've found nothing."

"Is Mrs. Milton aware of its location? Or one of the servants?"

"I asked her about it once, and she flew into a rage. The servants are all new and know nothing."

The magnitude of the task before him solidified in his mind. "Details can be determined later. We just need to get started. Today. I'll stay behind from hunting this morning."

Wainbridge exhaled, as if he'd been holding his breath for days. "One would assume such an inheritance would be a good thing. And it is. But so many strings are tied to it that I can barely see past them."

Lucas removed his coat and rolled up his sleeves. "Make an excuse for me. I'm much more use here anyway than on the hunt. You'd be surprised at what can be accomplished in a relatively short period of time. Leave it all with me."

Wainbridge finally cracked a smile of what could only be relief. "I'll tell the butler you're using the library and are not to be disturbed. I'd offer to allow one of the footmen to assist you, but I fear for confidentiality."

"Think nothing of it." Lucas grinned. "Believe it or not, this is a thrill for me."

"Very well. I'll stop in later to see how you're progressing."

Once Wainbridge left, Lucas moved to the curtains and pulled a dusty panel back, letting in a flood of gray morning light, which illuminated even more dust and cobwebs than he had first noticed.

It was something he saw often. One man's passion—a legacy—frozen in time. The accumulation of antique treasures had meant something to Mr. Milton during his lifetime. Perhaps it was an obsession. Perhaps it gave him a sense of purpose.

But now, what was it?

Lucas had seen some of the most incredible pieces in his lifetime—from Roman artifacts to Egyptian gold to Indian statues. Time and experience had taught him that every collection would, at some point, be sold and that items were merely objects that only meant something to those willing to pay for them. Because of this he could assess items clearly and without bias or envy. Even so, as he glanced around him, the sheer number of pieces that needed to be evaluated was overwhelming.

His thoughts turned, like they did so often, to his father, who would have relished this task and seen it as the pinnacle of his career. But he was not here, and it was up to Lucas to make sure he did his father proud.

Chapter 16

OLIVIA TURNED THE iron handle of the Blue Room's window and pushed the pane outward, then filled her lungs with the invigorating cool, clean air. Birdsong trilled, a cow lowed in the distance, and the breeze swayed the highest branches of the trees and rustled through the leaves.

In spite of the previous evening's turmoil, she'd slept well. Reinvigorated and rested, she clicked her small pocket watch open, noting the hour. She was due in Mrs. Milton's chamber in minutes. She quickly finished her morning preparations, opened the hidden door in her wall, and made her way through the series of smaller dressing rooms that connected the Blue Room to Mrs. Milton's chamber. Teague answered her knock and opened the door, revealing a chamber that made every other space within Cloverton's walls pale in comparison.

Gilded frames containing intricate sketches and paintings of every manner of flora and fauna adorned the painted sea-green walls, and rubber plants and massive ferns graced the space. A cylindrical Tunisian birdcage of wood and wire served as a home to a pair of songbirds, and a tall canopy bed of exotic teak with luxurious faint ochre brocade drapes anchored the chamber. Chest-high chinoiserie screens boasting pagodas, peacocks, and floral vignettes ornamented every corner, and the unexpected woody scent of agarwood incense perfumed the chamber.

"I'm pleased to see you ready for the day." Mrs. Milton's raspy voice drew her attention to a small breakfast table beneath a west-facing window. "The night was a long one. I feared you might sleep late."

"I don't believe in sleeping the day away." Olivia stooped to pet Louis, who'd jumped down from his mistress's lap and wagged his tail enthusiastically. "Besides, I am eager to get started."

Mrs. Milton stood from her breakfast table, shook the folds of her satin dressing gown, and crossed toward the marble mantelpiece. She lowered a rather large ceramic statue. "Do you know what this is?"

"Of course." Olivia accepted the outstretched piece and ran her fingers over the smooth celadon glaze. "It's a Chinese guarding lion. My father called them foo dogs. They protect against evil spirits and misfortune. But they usually appear in pairs—a male and a female. This one is male. You can tell because its paw is on a ball. The female lion always has her paw on a cub."

A rare smirk cracked Mrs. Milton's stern features, and she moved to the other side of the mantel and retrieved the female counterpart. "Impressive."

Without another word Mrs. Milton produced a key from a small box atop the mantelpiece and indicated for Olivia to follow her. She pushed up on a section of the paneled wall that matched the secret door in the Blue Room, inserted the key, and turned it, and the entire section of wall swung inward to reveal an extremely large alcove with two high windows at the chamber's end. "Go ahead then, Miss Brannon. Have a look."

Both sides of the alcove were lined with shelves displaying every manner of shell and stone, ranging in size from no larger than a walnut to a large pumpkin. Two intricately carved corner shelves displaying blue-and-white chinoiserie, from a ginger jar to a small dragon figurine, framed the two narrow south-facing windows. A lacquered table boasted a series of jade bowls and golden cups.

Olivia was used to collections of all sorts and was accustomed to being around valuable pieces, but she'd only ever seen them in the safety of a warehouse—never on display as they were intended to be enjoyed. To see them like this, shimmering in sunlight, gratified her.

"This is my China closet." Mrs. Milton's words rang with pride, and she straightened an Indian tapestry hanging on the wall just inside the door. "I suppose they've largely gone out of fashion now."

Olivia knew the term—a room or rooms in a lady's private chambers where one would display her beautiful collections. But she'd never actually seen one.

Mrs. Milton walked farther into the space, pausing to slightly adjust the angle of a jewel-encrusted chest atop a table in the chamber's center. "Everything in this room will need to be cataloged, of course."

Olivia nodded, desperately attempting to stay focused on Mrs. Milton's instructions, but a rare spider conch shell distracted her. Her fingers ached to touch its spikes, which had been dulled by the sea and time. "This is truly incredible, Mrs. Milton. I had no idea your collection was this extensive."

Mrs. Milton lifted Louis, who had joined them from the main bedchamber. "Each item holds one of my grandfather's stories. What I would have given to travel with him, or even to have been one of the sailors on his ships. To smell camelia and jasmine as they were meant to be enjoyed. To see the statues in the temples they adorned or even to feel the sand on a foreign shore. But as much as I love these items, I value autonomy more."

Many aspects of Mrs. Milton's character did not make sense to Olivia, but at that moment she felt an unmistakable kinship with her. Besides her own mother, Olivia had never encountered another woman with an affinity for the exotic, who longed for new places—to experience a world deemed suitable only for men.

Refocusing her thoughts, Olivia ran her finger over the lid of an Indian mother-of-pearl puzzle box. Not a trace of dust was visible. Not a piece seemed haphazardly placed. "I'm struck by how tidy and organized everything appears."

"You can thank Tabitha for that."

"The chambermaid?"

"Yes. She and Teague are the only two people I allow in here. I don't think any of the new staff are aware this chamber exists. I keep all my rooms locked when I'm away." Mrs. Milton motioned to the door. "Come, Teague will show you where the records are kept. You will join the other ladies this afternoon, and then we shall attend dinner tonight, but you should be able to at least familiarize yourself with the layout of things this morning."

Sensing the finality of her client's discourse, Olivia reluctantly left the China closet. She followed Teague to a massive mahogany armoire in another dressing room. Inside, receipts, bills of lading, transaction reports, lot sales, and journal entries were haphazardly filed. Even in its chaotic state, the armoire trunk containing it all was as much a treasure trove as the China closet itself. Each piece of paperwork was a piece to the puzzle that, once complete, would create a detailed account of exactly what Mrs. Milton owned.

How her father would have loved this process of discovery.

For the millionth time she wished he was with her.

This was what they had shared—this passion for the fantastic and captivating. And not only the pieces themselves but the stories behind them. It was a bittersweet sentiment. She wanted to travel, to see new things and meet new people, but it was a lonely goal. Laura wanted no part of her family's fascination, and the only other person she knew who shared her penchant was Russell.

The memory of their conversation the night before she quit London flared. He might share an antiquarian's knowledge, but not the passion. Was she destined to chase this dream alone? And if so, would it be worth it?

Chapter 17

ONCE OLIVIA STEPPED foot in the drawing room, there would be nowhere to hide. She might as well accept it.

The lighthearted chatter and dainty laughter flowed from the chamber in refined strains. The ladies sounded happy. Content.

She stifled a groan.

Olivia was used to interacting with men and, if necessary, making as little small talk as possible. The conversations that women would often engage in were, admittedly, not her forte. Her responsibilities left little time for female friendships. Even if she did have time, not many women understood her drive and passions. At least for the afternoon, Olivia needed to set all that to the side. She needed to be seen as an equal to these ladies—one way or the other.

She drew a fortifying breath, released it in a steady stream, and entered the drawing room.

All eyes turned to her. The beautiful Miss Haven, the genial Miss Stanley, and the effusive Miss Kline. Their respective chaperones were also present, and each lady held a piece of sewing or white-work embroidery. Miss Wainbridge was notably absent.

"Miss Brannon," Miss Haven exclaimed. "I'm so glad you have joined us at last."

"I do apologize that I'm late." Olivia sat primly in the indicated chair, feeling oddly out of place, just as she had when she attended the school for young ladies all those years ago.

"Is Mrs. Milton not joining you?" Miss Stanley lowered her embroidery hoop to her lap. "I was hoping to speak with her this afternoon. She seemed in quite an agitated state last night."

Keenly aware of the attention focused on her, Olivia straightened her posture. "She is quite well, no need for concern. She said she had a matter to attend to, but she would be here for tea soon."

Miss Kline, who was seated to Olivia's left, pivoted toward her, her almost-black eyes unnervingly direct. "You've come down at the most opportune time, for we've been discussing the Whitmores' ball."

"The Whitmores' ball?" Olivia echoed.

"Of course!" The volume of Miss Kline's nasal voice increased. "The ball we are to attend in two days' time! Don't tell me you've forgotten about it."

"Oh no." Olivia gave a little laugh to mask her mistake. "I've not forgotten about it."

"The Whitmores never fail to host the most exquisite events." The golden curls on each side of Miss Haven's face bounced with each syllable. "I'm sure it will rival any of those we attended in London this past Season."

Miss Kline lowered her sewing to a basket on the floor at her side. "I understand you're from London, Miss Brannon. What events did you attend this summer? Perhaps we saw you there."

She hesitated. She'd not lie, but neither would she divulge anything more than necessary. "I'm afraid I did not attend any balls this year, or really any events of significance. I've been much occupied with family obligations."

Miss Haven and Miss Kline exchanged a glance.

Miss Stanley, however, leaned forward. "While we were waiting for you to join us, we've come up with a surprise. We intend to produce a concert tonight for the gentlemen, but especially for Mr. Wainbridge, for his graciousness in inviting us all here. We've each already decided what music we will perform. You will, of course, participate with us. What musical skill will you contribute? Do you play the pianoforte? Harp?"

Olivia thought she'd be happy for a change of topic, but this development only intensified the anxiety gripping her.

Of course all of these women were likely accomplished musicians. They would expect her to be the same, and yet, on this topic, she could not even pretend to have knowledge. "You're kind to include me in your plans, Miss Kline. I do enjoy listening to others play, but I fear I'm not musical."

Miss Kline blinked. "You do not play? Anything?"

Olivia shook her head.

Miss Kline giggled incredulously. "Surely you sing at least!"

Olivia could almost laugh at the stunned silence that had descended upon the room. Was it really that difficult to believe?

She had no choice but to force confidence.

For it was true. They might have spent their lives chasing certain accomplishments, but so had Olivia. She was an expert in antiques and could rival any male in the business. And that was what she was here for.

Before she could respond to Miss Kline's question, commotion sounded in the corridor outside the drawing room. All attention shifted to the door, and Miss Wainbridge and Mrs. Milton entered with a newcomer: tall, dark, and extremely attractive.

Olivia thought Miss Wainbridge might burst with pride as she spoke.

"Ladies, a man who needs no introduction, I'm sure, but our esteemed guest has arrived. May I present Mr. Romano."

Olivia felt it as palpably as a gust of wind before a storm—a rush of excited energy surged through the chamber. Clearly the other ladies and chaperones knew details about Mr. Romano that she did not. She quickly assessed him: A sapphire ring glittered on his right hand, and his intricately tied cravat gleamed snowy white against his olive skin. Not a speck of dust or dirt marred his double-breasted sienna velvet tailcoat, and his black leather court shoes boasted a gleaming silver buckle.

"I recognize many of you." An entrancing Italian accent colored Mr. Romano's deep voice, and he bowed, dramatic and low. "A pleasure to see you again, ladies."

SARAH E. LADD

Miss Wainbridge continued, "You shall all have the opportunity to sit for him during the coming week, and he'll be offering instruction for those ladies who would like it."

As quickly as the man arrived, he excused himself, citing the need to get settled before dinner.

When all was quiet once again, Miss Kline clasped her hands before her. "What a thrill!"

Miss Haven fixed a pointed, uncomfortable stare on Olivia. "Surely you know of Mr. Romano, Miss Brannon. Even if you've not been in society much this Season, you've certainly seen his work."

Olivia recognized the veiled insinuation in Miss Haven's tone, and she hesitated to reveal yet another deficiency in her knowledge of social protocols. "I'm not familiar with Mr. Romano, no."

"How is it he has escaped your attention!" Shock creased Miss Stanley's smooth brow. "He is the most celebrated miniature artist, and he's been all the rage the past two Seasons."

Without giving Olivia the opportunity to respond, Miss Kline hurried ahead. "You do surprise me, Miss Brannon. Not musical, not familiar with Mr. Romano. You're a rare specimen indeed. But never you mind that now. You're in for quite a treat, I assure you. And to think my mother nearly forbade me from attending this party! Nothing against Mr. Wainbridge, of course, but he is still establishing his place in society. I shall write to my mother and inform her that Mr. Romano has joined us. It will ease her mind immeasurably."

Conversations raced on. Miss Kline turned to speak with her chaperone, and Miss Haven whispered with Miss Stanley. They were all aflutter with news of Mr. Romano's arrival and with plans for the concert tonight. Olivia participated in the conversation as much as she could, but the longer she was in the company of these ladies, the wider the gap in their refinement grew.

Perhaps there had been more truth to what her uncle and Russell had said than she'd given them credit for—she was nothing like these women, and she feared the differences were really about to make themselves known.

Chapter 18

NEVER HAD A conversation exhausted Olivia so.

As she and Mrs. Milton left the other ladies in the drawing room, her ears rang with the hidden questions and subtle slights that had been lobbed her way.

They'd intended to identify her social flaws. And they'd succeeded—to a point. Olivia felt judged. A little tricked. But if anything, the treatment made her more determined than ever to make this entire event a success.

Olivia turned to ascend the great staircase, but she was stopped by Mrs. Milton. "I've recently been informed that Mr. Avery did not attend the hunt today with the other men. He is up to something deceptive, I'm convinced."

Olivia frowned, concerned at Mrs. Milton's sudden change in demeanor. "I'm sure it was nothing. Perhaps after dinner we could—"

"No, no. I intend to deal with this once and for all. And you will accompany me."

Unsure of what awaited her, Olivia quickened her pace to keep up with Mrs. Milton as they trod along the broad corridor, past the great hall, past the dining room, and to Cloverton Hall's far end—a part of the house that Olivia had not yet seen. Mrs. Milton suddenly stopped in front of a paneled door, pivoted, and knocked.

"Enter."

The muffled response had barely been spoken before Mrs. Milton wrenched the door handle and thrust the door open. She stomped in, her arm still looped through Olivia's, leaving her no choice but to awkwardly follow into what could only be Mr. Wainbridge's study. Its state struck Olivia: It was chaotic and messy. Crates were piled up against the wall. Uneaten food sat atop the table.

Mr. Wainbridge jumped to his feet from behind a desk and reached for his discarded coat. "Aunt. Miss Brannon."

"I will not be put off, nor will I be deceived, George," Mrs. Milton blurted before releasing Olivia's arm and pushing her way farther into the chamber. "I know who Mr. Avery is, and about Avery & Sons. I demand to know why Mr. Avery is here."

Mr. Wainbridge only blinked in response. He looked from his aunt toward Olivia, as if she somehow held the explanation, and then back to his aunt. "Mr. Avery is a friend."

"Is he now?" Mrs. Milton drew closer, bold and brazen. "How dare you attempt to profit from my husband's death by selling off his antiquities collection. It's deplorable."

Mr. Wainbridge's expression twisted at the allegation. "I'm not exactly sure what you're accusing me of, but whatever your issue is, perhaps we should discuss it in private. Miss Brannon certainly does not want to be party to our conversation."

"No, no. Miss Brannon will stay." Mrs. Milton returned to Olivia's side. "I insist he leave immediately. Not a single item that belonged to my husband will be sold. Am I quite clear?"

Mr. Wainbridge donned his coat and stepped around the desk. "You've misread the situation. It's not my intention to dismantle what my uncle built. It is my intention, however, to see that the estate is productive and cared for. I'm doing what is necessary to secure a strong future."

"And you think throwing expensive parties and engaging extravagant entertainment helps matters?"

"I can only assume you are referring to this house party. And my answer is yes."

Mr. Wainbridge's amiable manner dissolved before her, and his dark brows lowered. He leaned forward and swept his arm out. "This entire event is a calculated investment, which you'd know if you'd but asked me about it. Cloverton's finances are in such a state that if I do not secure other forms of income, then the entire estate faces ruin. Not only that, but Isabella will require a dowry, and I've none for her. I fear for her future! Instead of offering condemnation, I would think that you of all people would understand the importance of prudence. I don't know how well you were acquainted with Cloverton's finances, but—"

"I'm very well aware," Mrs. Milton hurled back.

"Then you know that in order for Cloverton Hall to avoid fiscal ruin, things must change. It's not profitable, Aunt. It hasn't been in years. My uncle spent money on foolish things, without an eye toward securing the future."

Mrs. Milton lunged forward and slapped her palm across Mr. Wainbridge's face.

Olivia winced.

Mr. Wainbridge recoiled.

"How dare you speak of my husband in such a manner!" Mrs. Milton cried, her jowls shaking. "He was no fool."

He stared but did not retreat. He smoothed his hair, which had fallen forward in the slap, and sniffed. "I did not say he was a fool. I said the money was spent in a foolish manner, and that I will not apologize for. I will correct the financial situation of Cloverton Hall and its holdings, and you will not stop it, regardless of how many times you slap me."

Mrs. Milton's face flushed crimson and trembled with rage. "Will you then be the heir responsible for shaming the family's name? For bringing dishonor down on over half a century of prosperity and goodwill?"

He scoffed. "On the contrary, madam. I'll be the one to save it. You loved your husband and I've no doubt he was a kind man, but his decisions have had consequences. Yes, this house is grand, but what is that if the upkeep is unmanageable? It's on its way to ruin! Yes, I fully intend to sell what I can of the collection. And I hope against hope that someone sees value in it."

Refusing to concede, Mrs. Milton pointed her finger at him. "I will expose you for what you are."

"By doing so you would expose the truth of how your husband left this estate. Then what? I'd proceed with caution if I were you. I'm attempting to protect Uncle's reputation and going about this business as quietly as I can. If you cause a fuss, imagine what will be said! Tongues will not stop wagging with the gossip."

"Are you threatening me?"

"No, ma'am. You asked what my intentions were. And I have told you."

For several moments a painful silence reverberated around the room.

Then Mrs. Milton spun on her heel and stomped from the room, leaving Olivia with her host.

Reeling from the awkwardness of the encounter, she turned to Mr. Wainbridge.

He bowed but said nothing.

She curtsied and hurried to follow Mrs. Milton from the room at a distance, unsure of what to do or say.

If anything of what Mr. Wainbridge said was true, then he was truly in a difficult situation. Simultaneously, her view toward Mrs. Milton was shifting. She'd accompanied Mrs. Milton on this trip with the intention of looking over the woman's private collection, nothing more. Nothing should matter except the pieces she was evaluating. And yet, the cold manner in which the woman treated her nephew alarmed her.

It saddened her, but unfortunately heated discourse after a collector's death was common. As intriguing as any collection might be, they were really just items to be bought and sold. In this particular case, Olivia sensed Mrs. Milton was viewing these pieces as a way to keep her husband alive. To still feel him. Sense his presence. Mrs. Milton was grieving, and Olivia knew all too well that grieving did not often make sense.

Lucas remained still in the library. Should he intervene? He'd had no intention of eavesdropping, but it was impossible not to over-hear the argument between aunt and nephew.

When the shouting subsided, the footsteps retreated, and all was again silent, Lucas abandoned his position at the library's table and rapped his knuckles on the ajar door that separated the library from Wainbridge's study.

Wainbridge had returned from the hunt not a quarter of an hour prior. Mud had splattered his boots and buckskin hunting breeches, and his coat hung askew. His normal congenial expression had dark-ened, and he motioned for Lucas to enter. "We've been found out."

Lucas placed a stack of portfolios he'd been carrying on a table beneath the window. "So I heard."

"How that woman thinks she has any say over what I do with my property is beyond me." Wainbridge crossed the cluttered room to the sideboard, snatched up a decanter, and uncorked it. He poured two glasses, then lifted them. "Somehow she found out about you and what you do."

Lucas accepted the outstretched glass. He knew the most likely source of that information—a woman with eyes the color of topaz. In this moment he could expose the true nature of Miss Brannon's identity. But to what result? At the end of the day, based on what he'd overheard, Mrs. Milton was not interested in selling or dis-tributing the Cloverton collection.

"What a nightmare." Wainbridge, drink in hand, flopped into the chair behind his desk, propped his muddy boot up on the desktop, and took a swig of the amber liquid. "Why can't she see and understand that this must be done? If I do nothing, Cloverton Hall will be lost to debtors. Then what?"

The words resonated with Lucas. He knew far too well the fear that came with standing on the precipice of ruin. He sat in a wingback chair opposite the desk. "My opinion? She's mourning her loss and trying to hold on to the life she once knew. You're not the first man to attempt to sell parts of an inheritance and have family members resist."

Wainbridge shook his head and took another drink. "Would you believe that I never visited Cloverton Hall before I inherited it? I met my uncle once when I was twelve, and I'd never met my aunt. I was told that Cloverton was a massive estate, that it was fabulously wealthy, and that my aunt and uncle enjoyed a great deal of power and influence. Their influence has proven to be true, but other than that, nothing is as I expected."

Lucas leaned forward in the chair, rested his elbows on his knees, and held his glass in both hands before him, gauging when and how to respond. It was another thing his father had told him: *"Trust is built by listening, not speaking."*

"And then," continued Wainbridge, "imagine my surprise to learn the stipulation that my aunt be allowed to live out her days in this house! There is no escape from her! Taking a house in London was my hope of evading it, but now funds for such an escape are gone. And she's so angry that there is no telling how she'll behave."

Wainbridge jumped from his seat and began to pace. "And while we're on the subject, who is this Miss Brannon? No one knows anything about her, but she seems to be my aunt's most trusted companion these days. Why on earth would she bring the lady if she meant to confront me in the manner in which she did? To humiliate me? To threaten me?"

Lucas waited until the room was again silent, and then he kept his tone soft and steady. "Let's consider it rationally. Mrs. Milton would not risk shedding negative light on her husband's memory by saying a single word of this to the guests. I suspect she knows this must be done—she just doesn't like it. And as for Miss Brannon, I confess I don't understand that either, except she might feel outnumbered, or as if she needs a witness to be heard."

"You're right." Wainbridge moved to the window, stared outside for several seconds, then turned to the sideboard between the two windows. He picked up a Chinese *huluping* blue-and-white vase that was sitting atop the teak inlay. He held up the piece as if to study it and then shook his head. "All of this commotion over silly things. It's not even that attractive. And what purpose does it serve?"

Lucas stood and reached for the vase. "You might not care for it, but if you let me do my job, I will find someone who thinks the opposite."

Wainbridge scoffed and handed the item over. "Here, take it."

Lucas took it, fully knowing what to expect from the piece— the weight. The texture. The general feel of it. But when the porcelain hit his hands, he stiffened.

Something about it was not right.

It was too light. The texture was slightly grainy when it should have been smooth like glass.

Lucas chuckled to mask his concern about the item, and he glanced at the other porcelain pieces on the tiered corner shelf. "Tomorrow I'll spend more time in here. I think there may be more value here than in the library."

Wainbridge turned back to the window. "Be my guest. Tomorrow there's to be a picnic, though. The painter's arrived, and if the weather's in our favor, the ladies will spend the day painting on the lawn, and the men can watch or play lawn games or the sort. You should probably make an appearance so no one else begins to wonder where you get to during the daytime hours."

Lucas looked down at the peculiar vase in his hand, smoothed his hand over the cobalt-hued design, and then placed it back on the sideboard. "Come on. It's getting late. I need to get this dust off me before dinner, and you"—he motioned to the mud splattered on Wainbridge's breeches—"might want to deal with that if you are to convince any of the ladies that you are a worthy suitor."

Wainbridge cracked a smile. "It does not suit?"

"No. And be quick about it. If we're late, Tate will rob us of all the port, and then where will we be?"

The men exited the study, but as Lucas did, he cast one last look at the porcelain he had just held. It looked authentic from a distance, but the feel of it told another story.

Chapter 19

THE DUMBFOUNDED SHOCK in Mr. Wainbridge's expression.

The heated rage in Mrs. Milton's tone.

Olivia could not help but recount the scene she'd just witnessed. She should have listened to her uncle. She should have listened to Russell. She should have listened to anyone who told her that coming to Cloverton Hall might not be fruitful. Yet she'd forged ahead, stubbornly, obstinately, and now she was in a horrifically awkward situation.

How had she not considered the situation more earnestly before agreeing to this arrangement?

She'd been so eager to advance her own skills and situation that she did not allow herself any time to think of the possible drawbacks of accepting such an offer. It seemed the reasons to regret her decision were multiplying, and so far, witnessing Mrs. Milton's berating of Mr. Wainbridge was the worst offense. Never had she seen a woman slap another person.

It was behavior she could not tolerate—regardless of the reason.

"You're awf'lly quiet this afternoon," Tabitha chirped as she dressed Olivia's hair for dinner. The maid's cheerful nature was a balm to an atmosphere that otherwise seemed quite fraught. "I 'ope you're not fallin' ill."

"I'm quite well." Olivia smiled. "Merely lost in thought, I suppose."

Tabitha's normally buoyant expression sobered as she slowed. "I 'eard about what 'appened in Mr. Wainbridge's study. I 'eard you saw the whole thing."

"You did?"

"Teague told me o' it. Says Mrs. Milton's a'side 'erself an' fears she'll be unwell."

Relieved to be able to share her thoughts on the matter, Olivia handed Tabitha a ribbon to be woven into her hair. "I don't understand it. She's so angry. It's one thing to attempt to make a point. It's another to slap a man because he does not agree with you."

Tabitha swiped her frizzy ginger hair from her brow and accepted the ivory ribbon. "Mrs. Milton isn't a bad sort; she's just sad. All t' things they worked so hard t' accumulate will be scattered. It sounds silly t' most I'd reckon, but it's important t' her."

Olivia studied the young woman as she adorned Olivia's hair. She was a slender slip of a girl—petite and slight. Freckles dotted the bridge of her aquiline nose. Her sparse eyebrows matched the tone of her tresses and contrasted against her milky complexion. The bond between servant and mistress here appeared very strong. Tabitha might be in a situation where she was loyal without question. Or perhaps there was a reason for that loyalty. "You seem quite protective of her."

"Mrs. Milton's been good t' me." Tabitha lifted her thin shoulder in a shrug. "I 'ate t' think that Mr. Wainbridge might be takin' advantage o' 'er."

Olivia winced at the choice of words. "What do you mean, taking advantage of her?"

"People are not always as they seem, 'tis all." Tabitha smoothed her finger across the ribbon, straightened it, and then crossed the room to the wardrobe, signaling an end to the topic.

Unwilling to let go of the opportunity to learn more about Mrs. Milton, Olivia forged ahead. "How long have you been at Cloverton Hall, Tabitha?"

"Me whole life, I s'pose." She returned from the wardrobe with a gown of blush netted silk gauze folded over her arm. "Me mother was Mrs. Milton's chambermaid a'fore me, and I used to 'elp me mother in Mrs. Milton's chamber as a child."

Olivia had no idea the relationship ran so deep. "She must trust you very much. She said that you and Teague were the only ones she allowed in her chamber."

"'Tis true. Even with Louis she's suspicious. I'm t' only one permitted t' see t' his care and feeding, almost like a governess. For a dog! None of t' footmen are allowed near 'im."

"But why?" Olivia stood and stooped to allow Tabitha to slip the gown over her head. "There has to be a source of her suspicion."

"If ye ask me, she's afeared of what'll happen when she's not in authority. Mrs. Milton 'as experienced betrayal. She trusts no one. To make it worse, now that Mr. Wainbridge is master o' Cloverton Hall, she's had little more freedom than Teague or me.

I s'pose all t' money in t' world does not guarantee a life free from sorrow."

The words resonated in the still, silent room, challenging Olivia. She herself knew what it was like to want freedom and autonomy. To starve for it and chase it.

The door separating her chamber from Mrs. Milton's chamber opened, and Mrs. Milton swept in, as elegant as ever, in a brocade gown of shimmering deep aubergine that hugged her ample figure. Amethysts shimmered from a gold chain about her neck.

The polished woman's presence filled Olivia with dread. How could she pretend to be at ease after the exchange she'd just witnessed? Even so, Mrs. Milton's tone was unaffected, as if nothing had transpired. "I've arranged for you to be seated next to Mr. Avery at dinner. I want you to find out from him why he's here."

"Mr. Wainbridge told us why he's here," Olivia argued, pivoting to allow Tabitha to secure the small ties at the back of her neck.

"No, no. I want to know specifically what pieces he is interested in. Is it the chinoiserie? The statues? I must know."

"I can't do that, Mrs. Milton."

"Don't be ridiculous. Of course you can."

Olivia adjusted the lacy fabric on her crossover bodice and turned to fully face the woman. "If Mr. Avery is working with Mr. Wainbridge as a client, I know for a fact that he'd never discuss the details of such with anyone. Don't forget, he knows my family and their business. I think the more distance I can keep from him, the better."

"Oh, poppycock." She marched toward Olivia and, without a word, retied the ribbon at the high waist of Olivia's gown. "I will know what it is he is after."

Retreating from the physical contact, Olivia sharpened her tone. "I am not comfortable asking that. It would not be appropriate."

Mrs. Milton turned a hard eye on her. "You don't think it would be *appropriate?*"

"No. I'm not the person to inquire about such a thing."

"I think you are. You know him."

"I know *of* him, which is a different matter altogether. Mrs. Milton, you have engaged my services to evaluate a collection, but I—"

"I engaged your services, yes. And I have provided you with clothing and invited you to a party. All of this was done out of respect for your father. Do not fool yourself into thinking that you had anything to do with it."

The words shocked her. And stung.

"If you do not wish to assist me, then you are free to leave anytime you choose. But if you do, then I will definitely not partner with Brannon Antiquities to sell my pieces. It might behoove you to rethink what you consider *appropriate.*" Mrs. Milton spun on her heel and left the Blue Room.

Olivia clenched her jaw in the wake of what had been said.

It was becoming too much—all of this.

She loathed being told who to talk to and which gown to wear. What was more, she despised that the woman was threatening to take this job away from her.

Never had she expected such complicated emotions and odd encounters, but she would not compromise herself. She owed Mrs. Milton no loyalty other than to give an honest assessment of her collection. Other than that, Olivia was still mistress of her own thoughts and actions, her reservations and instincts.

And she suspected they were all about to be tested.

Olivia, now alone, paced the Blue Room. She'd be expected in the drawing room to mingle before dinner, but she had to gain control of her emotions.

The day—and all of its events—had confused her, infuriated her, frustrated her. And now she was about to be seated next to Mr. Avery for the duration of an entire dinner—the very man whose family had caused her own pain. And then, following dinner, she'd be the only lady without a musical piece to add to the concert.

Olivia stopped pacing, drew a deep breath, and glanced to her left at her reflection in a large cheval mirror in the corner.

Every so often, if she looked hard enough, she could see glimpses of her mother in her likeness. She saw it in her petite frame and her dimpled cheek, but the similarities went beyond the physical. Olivia's memory of her mother was always bitter-sweet. She could vividly recall her adoration for her mother and the way she made Olivia feel deeply cherished. She'd always en-couraged Olivia to follow her interests, even though they might not match society's expectations.

Her mother would be proud of her, she knew—proud of her for persisting and remaining steadfast in her pursuits.

Olivia lifted her chin. She was proud of who she was and how hard she had worked to develop her talents too. There was absolutely no reason for her to feel shy or nervous about whatever she would face this evening.

A knock interrupted her thoughts, and the door opened. Miss Wainbridge entered, as lovely as ever in a gown of Pomona green luster with a gauzy overlay of white netting. Her shiny tresses were piled high atop her head, and incandescent jewels glittered on her neck and ears. But her face grew somber, and she reached out her hands toward Olivia.

"Oh, my dear, George told me what happened." Miss Wainbridge's eyes narrowed. "How Mrs. Milton argued with him in your presence. The idea!"

It was a wonder that she already knew of the incident. "It's all right."

"No, it is not. It's intolerable! How difficult it must have been for you." Miss Wainbridge lowered her voice. "He also shared that you might be privy to some personal facts about him and the nature of the estate."

Olivia lowered her eyes. It was true. She was now aware of far more details about the Wainbridges' situation than she wanted to know.

Miss Wainbridge's words rushed out. "Such news could be devastating to my brother's goals. You're a good and kind person, I know. But if the others were to become aware of his situation, I fear—"

"I will put your mind at ease, Miss Wainbridge." Olivia softened her expression and patted Miss Wainbridge's hand. "I've no intention of sharing anything I've heard. 'Tis not why I'm here."

Olivia snapped her mouth shut when she realized what she'd said.

Confusion flashed on Miss Wainbridge's features. "What do you mean, it's not why you're here?"

Olivia faltered, chiding herself for not being more careful with her words. "I'm here as a guest, as a companion, to Mrs. Milton. Nothing more."

Miss Wainbridge tilted her head to the side. "Oftentimes people attend these gatherings intent upon finding a match. I can't help but wonder, has my aunt invited you here to further your prospects? Please do not be offended. That is the reason most of the women are here, me included. I am not a romantic, Miss Brannon. I cannot afford to be. My brother will provide for me the best he can, but you're aware of his finances. No, I must secure myself a husband with the means to support me. That is why my brother is hosting this party. For me, and for him."

Miss Wainbridge's words were clever—bringing her in, including her, stating her thoughts in such a way that left little room to refute them.

If Olivia was prudent, she'd do as Miss Wainbridge suggested and latch on to a wealthy young man. But that was not her goal. "I am not in search of a husband."

"You jest." Interest flashed in Miss Wainbridge's eyes. "Do you already have an understanding with someone?"

"No, nothing like that. But as with you, my situation is complicated."

"Well, I hope soon you'll feel comfortable to share your story with me, for I should very much like for us to be friends."

In that moment Olivia longed for just that—a companion, someone like her sister, to confide in.

Surely no harm would come from establishing a friendship with Miss Wainbridge. She truly did enjoy Miss Wainbridge's company. But then again, Olivia was not naive. Was Miss Wainbridge genuine, as she appeared, or was she attempting to secure Olivia's discretion? It was all disconcerting, and at the moment, she was tired. Worn. And she needed a gracious companion if for no other reason than to have someone to speak with when the evening's events became overwhelming. "I should like that too."

A smile brightened Miss Wainbridge's face. "Good! Then you must start by calling me Isabella. And with your permission, I shall call you Olivia."

They exited her chamber together, arms linked, and descended the great staircase to the drawing room, where the guests would gather before dinner. Already, voices and laughter echoed from the space, and despite the frustrations from earlier today and the obstacles before her, Olivia could not keep the anticipation from building.

In an attempt to strengthen their emerging amity, Olivia leaned toward Isabella. "You mentioned you were in search of a husband. Has anyone in particular struck your fancy?"

Isabella clicked her tongue. "My brother claimed he invited Captain Whitaker as a beau for me, but I refuse to be forced into any agreement, regardless of his wealth. But in truth, I think my brother would be content to simply see me settled with any of the men here. Except for perhaps Mr. Avery. He is, after all, in trade."

Olivia jerked. What would Isabella think if she knew the truth about *her*? "In trade? And that is a negative attribute?"

"Oh my dear, you are delightful!" Isabella threw her head back in a tinkling laugh. She then sobered. "But if we are to be friends, as I dearly hope we will be, I must come forth and tell you the rumor I heard about you."

"About me?"

Isabella lowered her voice. "One of the ladies believes Aunt invited you as a possible match for George."

Shocked, Olivia stopped and dropped her hand. "I assure you, that could not be further from the truth."

"That's why it was surprising to me to hear she'd argue with him in front of you. And I could understand if you were inclined to consider him; it's just that some of the other ladies fancy him. So if it is not true, I urge you to keep your distance. Trust me, there are some ladies here you might not want to cross."

Chapter 20

"EXCEPT FOR PERHAPS Mr. Avery. He is, after all, in trade."

Olivia could not shake Isabella's assessment of Lucas Avery. It was too amusing. Now, she spotted him instantly as she entered the drawing room to wait to be called for dinner.

Regardless of the difficult history that had occurred between their families, Olivia was again struck by his appearance. How different it was from the gangly youth she remembered. His dark hair, much darker now than it had been in his youth, curled away from his face, and side whiskers framed high cheekbones. His eyes reminded her of the color of sea glass, and the fact that they were fringed with dark lashes made them all the more striking. His smile, not to mention his manner, was genuine and affable, and he appeared completely at ease with the elite company. Miss Wainbridge might have begrudged the fact that he was in trade, but he spoke as equals with the gentlemen who most likely did not have to earn a wage.

Even so, she had been avoiding him, and probably would have continued to do so were it not for Mrs. Milton's impossible request. As indicated, Olivia was seated next to Mr. Avery at dinner. They exchanged cordial initial greetings as the guests were taking their seats, but he immediately engaged in conversation with Miss Kline, who was seated on his other side. The dinner, like the others, was *service à la française*, and for the first course the servants brought a variety of soups and fish and placed them around the table.

As was customary, the guests served themselves and each other whatever dishes were close, and it was at this point that Mr. Avery turned his attention to her. "Would you care for the artichoke soup?"

She accepted, and he lifted the silver ladle and filled her soup bowl before filling his own.

As she took her first bite of the creamy soup, she was aware that she had his attention, and she attempted to formulate a way to broach the topic of the Cloverton collection.

But he spoke first. "Miss Kline tells me that the ladies are quite pleased with the arrival of our guest."

Olivia followed his gaze toward Mr. Romano, who was seated next to Miss Haven at the table's end. He said something she could not quite make out, but Miss Haven, Miss Stanley, and a chaperone tittered in response.

Mr. Avery shook his head. "He definitely seems to charm the ladies. The gentlemen, perhaps not so much. But you know men. We do not care much for competition, and I'm sure not many can compete with a man so adept at capturing the female spirit on canvas."

"Oh, I don't know." She lowered her spoon and reached for her glass of water. "There are other ways to charm a lady, to be sure."

He laughed, took a drink of the brandy in front of him, and returned his glass to the table. "You're right, of course, but therein lies the quandary. Most men have no clue of what those other ways are."

Normally, Olivia would have surmised that his tone bordered on flirtation, but she knew better, for she knew men like him—men whose livelihoods depended upon making people feel comfortable and important. Her own father and uncle excelled at it. It was a hallmark of their profession. Mr. Avery was skilled in the art as well, for she'd observed his interactions with the other ladies. She didn't believe for a moment that he didn't know how to use his masculine appeal.

Olivia adjusted the napkin on her lap, and as she did so, she spied Mrs. Milton from the corner of her eye. The sooner she had this behind her, the better she would feel. She pivoted to face Mr. Avery more fully. "I am glad we have been seated next to each other, for I've been hoping to speak with you."

"What about?"

"Well, your business."

"Shh!" He lowered his voice and leaned closer, a playful twinkle glinting in his expression. "It's incredibly vulgar to work for a living."

Olivia could not help but release a little laugh. "I'm aware. Miss Wainbridge reminded me of that just today."

"Did she?" He leaned back in his chair. "Does she know of your family's legacy?"

Olivia shook her head. "No. No one does, except for you and Mrs. Milton. And I must thank you for keeping your knowledge of my family to yourself. Mrs. Milton is adamant that no one should know of it."

He winced. "Why on earth would she make such a request?"

"As you said, being in trade is nothing short of vulgar."

He indulged in a long laugh. "Is this your first time visiting Cloverton Hall?"

"Yes, it is. Why?"

He glanced over his shoulder to make sure no one was listening and then spoke to her in a low tone. "If I'm not mistaken, your father enjoyed a long and fruitful relationship with Mr. Milton. I thought perhaps you'd been here before, with him."

"My father did visit here, a couple of times actually, but that was many years ago."

"I wonder that you did not join him. If I recall accurately, you were always at your father's side."

"At the time I would have been far too young to be of significant help."

"Don't be so modest, Miss Brannon. I've heard that you're integral to the business."

Uncomfortable with the praise, she lowered her spoon.

"Oh, come now. Do not seem so shocked! I'd hardly be a man of my business if I didn't know such things about my competition."

She stiffened. Did he really think of her as competition?

His posture slackened and his voice lowered even further. "Russell Crane told me you had quite an eye for such things. He said that you have a hand in most of the transactions that go through your warehouse."

She frowned. "You know Mr. Crane?"

"Of course I do. I've seen him at the docks often meeting the ships as they come in."

There was no reason why Russell should have confided to her that he had spoken with Mr. Avery, but it still made her feel as if she was on the outside of things.

She had to regain control of this conversation. If she was going to say what needed to be said, she needed to do it now. "I have a confession, Mr. Avery."

Something had changed in Miss Brannon's countenance.

Was it something he'd said?

Lucas had done his best to maintain a congenial conversation, given the terse history between their families, and until this moment, her actions had exuded confidence: her eye contact, her posture, the steady, unaffected tone of her voice.

He repeated her intriguing word. "A confession?"

Her somber demeanor remained steadfast. "Mrs. Milton knows of your profession."

"That's not much of a confession, Miss Brannon," he teased, attempting to ease her concern. "Anyone may know it."

"There's more." Her voice lowered until it was barely audible over the humming conversations and clinking silver. "She's convinced you're here to exploit her husband's collection."

Lucas held her gaze, longer than he probably should, before responding. "I see."

"And I was not supposed to be seated next to you tonight, but Mrs. Milton rearranged the entire dinner so that I might talk with you and learn which items you're interested in. Even now she is staring at me, no doubt wondering what details I am getting from you."

He cast a glance toward Mrs. Milton. Sure enough, the older woman's watchful eyes were cut in his dinner companion's direction.

Miss Brannon continued, "I do apologize if this makes things difficult or uncomfortable for you."

He resisted a smile. When every other woman here was determined to pull at his heartstrings and toy with his emotions, her forthright deportment was refreshing.

He shifted in the seat. He still didn't know exactly why she was here at Cloverton Hall, but he surmised that regardless of the reason, she had her own difficulties to contend with. The other guests believed her to be Mrs. Milton's friend, but Miss Brannon's words implied otherwise.

"Well then, I have a confession of my own," he countered. "Mr. Milton's library is connected to Mr. Wainbridge's study. I was in there this afternoon and heard everything Mrs. Milton said."

Miss Brannon jerked. "And you didn't make yourself known? Is that not unethical?"

"Unethical? Come now, Miss Brannon. We are in the same business. It's our responsibility to broker sales and to ensure the legality of such transactions. It's *not* our place to question what is sold, when, or why. I'd be more than happy to entertain any questions Mrs. Milton might have, but at the day's end, Mr. Wainbridge is the rightful owner of the estate, and as such, he's who I must answer to."

"I don't disagree. And I told Mrs. Milton as much."

"You know as well as I do that there is no place for emotion in these dealings."

"On that point I must differ." A sudden flush colored her high cheekbones, and an impassioned sharpness flashed over her delicate features. "Emotion is the entire reason we do what we do, be it love, pride, affection, fear, or any number of motivations for why people amass things. What are any of us without emotion? Mrs. Milton is grieving, and her husband's collection is her last link to him. Once those items are gone, he will be lost to her all over again."

He sobered. "She told you this?"

"Not verbatim. But I can only assume."

When her words fell silent, he offered a smile to alleviate the topic's gravity. "I hope this does not sound presumptuous, but I must say I find your friendship with Mrs. Milton quite unusual. It does not seem as if you two would have much in common."

"Friendships come in many forms, Mr. Avery," she refuted. "She's known my family a very long time. And you? Are you friends with Mr. Wainbridge?"

Her masterful ability to turn the tide of a conversation impressed him. "Come now, Miss Brannon. There's no need for pretense. You may know I'm here on business, but no one else needs to know that. It would ruin the fun."

Her chest rose with a sigh, and her ardent aspect softened. "Well, if you'll not divulge what specific pieces you are considering, I cannot force it from you. But I can say that I envy you. You're spending time with the famed Cloverton collection—one of the greatest collections in all of England."

Lucas decided in that moment that he liked Miss Olivia Brannon. He liked her passion and her directness. He supposed he always had on some level. When she was a child, he'd been amused at her determination. As a young adult, he'd admired her perseverance. Even though she did little to hide her distaste of his family, he found her transparency refreshing. No, she was not as polished and cultured as the other women in attendance, but he suspected there was a depth to her—a sincerity—that intrigued him all the more.

The more he talked with her, the more he wanted to know about her. But he had to be careful. Just as with anything else, he would have to build trust before she'd let her guard down around him.

And he wanted her to trust him.

He supposed it would be easier for him to overlook the precarious past of their families than it would be for her. After all, it had been his father who wronged hers—not the other way around.

Under normal circumstances he would never presume to speak to a woman about his business. For not only would she not be interested, but it would be considered impolite. But Miss Brannon was different. "Have you seen the Cavesee Vase yet?"

"The Cavesee Vase." A soft smile curved her full lips, as if a memory had just been recalled. "I wondered if that might be one of the pieces you're eyeing. But to answer your question, no, I've not. Have you?"

"No, but I think it's in the gallery, in the room directly above us, where tonight's concert is to be held. Speaking of the Cavesee Vase, do you recall that day at the auction house, all those years ago?"

"How could I not? My father was so proud that day."

"And I seem to recall you being quite enthused at the prospect of seeing a tiger."

Her heart-shaped face flushed crimson. "I was a child."

"What were you? Fourteen? Fifteen? Ah, doesn't matter," he bantered. "And did you ever see your tiger?"

"I did not, but I did see the Cavesee Vase, which was the true spectacle. And no one could question Mr. Milton's tastes. Just looking around this chamber, I see a dozen pieces I'd love to examine."

"When I first saw you here, I assumed you were here to evaluate the Cloverton collection on your uncle's behalf," he admitted.

"No, no. You're quite mistaken." A small, playful grin tugged at her lips as she volleyed back a quip of her own. "Antiquities is a man's realm, as I've been told time and time again. Far too indelicate for a lady."

He laughed heartily at the subtle sarcasm in her tone. He could only imagine the sort of prejudice she'd encountered. "Well stated, Miss Brannon."

"In all seriousness, though, I'll put your mind at ease. I will not be evaluating Mr. Wainbridge's property. I'm a guest of Mrs. Milton, that's all."

A sparkle, which had been absent when they'd first sat down, now resided in Miss Brannon's eyes, and she reached for her wine with her long, slender fingers and took a sip.

He followed suit and lifted his glass, but he found looking away from her difficult. Like it or not, he was inexplicably drawn to her understated yet confident tenacity and the manner in which she challenged societal perceptions.

And he admired her for it.

Chapter 21

THE CAVESEE VASE.

If Mr. Avery was right, it would be through the gallery doors.

The giant vase, with its bright white background and the vibrant cobalt dragon wrapping around the entire circumference, had been her father's prized acquisition.

After all these years, Olivia was about to see it once again.

Dinner was complete, and all the guests were gathering for the concert, but music was the furthest thing from her mind as she stepped into Cloverton's gallery.

Then she saw it.

Her heart fluttered, and all else faded—the drama, the discomfort, the awkwardness. This glimpse of one of the largest pieces of chinoiserie in the country was a reward for her perseverance. It was perched on a sturdy, broad shelf in the gallery's southeast corner, away from any possible disturbances.

Unable to resist, she looked over her shoulder to find Mr. Avery not far behind her. The corner of his mouth quirked into a grin. And he bowed his head slightly.

In that brief space of time, she felt more connected to him than she'd felt to anyone in a long time. The look that passed between them communicated esteem for something beyond themselves, of which no one else knew.

"Miss Brannon!"

Olivia jerked at her name—the abruptness of which shattered the bubble she shared with Mr. Avery.

She turned to see Mr. Fielding approaching. In spite of his churlish conversation at the previous dinner, the tall, thin man did cut a striking figure in his bister wool tailcoat. His dark auburn hair was slicked back into place, and his meticulous sideburns framed his high Romanesque nose. "What are you doing over here all alone?"

She looked back to the Cavesee Vase. "I was just admiring this vase. Isn't it remarkable?"

The apathetic simper on his long face faded as he joined her in viewing the porcelain. "Yes, it's very interesting. Interesting indeed. And are you fond of exotic things like this?"

"Exotic things?" she gibed, attempting to downplay her amusement at his assessment. "I am. Very fond."

He hesitated, as if unsure what to make of her interest. "Well, the old man seemed fond of it, didn't he? He gave it the place of honor. There, on a shelf."

Olivia was gratified to know secrets that few others knew. She might not be acquainted with as many social graces as the other ladies, but she did have an area of expertise. And she was proud of it. What would this man say if he knew exactly how much this piece was worth?

"I was dismayed that we weren't seated together at dinner tonight." Mr. Fielding turned away from the vase and faced the others in the room, who were gathering around the chairs and instruments that had been set up for their concert. "I'd quite hoped to continue our conversation from the previous night."

"Oh?"

"I find you intriguing, Miss Brannon."

His expression seemed genuine, but his words rang hollow, as if they'd been practiced or, even worse, spoken before in a similar situation.

Whatever his intention, she would play the part. "Intriguing? How kind. But I daresay you only feel that way because you do not know me. I am a novelty, am I not?"

He laughed, the pitch of which rang unnaturally high, and wagged his forefinger in the air. "There, you see? Your candor. I'm inexplicably enticed by it."

He was flirting with her. And it was . . . surprisingly flattering.

"Did you enjoy your day today?" he continued.

The day flashed before her with all of its variety and unexpected occurrences, both pleasant and incongruous, but she merely smiled. "I did. It was a very pleasant day, sir. I understood the men were out on a hunt today. Were you successful?"

"Well, let's just say that no pheasant met its fate by my hand," he japed, and then he leaned closer as if to whisper a secret. "I've heard the ladies have organized a concert tonight. And how will you be entertaining us? Wait, let me guess." He tilted his head to the side and assessed her. "The harp?"

Olivia looked back to the bank of windows on the north wall, under which the candlelit pianoforte and harp were positioned, and endeavored to appear unaffected. "I hate to disappoint, Mr. Fielding, but I'm not participating. I'm an eager spectator, that is all."

He reeled back in emphatic disagreement. "Oh, now that I cannot agree to."

"I'm afraid you must, sir," she said with a little shrug. "I play no instruments."

"No instruments!" He winced, as if struck. "You are a rare creature, Miss Brannon. Rare indeed. I knew it the moment we spoke at dinner last evening."

"Then that only proves my earlier point. I am interesting to you only because you do not know me," she teased, indulging in a moment of harmless flirtation. "If you knew me, really knew and understood me, I fear you'd find me quite dull."

"That I cannot believe. Well, if you are not to perform, which I think is surely a travesty, then you must be my guest for the evening. Sit with me."

She beamed up at him and placed her hand on his extended arm, and he led her to the chairs. All around her, preparations were underway. Night had fallen, and soft candlelight cast a golden hue on all the guests. The windows were open, allowing a delicious cool breeze to waft in.

The excitement and eagerness in the room hummed, from Miss Stanley ordering the room's arrangement to Miss Haven testing the pianoforte keys. The general beauty of such elegance—

women clad in gauzy summer gowns, men in tailored clothing—seemed like a dream, one from which she did not want to wake.

———————————

Lucas was increasingly distracted. Not by the music. Not even by the Cavesee Vase. But by Miss Brannon.

She was seated, straight and tall, on the opposite side of the gallery. Her chestnut hair was swept up atop her head, and soft curls framed her face—one of which escaped the pearl-encrusted comb and trailed down her slender back. Her willowy arms were bare, exposing fair skin of alabaster, and a Vinci necklace around her neck—a different one than the previous night—glittered and sparkled in the candlelight.

Fielding sat next to her, puffed up and proud, chattering and laughing.

It shouldn't, but the sight of the man entertaining her irritated him.

Tate must have noticed Lucas's divided attention, for he leaned over and lowered his voice. "See there. It appears Fielding is wasting no time in being friendly with the new arrival."

Lucas did not respond. He'd not yet told Tate about his connection with Miss Brannon or disclosed her tie to the industry. Lucas *should* inform Tate, as his primary investor, but to what end? He didn't need Tate getting nervous about a possible bidding war for items in the collection. At present, no evidence existed that she was in any way attempting to buy or bid on the Milton collection, and whatever the reason for her friendship with Mrs. Milton, it should not concern them.

"I'm not surprised he's the first man to attempt to get in her good graces." Tate folded his arms over his chest, amused. "He told us at the hunt he found her unequaled in beauty and charm."

Lucas scoffed. "Well then, I feel for Miss Brannon. Fielding's sense of self-importance is unparalleled."

Tate chuckled. "He's convinced she's an heiress, citing her unaffected manners and aloof presence. Why else would she be counted among Mrs. Milton's friends?"

"Perhaps."

"Or maybe she's here as a companion or a favor to a family member or something of the sort."

Tate's last statement seemed odd. "What makes you say that?"

"Think on it. Miss Haven told me that Miss Brannon will not perform in the concert tonight, for she has no musical talent. Have you ever been to a house party where a lady did not have a talent she was prepared to boast? I'd be willing to bet that every one of the other ladies came here with a practiced song—no, *songs*—ready to perform at the mere sniff of a suggestion. But to not even play? At all? It's like a soldier stepping onto the battlefield without any armor."

Once the flurry of activity settled, Miss Haven was the first to entertain at the pianoforte, followed by Miss Stanley on the harp. In turn each female guest entertained, and each man dutifully praised and applauded. At times it seemed almost a ridiculous parade of unwarranted accolades, but this was what a house party was all about. To see and be seen. To show off and compete for the attention of the opposite sex.

And yet the procession of accomplishments could not hold Lucas's attention.

A strange protectiveness stole over him. It was not his business who Miss Brannon chose to speak with, but the truth was that one time their families had been close—very close. Their mothers had been the closest of friends. Their fathers—partners.

At the concert's conclusion it was decided that Mr. Romano should waste no time in sharing his talents with the guests. Chairs were cleared and instruments were returned to their original locations to allow the artist space to work. Miss Haven was his first muse, and once the paint, canvas, and easel were set up, the guests gathered around to observe the master engage in his craft. During this time Mr. Fielding stayed close to Miss Brannon, but eventually Mrs. Milton called Miss Brannon to her side. When Mrs. Milton was drawn into conversation with some of the chaperones, Lucas saw his opportunity and seized it.

"Will you be next?" he asked as he approached where Miss Brannon was standing at the back of the group, watching the artist at work.

Amusement danced in her expression, and she tilted her head to the side as she watched Mr. Romano. "No. He is talented, though. See how fast he works?"

"I'm sure that is the secret to his popularity," quipped Lucas. "His efficiency."

The sound of her laugh warmed him.

"And you?" She tucked a wayward lock behind her ear. "Will he paint you?"

He hesitated. The question reemphasized that she was not familiar with the popular happenings in London society. Romano never painted men. But Lucas would not call her on it. "I do not think I'd inspire Mr. Romano. No, no. But I wanted to inquire about your opinion of the Cavesee Vase. Tell me, what do you think of it now that you've seen it again?"

"It's exquisite, is it not? Do you not see the shading there at the base? Just magnificent. I do wish we could get closer to it."

He could not help but smile at the pure expression of wonder. Most people saw such items as nothing more than money, and he supposed he'd become jaded. "I saw you discussing it with Fielding when we entered. What did our friend think of it?"

She adjusted the paisley shawl around her shoulders and crossed her arms at her waist. "I do not think Mr. Fielding shares our opinion."

"No?"

"Decidedly not, but while on the subject of other guests, I do have a question, if I may. Is Mr. Tate related to Vincent Tate?"

"Yes. William is Vincent Tate's oldest son and heir. He has two other children—both daughters."

"I thought so. And his father brokered many art deals through your father, correct?"

"You surprise me, Miss Brannon." He chuckled. "I must say, I'm enjoying having someone to talk with who truly understands antiquities."

"I grew up with it, Mr. Avery. As you did," she stated frankly. "Did either of us really have a choice? But I am grateful to my father. He taught me everything. For instance, I can tell you with almost certainty that the harp is a counterfeit."

He could not resist the leading statement. He glanced back to the instrument in question. "What?"

"See? The harp. I may not know how to play it, but I do know that it appears, on the surface, to be a Ventcelli harp. But look at the ornament on the crown and the adornments on the pillar. Notice the angle? And the gilding is not correct at all."

Her point came into focus. No, he'd not noticed, but she was absolutely correct. Mr. Milton had probably thought it priceless, and to the untrained eye it would appear so. No doubt every lady present believed it to be a genuine version, but once the offending aspects had been seen, they could not be unseen.

"I don't suppose you and your father brokered this deal?" he joked to mask his surprise.

"I was about to ask you the very same question," she retorted with a wit sharp enough to rival any in the room. "But to answer you, no. We did not. We would have advised against such a purchase, but someone obviously convinced him of the authenticity."

Lucas straightened as Mrs. Milton reentered the gallery and her fierce gaze fell on him. "Your friend has returned."

She looked up, and he might have been mistaken, but he thought he saw a flash of something. Was it sadness? Disappointment?

"Have you received enough information on me and my intentions to satisfy her?" He attempted to revive the repartee he'd so enjoyed.

But his inquiry fell flat.

"I fear that when it comes to Mr. Milton's collection, she'll not be satisfied until she hears not a piece is to be parted with, but like you said, there is not a thing that you or I can do to change that."

With her statement, he knew their incredibly enjoyable but grievously short conversation had come to an end, so he bowed. "I'll bid you good evening, then, Miss Brannon. Please keep track of the treasures you come across, and perhaps we can compare notes tomorrow."

He bowed toward Mrs. Milton as she approached Miss Brannon, then left her to return to Tate, who was speaking with Miss Stanley. Part of him felt as if he should have stayed and assisted her. It didn't seem fair that she might have to bear the brunt of the widow's frustration alone, but he suspected she was quite capable of holding her own.

Chapter 22

OLIVIA COULD FEEL Mrs. Milton's annoyance as surely as she could feel the breeze wafting in through the open garden doors. In fact, she'd sensed the taxing scrutiny all evening.

Mrs. Milton had been watching her. Watching Mr. Avery. And now, as she approached, every muscle in Olivia's back and neck tensed.

"I'm about to announce that it's time for the ladies to retire for the evening," Mrs. Milton said. "I saw you speaking with Mr. Avery. I trust you had a productive discussion."

"Yes, ma'am."

Mrs. Milton fussed with her glove. "And?"

Olivia had known this question was coming, and still she was not comfortable with it. To complicate matters, she felt a strange, unanticipated kinship with Mr. Avery that she couldn't explain.

"It was as I thought it would be," Olivia began. "He does intend to broker some items, but he would not share details."

"Well, we'll just see about that." A flush reddened Mrs. Milton's otherwise pale skin.

Olivia did not like to be included in the collective *we*, but she would not argue. Not now. Not here.

"Come, let's gather the ladies. It is late."

As Olivia had quickly learned, when the hostess of the house party wished to retire for the evening, all the ladies and chaperones followed suit, regardless of the hour or the activity at hand. The gentlemen were free to cavort and be entertained as late into the night as they desired, but the women were at the mercy of the hostess. As it was, last-minute plans for a picnic and a painting lesson the following day were discussed, and then the ladies quit the increasingly animated company of the men for the quiet of Cloverton's corridors.

The day, and the interactions that had occurred, had not only given Olivia a great deal to think about but also exhausted her. Both her eyes and her feet felt heavy as she turned to make her way to the great staircase, but Miss Haven surprised her by calling her name.

Olivia slowed her steps to match Miss Haven's, even as the other ladies hurried on ahead.

"I do regret we've not had a chance to really speak this evening." Miss Haven's normally refined, singsong voice was barely above a whisper.

Olivia was not entirely sure how to respond. It was the first time the woman with the brilliant blue eyes had shown any interest in speaking with her the entire evening.

"In fact, I've been longing to speak with you a bit more privately since we arrived," Miss Haven continued. "Miss Wainbridge has been absolutely singing your praises. I hope we can become friends."

"I should like that too."

And part of her meant it. What would it be like to be friends with these people, to be like one of them?

"You are joining us, aren't you?" Miss Haven's scent of jasmine was overwhelming as she tightened her arm around Olivia's. "At the picnic tomorrow?"

Olivia spied Mrs. Milton several paces ahead of them. "I believe so. It is Mrs. Milton's decision."

"Oh, Mrs. Milton would not miss this, not for anything! It is not often one has the opportunity to be instructed by such an esteemed artist as Mr. Romano. I know you do not play music, but do you enjoy painting, drawing, or anything of the like?"

How boring she must seem to these women, each of whom boasted a long list of skills and accomplishments. She forced out the words. "No, not really."

Miss Haven's demure laugh echoed from the paneled walls. "You are a strange creature, Miss Brannon. Fascinating, yes, but strange. No music? No art? How do you spend your days?"

When Olivia did not answer her question, Miss Haven continued. "I must say, I've overheard more than one gentleman speaking about you. Everyone is curious, including Mr. Wainbridge. I heard him say as much myself! But then again, I could not help but notice Mr. Avery and you spoke several times this evening. You seemed quite captivated at dinner and then again after the concert. Could a match be afoot?"

In a sudden burst of energy, Miss Haven stopped and whirled toward Olivia and grabbed her hand. "You should leave your matchmaking in my hands. I have a gift for sensing what personalities are compatible. I adore it."

Dread raced through her. "I don't think Mrs. Milton would—"

"Mrs. Milton is well respected, yes. Considering her shift in circumstances, though, is she really the best person to be leaving such matters with? No, la, no. Her time as a society matriarch has passed, I fear. Leave it with me. I shall make it my sole objective during our time here to identify which gentleman you are most suited to. And if nothing comes to fruition, then no harm is done, right?"

Without giving Olivia an opportunity to respond, Miss Haven squeezed her hand, kissed her cheek, spun on her heel, and was on her way down the corridor toward Cloverton's east end.

The other ladies and chaperones were dispersing, and before long, she and Mrs. Milton were once again alone as they headed down the corridor to their chambers. As they walked, the candlelight from the wall sconces flickered and danced, giving life and movement to the odd assortment of paintings lining the wall and the artifacts displayed on the narrow tables.

As the men's voices and laughter echoed from the distant gallery, Mrs. Milton muttered her dissatisfaction with Miss Stanley's coquettish behavior and her disapproval of Miss Kline's musical abilities.

But Olivia paid little attention. She was more focused on her own mounting grievances. Despite her frustrations with Mrs. Milton, Olivia disliked how the other guests spoke of their hostess. She understood their point, but regardless, Mrs. Milton was here to be the respected voice of reason—to oversee manners and virtue. It was a farce, really. These women and men seemingly had the world at their disposal, and yet they were cruel in their mocking of her. Neither party was without fault.

This was a world she had glimpsed only from the outside, and those glimpses had formed her opinions and prejudices. Now that she was seeing it from a different purview, her opinions were strengthening. Even seemingly kind people like Miss Wainbridge or even Mr. Avery—everyone here had an ulterior motive. If they were so discourteous to those with whom they were acquainted, she could only imagine how their treatment of her would change if they knew the truth about her background.

She had to keep her guard up, now more than ever.

Chapter 23

OLIVIA LIFTED A bronze *gu* vase and pivoted toward the light from the alcove's high window. Patina shaded the metal, but the phoenixes and leaves etched on the neck were spectacular. She smoothed her finger over the curved handle. Not a trace of dust or dirt. It was a fairly small piece as far as these vases usually went, but it was heavy—a good sign.

"Definitely seventeenth century," Olivia said to Tabitha, who was making notes for her. "Early Qing dynasty. Condition, excellent."

Mrs. Milton, who had joined her for the morning assessment, had not yet dressed for the day. She appeared quite frail in her deep carmine-hued wool dressing gown. A white cap covered her graying hair, and without her powders and rouge, her aged complexion looked wan. The last two eventful days had been rife with emotional displays and defensive posturing, but here, surrounded by her belongings and only Teague, Tabitha, and Olivia for company, she seemed quite at ease.

"My grandmother always put lilacs in that vase in the spring." Mrs. Milton gestured toward the vase as she sat with Louis in a tall wingback chair in the corner of the alcove. "My grandfather always protested, citing its rarity and value. But my grandmother insisted. She said there was no point in having such things about the house if they were not to be used."

Olivia lowered the vase to the table. "I think I'd have liked your grandmother. I often said something similar to my father when he'd pack things away or place them in storage."

"It doesn't matter now, though, does it? I only hope the next person who owns it finds the same beauty in it."

Olivia liked this side of Mrs. Milton—a side void of anger and defensiveness. She'd not even brought up Mr. Avery or her nephew once. Additionally, seeing Mrs. Milton engage with the pieces she so ardently adored incited sympathy.

A moral battled flared within Olivia. Who was right—Mrs. Milton and her desire to respect the past, or Mr. Wainbridge and his sights for the future?

Was one objective more viable than the other?

And how did one tell?

After another hour of matching documentation to the pieces and recording notes in the ledger, Mrs. Milton stood, adjusted Louis in her arms, and moved to the window that overlooked the back garden. "They're already gathering, as if none of them have a care in the world."

Olivia lifted her gaze through the window to the south garden, where liveried footmen were setting up easels in various sections and tables closer to the house. She recognized the opportunity to learn more. "Did you and Mr. Milton entertain often?"

A slow, wistful smile cracked Mrs. Milton's hard expression. "When we were young, we entertained lavishly! Our gatherings were the envy of every member of the ton. But that was long ago. Everything was so different then. So . . ." Her words faded off. "I can only imagine what my Francis would think of this. Of *that man* touching and assessing his personal things as if they were naught but twigs or debris. My only comfort is that he will never know what this has come to."

Olivia recognized the look of longing—of sadness—in Mrs. Milton's visage. Her father used to wear it as well, thinking of his wife. "I'm sure Mr. Milton would only want your happiness. I doubt he'd want you to agonize over something out of your control."

Mrs. Milton did not immediately respond, only stroked Louis's fur for several seconds. "I hope against hope that you never find yourself in such a situation, my dear. I'd gladly trade every single party I have ever attended to have my Francis back with me."

Olivia's gaze fell back to the items she was documenting. She understood wanting to honor someone's memory. After her father had died, her uncle had been merciless as he went over his business records. He'd been critical in his review, and Olivia had jumped to her father's defense. This seemed, in some way, quite similar.

After finishing the morning's work and dressing for the picnic, Olivia and Mrs. Milton made their way down from their chambers to the south lawn and gardens. White fluffy clouds, friendly and bright, floated across an azure sky.

She'd seen the two white tents from the alcove window in Mrs. Milton's chambers, and a team of servants carried trays and crates back and forth to the house. It seemed an extravagant endeavor to eat out on the lawn instead of inside, but the spectacle of it, no doubt, was the plan.

The gentlemen were already engaged in a boisterous game of cricket on the open lawn just past the formal garden, and the ladies were positioned at easels under the shade of the garden's majestic sprawling oaks. Everything here was so clean, so meticulous, so untouched by soot and smoke and the effect of too many people crammed closely as in London. She could see how the ladies would vie for the opportunity to make this their permanent home. Would surroundings like this ensure happiness?

"Mrs. Milton! Miss Brannon! Please, you must join us." Mr. Romano's heavily Italian-accented English echoed as the two women stepped from the stairs to the paved garden.

"No, no, Mr. Romano. I've not the patience for it." Mrs. Milton barely looked in his direction as they traversed the uneven brick pathway. "I've no desire for such pastimes. I will stay here in the shade, where it suits. Miss Brannon may accompany you, if she wishes."

"We shall miss your company, of course." He bowed dramatically before turning his attention to Olivia. "But I will be honored to escort Miss Brannon to her easel."

Mr. Romano made a great display of offering her his arm and of flashing a brilliant white smile at her, and she placed her arm gently on his.

Mr. Romano's eyes were very dark—the color of strong coffee—and yet they exuded brightness and warmth. His enthusiasm never faded. He seemed captivated by whomever he spoke with, and his confidence was palpable, as if he was aware of the effect his presence had on the fairer sex.

And now, that good-humored attention was focused entirely on her.

"We've not met before our time here." He escorted her down the paved path to the section of the garden that overlooked the pond, where swans and ducks moved over the fairly still water and among the cattails.

She sensed the eyes of the other ladies watching them. "No, sir, we have not."

"I've encountered the other ladies at various parties over the past two Seasons, but you've somehow eluded me. Where do you call home, Miss Brannon?"

"London, sir."

"Ah, London. It is a very great city. I spend much time there. It's truly a wonder that I have not seen you. At least we will remedy that now, for it is a shame that such beauty should not be captured on the canvas. I delight in a lovely new muse."

The unmistakably flirtatious quality of his tone, combined with the rolling timbre of his voice and the unique and lovely atmosphere, almost made her forget why she was at Cloverton Hall in the first place.

They stopped at an open easel at the edge of the hawthorn shrubs, and after she sat down, he opened the box at the base of the easel and arranged her supplies. "I do hope you'll allow me to paint your portrait while you are here at Cloverton."

She accepted the brush from him. "I've never had my portrait painted before."

"How is that possible?" He leaned closer to her, his scent unrecognizable but not unpleasant, and stared at her face.

She resisted the urge to withdraw at the scrutiny.

He nudged his finger against her chin, inching it upward slightly and to the right. No man had ever touched her face before.

"There. See?" A smile crept over his distinct features. "How the light falls across your face? I have noticed your eyes, the shape of your nose, since my arrival, and thought to myself, that is a woman I must paint."

She very much doubted he would think her a viable muse when she was dressed in her work apron with a dustcloth covering her hair, but it was lovely to be thought of just the same.

"That Romano is wasting no time, is he?" Tate exclaimed as he and Lucas exited the drawing room doors to the back garden to join the others for the picnic planned for the afternoon. "Now all the ladies will prefer to spend all their time with him. And what will that do for us?"

"I spy an open easel." Lucas pointed across the lawn. "You should try your hand."

"That's not a bad idea. I just might find my life's calling. Wouldn't that set my father into fits?"

Lucas laughed. Whereas he'd enjoyed a respectful relationship with his father, Tate and his father rarely saw eye to eye. "I wholeheartedly encourage the pursuit."

"Ah, look, Miss Brannon has joined the flock."

Lucas did not respond as they traversed the stone veranda to the grass below. He and Tate might be friends, but he wasn't sure he wanted to share his thoughts on Miss Brannon with his friend.

"I've known you a long time, Avery. A very long time. I can't recall the last time you seemed to enjoy a conversation as you did last night with Miss Brannon after the concert."

There would be no avoiding this topic. "She's pleasant company, that's all."

A welcome reprieve in the form of an approaching footman arrived. The liveried man crossed the yard and extended a tray toward him. "A letter for you, Mr. Avery."

Lucas took it, and as he continued down the path, he slid his finger beneath the seal, popped it open, and unfolded the paper.

Mr. Avery,

I saw Russell Crane at the Thames docks. He mentioned that Miss Olivia Brannon was attending an event at Cloverton Hall and was assessing a collection belonging to Mrs. Agnes Milton. He did not seem to be aware that you were in attendance, and I did not tell him, but he seemed very enthusiastic about Miss Brannon's prospects. If she is indeed there, then you already know, but I wanted to tell you what I have learned. I will write again if I hear more.

Clarence Night

Lucas read the letter again. Then again. He looked over to Miss Brannon, who was still seated at an easel in the far corner of the garden.

She'd deceived him.

She'd claimed she was not there to purchase anything from the Cloverton collection, but she'd never said anything about purchasing items from Mrs. Milton.

She was a clever one.

"What's that you're reading? A love letter?"

Lucas tucked it away. "The second one today."

"I knew it! We'll see you married off yet."

"Not me," Lucas objected. "Not for a long time. I haven't the time or the inclination for that."

It was true—he did have too much on his mind to think of romantic pursuits. He was a man of business, after all. His entire livelihood and future hung upon his success with the Cloverton collection.

But it wasn't entirely true.

There had always been a part of him that expected to be married and have a love like his parents had. His father had been far from perfect, but he'd loved his mother. And she'd loved him. When his brother died, then his father, every ounce of Lucas's energy had been devoted to his mother and the business.

But something about Miss Brannon had those thoughts churning again in his mind.

And the notion was enticing.

Chapter 24

HOW COULD THE other ladies find this enjoyable?

Olivia groaned and jerked her paintbrush away. Each time she pressed the bristles to the canvas, the watercolor bled and spread. How was one to get the paint to stay in one place?

Olivia clamped her teeth over her lower lip, tapped her paintbrush against the paint once more, and hovered it over the canvas for several seconds before pressing it against it. Patience had never really been her strength, but this was maddening.

Miss Kline was seated to her left, and Olivia cast a sideways glance over toward the lady's canvas. Olivia could clearly decipher her subject matter: the swans on the pond. She looked back to her own canvas. Mr. Romano had instructed her to imitate the magenta roses in front of her.

Her painting looked nothing like flowers.

Laura had always possessed a talent for such things—she was always drawing or sketching—but she'd also always obeyed her governess and done her lessons. Laura also knew how to embroider, play the pianoforte, and perform all the tasks that the other ladies engaged in.

Determined not to fail, Olivia wiped her hair away from her brow with her bare forearm and tipped her brush in the paint once more.

She could do this. She *would* do this.

Approaching footsteps broke her concentration, and Mr. Avery appeared at her side.

And her mortification was complete.

She resisted the urge to turn the easel and hide her dismal failure. But she straightened her shoulders. She'd show no embarrassment. Her pride would not allow it.

"Miss Brannon." Mr. Avery drew near and put his hands on his hips, squinting at her canvas. "What are you painting?"

She pivoted in her seat to face him more fully. "Can you not tell?"

He lifted his gaze to the garden bed beyond her easel. "The roses?"

She smiled, noting how the breeze lifted his hair. "Did the color give it away?"

"Absolutely."

Her shoulders relaxed slightly, and she lowered her brush. He'd seen her painting. And it hadn't been as embarrassing as she'd anticipated. She hated the thought of being seen as incompetent in anything by the other guests, but Mr. Avery was different.

Perhaps it was because she, in some way, knew him, and he was not such a mystery. Perhaps it was because he knew the truth about her—her family and where she came from.

There was freedom in not needing to hide such things.

But there was another element—something about his manner that made her comfortable. She liked the way he talked to her—as an equal.

He came closer, and the breeze caught an alluring scent of sandalwood and smoke. Yes, he made her comfortable, but there was also an aspect to him that made her heart trip within her chest and her breath feel light.

"I've come across something that might interest you."

The idea that he had been thinking of her shot a bolt of excitement through her, like a streak of lightning across the sky.

"It is nothing untoward, I assure you, but it does require discretion," he continued. "Would you meet me privately in the library after we are done here? I would understand if you do not wish to, but there is a particular item on which I should like to get your opinion."

She hesitated, for it did seem untoward . . . an unmarried lady should not be alone with an unmarried man. Was that not the reason for all the chaperones?

Her heart responded before her head. "I should be happy to. I'll meet you there before we all gather in the drawing room, if Mrs. Milton can spare me."

"Good." He reestablished a greater distance between them. "I'd best go and compliment the other ladies on their artwork."

She liked the hint of laughter and amusement in his tone. "By all means, Mr. Avery. I would not deny that for the world."

Olivia knew better than to do what she was doing. It did not matter who she was or which social class she belonged to. She should not be meeting Mr. Avery secretly.

But she couldn't resist the invitation.

Upon returning from the picnic, Mrs. Milton had decided to rest before dressing for dinner. The other ladies were also making dinner preparations, and the men had embarked on a ride to the nearby village. It would be at least an hour before they returned. Olivia took advantage of the quietude, slipped out from her chamber, and made her way to meet Mr. Avery.

Once at the library she opened the door to what had to be one of the largest rooms in Cloverton Hall. The thick damask curtains were drawn over tall windows, but daylight seeped in around the edges of the fabric, illuminating dust motes hovering in the air. Shelves of books lined the walls from floor to ceiling, filling the space with their unmistakable scent. A large corner shelf covered with pottery and ceramics summoned her to explore. In the center of it all stood a full-size marble statue of a feminine figure, like a sentinel keeping watch over the treasures.

"You're here."

Mr. Avery was standing next to another door with a stack of crates piled next to him. He wore no coat, and his white shirt-sleeves were rolled to his elbows, revealing muscular forearms. His navy checked waistcoat hugged his athletic torso.

Each time she encountered him, his effect on her intensified. The reality that she was meeting him—alone—raced through her mind.

She feigned composure. "This room is impressive. It's even larger than our storeroom." She drew closer to the statue in the room's center. The worn, smooth marble called to her. She reached out and touched the hand. "It is a statue of Venus?"

He joined her next to the piece. "I'd say."

She marveled at the detail of the fingernails. The intricate carved draping of the fabric. The locks of hair. "Normally I only see items like this in my uncle's warehouse. I rarely see them in a home. Like this."

"Well, I've seen a lot of parlors, libraries, and studies stuffed to the brim, and I can say with certainty this is a rare collection indeed."

She shook off her awe and refocused. As much as she would like to stay and get lost in the pieces here, she needed to be mindful. "You said you wanted to speak with me?"

"I do." He crossed the broad space and picked up a small chinoiserie urn adorned in blue-and-white vines. "What do you think of this?"

She accepted the piece from him. Immediately something felt off.

It was far too light.

She carried it to the window, pulled the curtain away, and held it up to the light. The piece should be somewhat translucent, but the amount of light coming through was off. She angled it so the light hit it directly. The blue pattern had a slightly greenish hue. The shade of white was too warm.

She flicked her eyes back to Mr. Avery. "This was in Mr. Milton's collection?"

He nodded.

Her chest grew tight as the reality rushed her.

This was not an authentic piece.

Surely Mr. Milton was enough of an expert to be able to spot the difference. What was more, her father was the one who worked with him to build his collection. He most definitely would have known the difference.

She looked back to Mr. Avery and his expectant expression.

She was confident in what she was doing. Why should she feel shy? "There's something amiss with this."

His forehead furrowed. "You see it too?"

Relieved that his assessment matched hers, she turned it over in her hands. "It is a very good likeness, but it is not Chinese. Or Japanese, for that matter. I think it's bone China."

"Exactly what I thought. Made somewhere here in England. And fairly recently." He took it back from her and placed it on the table next to him. Then he reached up and took two more off the stair-stepped shelves and handed one to her. The piece in question was almost identical in weight and material to the first. Her stomach clenched within her as her mind raced to map the implication. "Are they all like this?"

He shook his head. "Not all, but several are."

"That doesn't make any sense." She frowned. "Mr. Milton was an experienced collector. He surely would have known."

"The way I see it, either Mr. Milton bought counterfeit pieces, which I highly doubt, or somewhere along the way the original pieces were exchanged with these to make it appear as if the collection was intact."

She was glad to hear that he did not suspect that Mr. Milton acquired the pieces from her father in this condition, but the alternative he offered was grim indeed. And she could not argue with his logic.

"Does Mr. Wainbridge know yet?" She returned the piece to him.

"No. I intend to get a better handle on what it is we're dealing with before I do. In fact, you're the first person I've told."

Again, that strange sense of kinship flared within her. He took her seriously—and that fact alone drew her to him even more. "Do you suspect foul play by Mr. Milton?"

"It's hard to tell, but regardless, someone who understands these pieces is attempting to deceive another." Mr. Avery lowered the piece he was holding to the table. "I need to tell him soon, though. I know he was counting on this, but I can't sell these. Not as Chinese porcelain." His tone sobered. "There's one other thing I'd like to show you."

"Goodness," she exclaimed, "this is quite a bit of information as it is."

He pulled a letter from his pocket and extended it to her. "Go ahead. Read it."

She accepted and unfolded it, then angled the letter toward the light to read it.

Olivia thought she would be sick.

In a single moment, everything she was attempting to do discreetly came crashing down around her.

"So you *are* here on business," he said, more a statement than a question.

She was not a liar. And she'd not start now. "Yes. I am, but not in the way you suspect."

He said nothing, leaving a wide, empty moment of silence.

"Mrs. Milton stopped by our shop a couple of weeks ago and said she had a collection of her own that she wanted to sell, but she did not want to draw attention to it. She thought that if I masqueraded as a guest I could evaluate and catalog it, and then my uncle would broker the deals. She feared that if her nephew found out about the collection, he'd attempt to claim the pieces as his own."

"And do the pieces belong to her?"

"Yes. Most of the paperwork is in order, and for items without a bill of sale, she has dowry papers to support it."

His questions came quickly. "What's in the collection?"

The more she talked, the easier it was to confide in him. "Jewels. Stones and shells from India and the Orient. Bronze sculptures. Porcelain."

He lifted the porcelain once more. "Was there anything like this in there?"

"Not that I've seen."

She extended the letter back to him and waited for his reaction. She had, after all, deceived him, in a manner of speaking.

He tucked the letter back in his pocket. "Perhaps we should keep this information between us until we understand a bit more. I'll try to find out the extent of the counterfeit items, and then we can figure out what to do."

"We?"

He lifted a shoulder in a shrug. "The way I see it, I need your help—help from someone who understands this business. And maybe you'll need mine."

Since first arriving in the library, she managed a genuine smile. She liked the idea of working with him. She liked the idea of being taken seriously as an antiquarian. But above all, if any deception was transpiring, she wanted to expose it, not let it continue.

Footsteps sounded outside, and muffled voices followed.

"I should return," she said.

"You certainly don't want to get caught alone in the library with a rogue like me. What would the others say?"

She could not help but laugh at his poke of the overly rigid rules of the gathering. "I can only imagine. Good evening, Mr. Avery."

He bowed in parting. "I'll see you at dinner."

Chapter 25

OLIVIA COULD DIE of mortification. She could admit that her pride caused problems for her at times. But this—this was cruel.

Her steps slowed as she entered the drawing room to gather with the other guests before dinner. All around the space, the canvases from earlier that day were displayed—lovely depictions of the pond and the forest, the gardens and the topiaries, all painted by artists who had been instructed, at least informally, in the art of watercolor.

And then there was her painting of roses.

Chatter and laughter abounded around her. It felt as if everyone must be staring at her sad representation. Surely her face had flushed as florid as the salmon-colored gown she wore.

A light gloved hand rested on her arm, and she turned to see Miss Haven. A gown of chartreuse silk adorned the lady's graceful frame, and her flaxen hair was elegantly styled up in curls and twists. She fixed her brilliant cornflower-blue eyes on Olivia, and a smile curved her lips. "Did you enjoy the painting earlier today, Miss Brannon?"

"I did." Olivia turned away from her easel, trying to pretend her hideous painting was not in the room. "And you?"

"Oh, I always enjoy time spent with Mr. Romano. He's nothing short of a genius! Now that you've seen him work, do you not agree?" Miss Haven linked her arm through Olivia's and directed her along the line of easels, then paused in front of Miss Stanley's piece. "See how Miss Stanley captured the sunlight reflecting there on the pond? Just lovely."

Miss Haven dropped her hand and intimately lowered her voice. "I am glad I have a moment to speak with you privately, for I wanted to follow up with you on our conversation from last night."

Olivia's stomach tightened, and she steeled herself for what she would hear.

"Mr. Fielding was watching you paint earlier today. I daresay he's quite smitten."

The mention of Mr. Fielding added to Olivia's increasing trepidation. His attention had, at times, been flattering, but now it seemed bothersome, even superfluous.

"I heard him tell Captain Whitaker that you were spellbinding. Could there be a more romantic sentiment?" Miss Haven continued eagerly, as if divulging a great secret. "I took it upon myself to speak with him on your behalf."

Olivia shook her head. "Oh no, Miss Haven, I really wish you—"

"Do not thank me. I told him that you and he would make a fine match, and I encouraged him to pursue it. Is that not wonderful?"

Olivia's face burned as she looked to the man in question, who was standing at the far side of the chamber speaking with Mr. Avery.

For the first time since she arrived, she truly did not know what to say. She'd managed to handle every odd instance and erratic request to this point, but this—the idea of flirting and making a *match* with a man she'd met two days prior—was too much.

Miss Haven, excited and bubbly, pressed a kiss to Olivia's cheek and spun on her heel, completely unaware of the turmoil that she had incited.

Or perhaps she was completely aware.

Olivia could only stare at Miss Haven as she retreated to speak with Mr. Wainbridge and the captain.

All around her, the guests were laughing, chattering, conversing. How was one to respond in such a situation?

In that moment she felt more alone, more like an outsider, than at any other point.

She barely noticed when Isabella appeared at her side.

"You appear as if you've seen a ghost."

Olivia's breath shuddered, and she looked to Isabella's sympathetic dark brown eyes.

"Let's walk." Isabella took her arm and guided her away from the other guests to the open veranda doors, where the drawing room opened up to the back gardens where they had just passed the afternoon. A few of the chaperones were on the veranda, but otherwise they were alone. "I couldn't help but overhear Miss Haven's declarations. About Mr. Fielding. She wasn't exactly being discreet, was she?"

Once they reached the balustrade, Isabella leaned against the railing. "That was uncalled for, but I'm not surprised. It's not the first time she has acted in such a way. I do believe she feels threatened by you."

"By me?" Olivia laughed. "Believe me, there is no reason for her to feel threatened."

"Is there not?" Isabella arched her brow. "Miss Haven considers my brother a suitor, but I think she worries he will find you more interesting."

Olivia scoffed and gazed back to the blonde beauty. "She is quite mistaken."

"Is she? You are a mystery, my dear. To everyone here. Do not underestimate the allure in that."

The conversation fell silent for a moment, but then Isabella spoke again. "I do wonder, dear, if it would not make things easier if you were to share a little more about yourself. Perhaps by doing so, you might alleviate some of the questions around you."

Isabella's suggestion held merit, but how could she explain her situation in a way that both protected her truth *and* satisfied the questions?

"It does seem odd that we know so little of you," continued Isabella, almost with trepidation.

Guilt engulfed her.

This was her own fault. All of it. By attempting to fade into the background and be nonexistent, she was actually drawing attention to herself. If she shared the truth, she'd be shunned immediately. She thought she'd be unaffected by such a situation, but she'd underestimated how much time the guests spent with one another.

Isabella sighed. "Every person has the right to privacy, and I suppose we all have reasons for discretion."

Her hostess's kind patience made Olivia feel worse.

The rest of the evening felt contrived. And it made her miserable.

She laughed at Mr. Fielding's jokes at dinner. She hung on to Mr. Romano's stories of his childhood in Italy. She added her voice to the others and pleaded with Miss Haven to regale them with another musical performance after dinner.

All the while she was distracted.

Mr. Avery was seated far away from her next to Miss Stanley, and judging by their laughter and smiles, he seemed quite content with his dinner companion.

When the ladies withdrew to the drawing room and left the men to their port, Mr. Romano joined them, and it was Miss Stanley's turn to sit for a portrait. Olivia watched as the artist used his paints to re-create Miss Stanley's likeness, but the longer she was in the room, listening to the other ladies, the more her neck muscles ached and her head began to throb.

The burning candles added a dense heat to the room. The air felt too thick. Floral perfumes, heavy musks, and the scent of too many bodies in one small space hovered over them all. By the time the gentlemen joined them, the wine had been flowing freely, as was evident in the men's behavior.

Olivia was out of her realm . . . and she knew it.

And what was worse, she felt completely alone. She was no stranger to solitude, but here she lacked the confidence afforded by her usual environment. Everyone else seemed content, if not thrilled, with the tight quarters and intimate conversation. Even Mrs. Milton was speaking with two of the chaperones.

She glanced quickly in Mr. Avery's direction, just as she had several times since the men joined them. He was speaking in the corner with Miss Kline and Mr. Tate. The sight of him incited an unsettling sense of disquiet in her. In the span of two days, she'd gone from considering Mr. Avery the enemy to viewing him as one of the only safe people present. She found herself drawn to the warmth in his expression, the dry humor of his personality, and the sense that they shared a secret—an understanding—that only a mutual background could afford.

She hoped he would look her way, or that he would seek her out for conversation. How had everything she thought she knew about herself and her beliefs shifted so radically?

She caught a glimpse of Miss Stanley, who was speaking intently with Miss Haven. The elegant ladies cast glances toward her and resumed whispering. A pang of homesickness clapped hard in her heart, and she longed for the peace of her home and the companionship of her sister.

Fearing she might cry out of sheer frustration, she inhaled a deep, shuddery breath. This was not an idyllic visit to the countryside as she had envisioned in her naive daydreams. It was a place where bargains were struck and deals were made. The sights around her, the opulence, made her feel sick, and the heavy dinner felt unsettled in her stomach.

She spied Mr. Fielding walking toward her from the corner of her eye. The thought of speaking with him now seemed more than she could bear. Suddenly, it felt as if the air had thickened and there wasn't enough to breathe. She gasped for air once. And then twice. She had to get away from here—somewhere the air was fresh and silent.

The other guests were blocking the path to the corridor, so she pivoted and darted through the open doors to the veranda. Outside, torches illuminated the garden and the intricate paths. Voices and laughter wafted on the night breeze. But for the moment, the veranda was empty, and at the far side of it, she leaned against the cool limestone railing and let the breeze rushing around the corner calm her frayed nerves and soothe the hot tears welling in her eyes.

She wanted to go home. She wanted her sister. Her small bed. Even Russell's company seemed preferable to what she was experiencing here.

Chapter 26

IT WAS BECOMING . . . uncomfortable. And Lucas was not the only one to notice.

Tate joined him on a sofa in the far corner of the drawing room. The men had reunited with the ladies after dinner not fifteen minutes prior, and already he was out of sorts.

"You know I enjoy a good bit of entertainment, but this is disturbing even for me." Tate dropped to the chair next to Lucas. "Your charm must be irresistible. Miss Stanley cannot resist it."

Lucas scoffed and raked his fingers through his hair. His blood still rushed through his veins—a result of the possessive manner in which Miss Stanley had just clung to his arm. He all but had to force her to loosen her grip. "Is it that obvious?"

"Don't look so sour, Avery. After all, congratulations are in order," ribbed Tate. "There can be no doubt you're the man she's set her eyes on. And to think you said you weren't interested in matrimony."

"And I'm still not," Lucas hastened to add.

"You might want to tell her that."

News of Miss Stanley's misfortune had spread through the gathering, and now it was the premier topic of nearly every conversation.

It was heartbreaking to see someone whom he'd counted a friend come under such distressing circumstances, but even though he harbored empathy for her, he would not be the man to swoop in and save the day.

"Likely she sees me as the easiest target." Lucas stretched his booted leg out and leaned against the back of the chair.

"Oh no. Why would you say that?"

Lucas only glared at Tate. Seeing as Miss Stanley had no fortune, none of the other men would consider her. Lucas, however, likely seemed a more realistic option. He was established but did not have enough to tempt the wealthier ladies. This entire situation was not a game of hearts. It was a game of numbers.

"Is that pessimism I sense? From you?" Tate challenged. "Never thought I would see the day."

Lucas supposed Tate was right. Normally he bucked pessimism in any form. He simply didn't have time for it. But the discovery of the fake chinoiserie had rattled his normally steady outlook. Cloverton Hall was bursting with all sorts of artifacts other than chinoiserie that would bring in a fortune, but if word got out that the chinoiserie was, in fact, counterfeit, it would cast a bleak, unforgettable shadow on every other piece. The validity of everything under this roof would face even more scrutiny.

What was more, the scandal that his father had been involved in had already dealt a serious blow to Avery & Sons. If Lucas was involved in uncovering the counterfeits, it could throw him into another scandal—one he was not sure his business could survive.

He yanked at his cravat and adjusted the lapels of his tailcoat. The fire in the broad hearth was burning much too warm, and the weight of Miss Stanley's gaze on him—again—was inescapable.

If he was honest, though, it was more than just Miss Stanley's forwardness or the chinoiserie debacle contributing to his chagrin. The atmosphere was different tonight. Everyone laughed louder. The wine flowed more freely. Looks were more brazen, and behavior was laxer.

He looked for *her* . . . again.

Miss Brannon had dominated his thoughts. He'd sought out opportunities to be near her ever since they all converged in the drawing room before dinner, but to no avail. Her reception to him earlier in the library had ignited a hope in him that even though other areas of life seemed to be sputtering, she might become a part of his life that would flourish.

But she'd seemed unusually elusive this evening. Her manner—her darting glances and the subtle twitch of her jaw—suggested that she, too, was uncomfortable with something.

He spied her. She was hurrying toward the veranda door.

He would not sit around and wait.

Lucas jumped from the chair. "I'll be right back."

"Where are you going?"

Lucas didn't respond to Tate but followed Miss Brannon through the open doors to the veranda and found her standing at the thick limestone balustrade, staring into the night's blackness. The weather was changing, and a cold, damp gust swept in from the garden, disrupting the loose curls that had escaped her chignon and rustling the tassels on the shawl pulled taut about her narrow shoulders.

She did not turn as he approached, so he stepped next to her, shoulder to shoulder. He leaned forward to rest his hands on the balustrade. "I have another confession, Miss Brannon," he said, not looking in her direction.

"What, another one?" A hint of amusement tinged her tone.

He chuckled at the continuation of their ongoing jest. "I fear so. I saw you come out here. You seemed troubled, and I was concerned."

She tightened the shawl around her shoulders and lifted her hand to still the strands of hair. "No need for concern, Mr. Avery. I only needed some air."

The silence returned, but it was not uncomfortable, as so many bouts of silence tended to be. Instead, an unspoken sense of solidarity simmered between them. "Cloverton Hall is quite different than London, isn't it? Sometimes I come to these things, and they're uneventful. And other times I feel like I've entered a different world."

She still did not look at him, but her chest heaved in a small sigh. "I think it was a mistake for me to come here. I don't fit into this at all."

He wanted to protest, to reassure her, but in some aspects, she was right—she didn't belong among these women. She was a cut above them in so many ways. "Many people do fit in with this sort."

"And you?" She at last turned toward him. "Do you?"

He hesitated. Had that not been the very question that defined his youth? His school days? His efforts to make his business successful? "I suppose that depends on what you consider fitting in. I went to school with them. I interact with them on a daily basis, but our views on life are quite different. As are our goals. Take Tate for example. I count him a great friend, but we will never truly understand each other."

A shadow fell over her face, concealing her expression. "You play the role well."

He smirked and cocked his head to the side. "I will take that as a compliment."

"I meant nothing negative by it," she added quickly. "It is just that you seem so at ease. I feel my discomfort is written all over me, and I don't know how to conceal it."

"It's a practiced skill. I've had to fine-tune it if I ever wanted to have a client trust me," he said matter-of-factly with a shrug. "I never really knew your father, but I'm sure he was quite at ease with this set as well. It is part of the business."

"A part of the business I'm clearly not acquainted with."

He looked at her again—*really* looked at her. Physically, she appeared so delicate, but her personality seemed too big for her small frame.

How odd it must be for her.

If she were a man, she'd undoubtedly have a flourishing business of her own. But as she was a woman, those doors were firmly shut for her. He thought of his travel and the experiences he'd had. If he'd been born a lady, those opportunities would have been closed to him.

"You've not asked my advice, yet I will tell you just the same," he offered. "Everyone here—every single person in that drawing room—is driven by fear. Fear of being alone, fear of not being accepted, or fear of being without money. For the most part they all enjoy financial security, but at any moment it could all be snatched away from them.

"Mrs. Milton, for instance. She was one of the most respected, wealthiest women in society, and she and her husband poured their entire lives into building this place, only to have it pass out of her hands. If you're able, try to find the humor in it. They are all vying for attention, and whether you believe me or not, *you* are the foremost threat to them all."

She scoffed adamantly. "I'm hardly a threat."

"Well, from what I've heard, no one knows if you are a rich heiress, a nobleman's illegitimate daughter, or a stowaway."

She finally gave a little laugh. "I'm none of those things. And only you and Mrs. Milton know the truth."

"Well, we know the truth about each other, then." He tried not to stare but noticed how the breeze caught a long lock of light brown hair and blew it over her forehead. How he longed to smooth it back into place.

"Do you remember the night our fathers parted ways?" Lucas asked, unwilling to let their conversation end.

"How could I not?"

"You were very young." He adjusted his position to lean with his elbow on the railing's edge.

"I wasn't so young that it didn't leave an impression. I'd never heard my father shout prior to that night. And I never heard him shout after it."

"No doubt you also recall the source of that argument," he prompted. "The Vienna painting."

Miss Brannon shifted, making it difficult to read her reaction. "Yes, I've heard it mentioned a few times."

The sarcasm in her tone amused him. "I'm sure you have."

It was an odd sense of connectedness, to share such a poignant memory. Did she feel it, too, or did he alone struggle to resist the magnetic pull between them? "I suppose we'll never know what that partnership could have grown into."

"It happened so long ago. Everything that has happened since then has made us who we are."

A sharp bout of laughter echoed from the drawing room. Her preoccupied expression returned. "Mrs. Milton will notice I'm gone. I should rejoin the party."

She turned, as if preparing to leave the veranda, but he could not resist one last thing.

"For what it's worth, you say you don't belong here. But I believe you are the rival of any woman in the room. And I daresay you are infinitely more interesting. There is something about a woman who can think for herself that is quite intriguing."

Chapter 27

WAS IT POSSIBLE for a person to change the core of who they were in just a few days' time?

The question rattled around Olivia's mind when she awoke the next morning, challenging the sound of autumnal thunder and pelting rain just outside the Blue Room's windows.

The events of the last few days—not to mention her conversation with Mr. Avery the previous night—were conjuring doubts about things she'd always accepted as truths. They'd challenged her perception of right and wrong and her view of herself and her abilities. In such a short time she'd witnessed coldness and selfishness, but she'd also encountered benevolence.

How odd was it that an Avery had been one to show kindness—who offered support without taking advantage? He had nothing to gain by being kind to her. But other people, like Mr. Fielding and Mrs. Milton, behaved as if Olivia owed them something, merely because she was here.

With her thoughts as her companion, Olivia spent that morning with Tabitha, Mrs. Milton, and Louis in the China closet, keeping a close and careful eye on the paperwork and matching it up to the items as she evaluated them. Because of the incessant morning rain, the ladies' afternoon activity of archery had been canceled, so Mr. Romano requested to paint Olivia's miniature during that time. A headache, brought on by the change in the weather, confined Mrs. Milton to bed during the afternoon hours, leaving Olivia to make her way down the corridor to meet Mr. Romano alone.

On her way to the formal parlor on Cloverton Hall's first floor, Olivia passed the gallery. She'd not been by the space since the night of the concert, and through the open doors she spied the Cavesee Vase.

She slowed her steps.

Mr. Avery had shown her counterfeit porcelain—pieces she would have expected to be authentic. Everything within her resisted the idea that there might be something amiss with the Cavesee Vase. After all, she had personally witnessed it being unpacked from its crate, but a great deal could have happened in the years since she saw it last.

Interest flaring, Olivia glanced to her right and then to her left. All was quiet and still. Not a soul was in sight. She'd been told that the men had gone to the village for the day and the women would be in the parlor, so she took advantage of the solitude to enter the gallery undetected. Her footsteps were light on the polished wooden floor, and she made her way to the far wall and looked up at the shadowed space.

The vase was a few feet above her and out of reach. If she could only tap it with her fingernail and hear the resulting sound, she'd be able to gauge its authenticity.

A small ottoman was in front of a chair by the window, so she dragged it near the piece. As she prepared to step up on it, a noise cracked.

She jerked toward the door.

Mr. Wainbridge stood in the threshold, staring at her. Surprise, or perhaps confusion, tweaked his features.

"M-Mr. Wainbridge," she stammered. "I thought the men were to go to the village today."

"Change of plans. We decided it would be much more pleasant to stay indoors." He cleared his throat. "Is there something I can help you with?"

A nervous laugh escaped. "No, no. I was just admiring this vase."

He clasped his hands behind his back and looked up. "That is the Cavesee Vase. It's nearly two hundred years old, or so I've been told."

At least four hundred, to be more exact.

She thought it best not to correct him.

Grateful for the dreary shadows to hide the flush she knew was tinging her cheeks, she knitted her fingers before her. "It really is spectacular."

"You witnessed my conversation with my aunt, so you know my uncle dedicated his life to these things." He picked up a small carved jade Pixiu beast from another shelf on the wall.

She bit her lip.

He was lifting it by the tail.

She resisted the urge to take it from him and return it to the safety of the ledge. "And do you share Mr. Milton's passion for such things?"

"Egad, no. Not at all."

He returned the statue to the shelf, and she exhaled in relief. Sensing the opportunity to help bridge the gap between the relatives, she nudged the ottoman back into place. "Your aunt is quite fond of it all, you know. I think it brings her comfort."

"I'm well aware."

She ignored the flatness of his tone. "I don't believe she intends to be so cross. Memories of loved ones are powerful, and all of these remind her of her husband."

He narrowed his gaze at her and smiled strangely, as if awed. "You are quite a sentimental creature, aren't you?"

"I suppose." She moved toward the door. "Again, I apologize for intruding where I should not have been. I am due in the parlor. Mr. Romano is to paint my portrait."

"Ah, I see." He clasped his hands before him. "Then by all means, do not let me keep you."

Olivia could feel the weight of his attention as she swept by him and into the corridor. Eager to put the awkward encounter behind her, she rushed to the parlor. She expected to see the ladies gathered but was shocked to see the men present as well. Mr. Avery, Mr. Tate, and Mr. Fielding were interspersed with the ladies, and tables had been set up for games of cribbage and chess.

"Miss Brannon!" Mr. Romano's exclamation captured her attention. His customarily bright expression eased her, and he extended his long arms in her direction. "I am so glad you could join me on such short notice. I know many thought the rain was a damper to our day, but I consider it fortuitous, for look at the time it has afforded us. I've been waiting for you. Please, sit."

Olivia did as she was bid, cognizant that the other guests' focus was drifting to her.

"As I told you in the garden, I've been most eager to paint you from the moment I laid eyes on you." He motioned for her to move at certain angles and tipped her chin up slightly before retreating to his spot by his easel.

She glimpsed motion from the corner of her eye, and she cut her gaze to her left while keeping her chin still. Dread trickled through her when she saw Miss Haven sauntering toward her.

"My dear, how lovely you look. Oh, to have such a natural beauty, such a natural presence!"

The chintz fabric of Miss Haven's gown rustled as she moved closer. "I spoke with Mr. Fielding earlier this morning. The poor man was beside himself. I blame myself entirely, of course."

Olivia feared that any response she might offer would lead to some sort of trap, yet Miss Haven's ensuing silence demanded she speak. "What do you mean?"

"When you and I spoke the other night, I offered to find you a match and happily took to the challenge. But I fear I've been misguided. Mr. Fielding was so captivated by you, and based on our conversation I believed you to feel the same. Imagine my surprise when he told me that you were quite cool to him last night in the drawing room after dinner! He said that he tried to approach you, but you turned and fled out the door. Surely he must've been mistaken."

Olivia's defenses flared, but she determined to remain in control. "I'm not here to find a husband, Miss Haven. I do apologize if I made you believe otherwise. When I do find a match, it will be entirely of my own making."

Miss Haven straightened in obvious annoyance. "Does that extend to Mr. Avery?" Her pointed question smacked of an accusation, and she narrowed her vibrant eyes toward Olivia. "Mr. Fielding said you seemed to be quite friendly with him on the veranda. We must be very careful, mustn't we, Miss Brannon? How quickly one's reputation can be blemished by careless actions and words."

The statement—and the insinuation behind it—struck.

Never before had anyone accused her of loose behavior.

How was one to respond?

Without another word Miss Haven flounced away.

Heat rose from Olivia's bodice to her neck, her cheeks. She was not prone to tears, yet the searing sting of tears gathering in her eyes pricked.

She sniffed and reminded herself that her goal here was not to make friends.

She was not here to impress others.

She was here to prove herself—prove her abilities.

But the cruel nature of Miss Haven's words still hurt.

After several minutes, Mr. Romano adjusted his easel so he was seated closer to Olivia. His accented voice was barely above a whisper. "You have a secret, Miss Brannon."

She eyed him.

"I find you interesting. And not just because you are a pleasant muse for my paintbrush. You see, I firmly believe that confidence, knowing one's worth, is the most beautiful trait a woman can possess." A hint of amusement curved his lips, and his dark eyes did not leave his work. "Does this surprise you?"

She considered his actions since his arrival—his praise of beauty, his flirting. She lifted her face in response. "Perhaps."

"Ah, ah, ah! Leave your chin just like that." He dipped his brush in fresh paint and his dark eyes never left his canvas. "I see many people. Many women. Very few hold true to a conviction, for it is easiest to do what is expected and easy. But you, I think, are different. You have a secret, and because of that you refuse to sacrifice the most essential parts of your soul."

She warmed at the vote of confidence. This was a difficult game to play—to be an impostor in such a world. Perhaps he knew it too.

"That is perhaps one of the loveliest compliments I have ever received, Mr. Romano. I fear I will revisit those words very often. Thank you."

He grinned. "It is my honor, Miss Brannon."

Chapter 28

WAS HE . . . JEALOUS?

Lucas tore his focus away from Romano. The painter was sitting quite close to Miss Brannon, and he must have said something entertaining, for a soft smile curved her lips.

It was not his business, of course. And he refused to be the sort of fellow who would even harbor envious thoughts, but if Miss Brannon were to smile at him the way she was smiling now, it would be the pinnacle of his day.

"Why did you leave the cribbage table so abruptly? I thought we might play another round."

Lucas resisted the urge to cringe at the familiar feminine voice and looked up. Miss Stanley, Wainbridge, and Tate had gathered near him. Lucas bolstered his attitude, for if there was one truth about a house party, it was that one was never alone.

Tate clapped Lucas's shoulder as he passed him to drop into a nearby chair. "Never mind Avery, Miss Stanley. He's upset he lost, 'tis all. Avery can't stand a loss."

Lucas smirked. "You've found me out."

"No, it isn't that," Miss Stanley stated thoughtfully as she sat next to Lucas on the sofa, quite close. Her downcast lips formed a pretty, coquettish pout, convincing enough that he could almost believe she was concerned. "You look positively sour."

"Yes, did you have too much fun last night, Avery?" Wainbridge quipped, sitting in the remaining chair.

Lucas chided himself for not being more on guard and forced a good-hearted chuckle. "Hardly. I'm just trying to figure out how on earth Tate managed to best me at billiards this morning."

Wainbridge snorted at the joke.

Tate shook his head. "You may be a great deal smarter than I am on many fronts, Avery, but beat me at billiards? Never."

"A rematch, then," suggested Lucas.

"I'd take that bet," added Wainbridge.

Tate guffawed. "Challenge accepted."

Miss Stanley shifted next to him, making a great display of adjusting the folds of her pale pink skirt. She never was one who liked to be left out of a conversation, and talk of billiards did just that. As the men's laughter subsided, she redirected the conversation.

"What a thrill that you included Mr. Romano as a guest, Mr. Wainbridge." Miss Stanley straightened her posture as she perched pristinely on the edge of the sofa's cushion. "I wrote to my mother just this morning and told her what an exciting addition he was to the party. I cannot wait to share my portrait with her."

Wainbridge beamed proudly, unfazed at the conversation's new direction. "I'm glad his presence has made your time at Cloverton that much more enjoyable."

"Oh, it has! And the profiles last night. Just wonderful." She turned her attention to Mr. Romano and, by association, Miss Brannon. "How lovely Miss Brannon looks in that shade of blue. I have no doubt the portrait will be stunning."

Lucas followed her direction. Miss Brannon did look lovely, but it was unlike Miss Stanley to draw attention to another woman's charms. There had to be a motive, and he could only guess it was an effort to keep the focus from her own crumbing financial situation.

"What an interesting creature she is," Tate mused. "And such a mystery! Who is she really, Wainbridge? I think you know and are keeping it a secret from us."

Wainbridge held his hands out as if to declare his innocence. "Honestly, I wish I knew, but I know nothing more than you do. Actually, the oddest thing just happened. Not even half an hour ago, I encountered Miss Brannon. She was alone in the gallery, just staring at one of Uncle's giant vases. She had an ottoman, and I can't be sure, but I think she was going to climb on it. Surely I was mistaken, but it was strange. Very strange indeed."

Lucas stifled a chuckle. Of course Olivia Brannon would attempt to climb on an ottoman to get a better view of the Cavesee Vase.

Miss Stanley frowned. "That is odd. But if she is a friend of the Miltons, perhaps she is fond of all those old things just as they were."

Wainbridge shrugged. "Whatever the reason, it's beyond me."

Tate leaned back contemplatively in his chair. "I can't help but wonder if she is merely a companion. If she were wealthy or related to someone of importance, someone here would certainly know."

"I think you might be right." Miss Stanley's plummy tone was almost mellifluous. "After all, Mrs. Milton is the sort of woman who could pluck a person out of obscurity and make her a celebrity overnight. Consider that Miss Brannon is not musical, nor does she paint. Why, she does not even sew!"

"Ah. The hallmarks of every truly worthy woman," teased Tate. "Perhaps she does not like those things. They all sound dreadfully dull."

"Don't be ridiculous, Mr. Tate. It isn't about *enjoying* them. It is about *succeeding* at them. And you—you're awfully quiet on the topic, Mr. Avery." Miss Stanley sounded accusatory as she pivoted toward Lucas. "She seems to like you. I've seen the two of you talking frequently. I know you must have an opinion."

Lucas drew a sharp breath. Now they were getting to the heart of it. Miss Stanley did view Miss Brannon as competition.

"To answer your question, I do have an opinion." Lucas forced a casual tone to his voice. "It matters not to me if she's a companion or an heiress or anything else. I enjoy her company. Shouldn't that be the benchmark for whether she's worthy to be part of our group?"

Miss Stanley rolled her eyes. "I'm not surprised to hear you, a man, say as much."

"And if she was from lower means," Lucas continued, "what would we do? Throw her from the premises? Refuse to speak with her?"

"Well said." A twinkle sparkled in Tate's light blue eyes. "And I'm certain those large hazel eyes and bright smile have nothing to do with such an opinion."

———————

The next day was Olivia's fifth day at Cloverton Hall—and the day of the Whitmore ball. Each day had provided deeper insight into a collection that was proving more extensive than she'd ever have anticipated. The fact that so many of the pieces were together and Mrs. Milton had such complete documentation only added to the fact.

Her opportunity to complete the evaluation would be over before she knew it, and the task was taking longer than she had initially calculated. With each new piece of the collection, she had to match it to any existing paperwork, write both a description of the piece and an assessment of its condition, categorize it, assign it a preliminary monetary value, and then record it all in a ledger. It was a slow, tedious process, and one that had been made slower by the demands of the party.

Even so, Olivia was confident in her ability to be seen as an antiquities purveyor in her own right—each step forward moved her that much closer to her goal. Perhaps she could even travel to make her own purchases. It was a lofty dream, and many obstacles stood in the way. But maybe, just maybe, if she could prove herself here, doors might start to open for her.

"Merciful heavens!" cried Tabitha. "Would ye listen t' that wind?"

Olivia lifted her head from her work and looked to the China closet's windows. Rain streaked down the panes, and the impenetrable clouds darkened the entire landscape by several shades. She frowned. "I hope the weather will cooperate for the ball tonight. I fear for the roads."

"La, Whitmore House is not a mile from here." Tabitha returned the silver bowl she'd been polishing to the completed pile and picked up another piece. "Mrs. Milton used t' walk it t' take tea with Mrs. Davies, t' former mistress o' Whitmore, nearly every afternoon—it's that close! T' weather shouldn't interfere."

Olivia tried to imagine what Mrs. Milton was like before her husband died. Had she always been cantankerous and defensive? Surely at some point she must have been happy here at Cloverton. Why else would she be so determined to continue her husband's legacy?

Tabitha continued, "T' Miltons and t' Davies were quite thick in those days. But t' Davies are gone now. Moved to London years ago. I imagine this'll be difficult for Mrs. Milton. T' Whitmore House she knew is no more."

Olivia was always surprised at how much Tabitha knew about Mrs. Milton, and yet never once did a criticism of any kind cross her lips. In the last few days Olivia had spent a great deal of time with the maid. A friendship was forming, but so many questions remained.

"May I ask what happened to your mother? You mentioned that Mrs. Milton was good to her."

Tabitha tucked a frizzy lock of hair behind her ear. At first Olivia thought she wasn't going to respond, but at last she spoke. "She was taken advantage of while in service t' Mrs. Milton, an' she became with child. *Me.* But instead of throwin' her out, as she'd 'ave every right t' do, Mrs. Milton kept me mother on an' saw I was taken care of. She even made sure I learned to read 'n' write. Everyone 'ere knew t' truth o' me mother's situation, but

Mrs. Milton threatened t' dismiss anyone who breathed a word o' it. Then, after me mother died, she made me 'er personal chambermaid, and 'ere I've been e'er since."

"Goodness," Olivia exclaimed. "That's quite a tale."

"Isn't it? Can ye even imagine what would've 'appened to me if she'd dismissed me mother?"

Olivia was quickly learning that loyalty was an important trait to Mrs. Milton. "Do you think that Mrs. Milton will ever be able to coexist with the Wainbridges?"

Tabitha stood from her seat, retrieved another box of combs, and returned to the small table. "I don't think so. But times change, don't they? She'll miss Cloverton, but she'll be 'appier on 'er own."

"Will you go with her when she leaves? You and Teague?"

"I'll stay wit' her 'til one o' us is put in t' earth, I reckon."

Olivia stiffened. "I'm not sure I have ever heard such a statement of loyalty before. I don't even know if anyone would say that about me, with the exception of my sister."

A knock on a distant door sounded. Tabitha left to go answer it and returned a moment later. "This is for you."

Olivia looked at the note. "For me?"

"Aye. T' maid brought it up. Aren't ye goin' t' open it?" Tabitha laughed as she held it out toward Olivia.

Surprised, Olivia accepted the missive. There was no post marking on it, nor address. It had to have come from someone inside the house.

"Who's it from?" A teasing glint sparkled in Tabitha's eyes. "A gentleman?"

Olivia waved her hand playfully to dismiss Tabitha's suggestion, but almost immediately her mind raced. Was it from Mr. Fielding? Or Mr. Avery? After excusing herself from the China closet and returning to the privacy of the Blue Room, she slid her finger beneath the seal, popped it open, and sought out the signature.

Lucas Avery.

A thrill shot through her.

She lifted the note to the light filtering through the window.

I've gathered a few more pieces I should like you to take a look at. If you are interested, meet me in the library. I'll be there all afternoon.

Olivia didn't know what to make of the giddy, girlish feelings that enveloped her. He wanted to meet with her! It was exhilarating, mystifying, new, confusing.

Surely it was a mistake to feel this way. In mere days she'd return home to Kingsby Street—back to her uncle and her sister. Mr. Avery would return to his home as well. Their normal lives and routines would resume. Memories of their time at Cloverton Hall would fade.

If she was not careful, she'd be setting herself up for many pain-ful moments.

After shrugging her work apron from her shoulders, she retrieved her pocket watch and clicked its latch. Time was of the essence if she wanted adequate time to prepare for the ball. She smoothed her hair into place and drew a fortifying breath. Perhaps she was setting herself up for trouble by meeting him, but if she didn't, she might always regret it.

Chapter 29

LUCAS FULLY UNDERSTOOD the implication of sending Miss Brannon a message directly. Normally, secret notes sent at a house party were tokens of love or romantic intention, but how else could he get a message to her on such short notice? Then the library door creaked open slowly, and she appeared.

And the risk had been worth it.

Miss Brannon was clad in a simple, drab, printed calico gown with long sleeves and a high neckline. The modest design boasted no ribbons, no frills, and her hair was gathered low in a chignon at the base of her neck. But even in the darkness, her eyes were vibrant and alert, and the angular shadows that fell on her face accentuated the fullness of her lips, her high cheekbones, and the dimple in her cheek that appeared with every facial movement. He wasn't sure how it was possible, but she seemed more beautiful now than when dressed in her dinner finery.

He cleared his throat and refocused his thoughts. "You received my note, I take it."

"I did." She let the door close behind her.

"I'm glad, for I want to show you something." He motioned for her to follow him to a long rectangular table centered beneath the window. He drew back the curtain, and a silver light tumbled through the rain-streaked windows onto the dozens of counterfeit pieces he'd encountered.

At first she said nothing. She lifted one of the bowls with her slender fingers, held it to the light, then turned it over to examine the bottom of it. "Are *all* of these bone China?"

"I'm afraid so. And if you'll notice, most of these pieces are small and of a fairly simple design. Even so, whoever made these knew enough about Chinese art to capture all the pertinent details."

She moved down the table, picking up pieces and studying them. "They are all a remarkable likeness, aren't they? I wonder where it all came from."

"And I can't help but wonder where the original pieces are." He retrieved the portfolio he'd placed on the table's edge and handed it to her. "I located Mr. Milton's chinoiserie inventory list, and each of the pieces on this table matches a visual description on a sales sheet."

She lowered the bowl back to the table, accepted the portfolio, and opened it. As she thumbed through the papers, her movements slowed. She stopped, read the paper more carefully, and then touched one of the signatures at the bottom of the page.

Her father's signature.

"My father would be sickened by this. He never would have sold pieces that were not authentic. Whatever happened here happened after my father sold them."

Lucas reached out to take the portfolio back. "I think so too."

And it was true. Edward Brannon was known for his honesty and integrity.

Unlike his own father.

Her brow suddenly furrowed, and she turned on her heel. "Do you remember the story about the artwork at Bentcress Manor from a few years back?"

"Bentcress Manor? I don't recall it."

"It's a large estate in the very south of Devon, with an impressive collection of Italian artwork. A young artist, I think his name was Fallow, learned about this collection, and when the family was in London for the Season, he broke into the house and stole a single piece of art, frame and all. He then painted a duplicate image, placed it in the original frame, and returned it before the family returned in late summer. Then he sold the original. No one noticed. This went on for a number of years until a friend of the family encountered one of the original paintings in a sale. One clever agent connected the two and the forger was eventually arrested."

"I'd not heard that." Lucas considered the story as he picked up one of the pieces. "I'm not aware of anyone in England who would have the skill to re-create this chinoiserie. It's beautiful. But unfortunately for Wainbridge, it's utterly useless."

She folded her arms over her midsection. "When are you going to tell him?"

"I plan to wait until after the ball. I'd like to finish assessing some of the other pieces so I have pleasant news to counter the bad."

Silence fell over the darkened room until only the crackling fire and the rain pattering on the windows could be heard. The candles in the lantern sputtered, flickering their light over the contents and mingling with the afternoon's moody light.

She bent her head over the table again, and he was struck afresh by her demureness. Her loveliness. The sentiment prevailed over concerns of chinoiserie or an upset client.

"I'm glad you came to meet me." He stepped closer to her. "I wasn't sure if you would."

She flicked her topaz gaze toward him. "Why would I not?"

"Well, I can think of a couple of reasons, but the most likely is that our families have not been on speaking terms for over a decade."

She shook her head—completely unaware of how the candlelight glinted on the glossy strands of her hair—and grinned. "I can't help but wonder what our fathers would say if they saw us here, in the Cloverton library, looking at a collection of counterfeit chinoiserie."

He liked her sense of humor. "Your father would be furious that you were speaking with an Avery. My father would be furious that it was taking me so long to finish this evaluation."

She let out a sweet, charming laugh.

He wished he could erase every barrier that had separated them. Never had he met a woman who intrigued him so. But the attraction went beyond merely enjoying her company. He was inexplicably drawn to her uniqueness. Her clever wit and inquisitiveness. Her self-assuredness. Her beauty. Her very presence was awakening a part of him he never realized existed. He'd set his goal so firmly on business that he'd not considered much else. But now, what good was business and the success it could generate without someone to share it with?

She was close—he could reach out and touch her. Would she welcome an embrace? At this moment, he desired nothing more than to be the source of her happiness. He wanted to be the first person she sought when she entered the room. He wanted her to hold him in high esteem. Could she do that given their past? Given how his father treated hers?

He needed to make it right.

He did not think. He simply blurted, "I owe you an apology."

Her smile faded. "Whatever for?"

"Well, perhaps not me specifically, but on behalf of my father."

"I still don't understand what you mean."

"Last night we spoke about our fathers' argument. They were both so stubborn, and our families have keenly felt the effect of it. I would like to think that you and I could mend the rift that our fathers could not."

"That was our fathers' argument." She offered the slightest hint of a smile. "There is no reason why it should continue to be ours."

Encouraged by her words, he drew nearer to her, as if by closing the distance between them, he could strengthen their bond. He was close enough now to see the specks of gold in her eyes as she looked up at him. He took a moment to take in her long lashes, which were just a few shades darker than her chestnut hair, and noticed how the wisps of hair curled at her temples. She was lovely—lovelier than any antique, any painting.

This was what he should be seeking—this sensation of closeness and intimacy—being close to *her*. The feeling of building a life with someone instead of merely existing to reach a goal. Everything within him screamed that Olivia Brannon was the lady who would capture his imagination and make him see his future in an entirely different light.

The mantel clock chimed the hour, snapping the moment that seemed to be suspended in time. Miss Brannon pressed her lips together, stepped back.

"I should be going."

Lucas wished he could come up with an excuse to extend their time together. "Yes. It will be time to depart for the ball soon."

As he watched her curtsey and withdraw from the library, a fresh new optimism flared. He'd come to Cloverton Hall hoping to change his financial circumstances, but as the event went on, a new hope was forming . . . one that was more powerful than money could ever be.

Chapter 30

MISS HAVEN HAD declared several times that Mr. and Mrs. Whitmore held a ball that would rival any ball thrown in London, and she was right.

Lucas accepted a glass of champagne as he exited the gaming room and entered the ballroom. Hundreds of candles and lanterns illuminated every inch of the massive space and reflected from the mirrors paneling each wall. All around him, laughter and music floated in lighthearted strains. The Whitmore ballroom was bursting with people who would not be deterred by the incessant rain and cool September wind.

He'd arrived with Tate and Wainbridge over an hour prior, but his comrades had settled in at the gaming tables, where they would likely be for the rest of the evening.

But Lucas had other plans.

He wound his way through the throngs of people and around the vivacious dancers, intent upon one thing: finding Miss Brannon.

He knew she'd be arriving with Mrs. Milton, but he'd yet to see her. The memory of their auspicious conversation in the library fueled his every move, flooding him with an energy he'd never quite experienced before. He mulled the entire interaction over and over in his mind: her reactions, her statements. All he knew was that their time together had ended too soon, and waiting to see her again was nearly driving him to distraction.

He located a spot just at the edge of the ballroom where he could keep an eye on those entering. He'd gladly wait here all night if it meant being able to greet her.

"You look lonely, Lucas."

Lucas jerked at the unusual sound of his Christian name.

Only his mother ever called him by it.

He pivoted.

Miss Stanley was sauntering toward him. The light from the candles shimmered off the golden strands embroidered in her lustrous dress and sparkled from the tiara atop her tresses.

He stifled a groan. This could not go on. "Not lonely. Just watching."

"Then I hope you will not object to my company." A satisfied simper tweaked her rouged lips, and she flipped one of the long auburn tendrils purposely left free of her chignon over her shoulder. She took his arm as if it had been offered and then sighed as she made a display of watching the dancers. "Look at all those people. Beautiful ladies. Handsome gentlemen."

Lucas did not like this side of her—and he was growing to dislike it more and more by the day. He missed the old version of his friend, when they would poke fun at the overly pious or find amusement with those attempting to make a conquest. Never would he have thought that he would become one of them.

On some level he understood. With her father's change in circumstance, she needed to act quickly to secure a future for herself, but she'd set her eyes on him. And that would not do.

Another guest was announced. He needed to find a way to separate from her. "I seem to recall that you enjoy dancing. Why are you not out there with them?"

She tightened her grip on his arm, but instead of flirting, her posture slackened and her easy smile faded. "Let us not pretend. I know you've heard about my father. Miss Wainbridge told me that you and her brother were discussing it. And now it seems as if everyone knows of it. No one will be asking to dance with me tonight, I fear."

Relief surged through him. He was glad to have the topic finally out in the open so it could be addressed. "I do know of it, and I'm sorry to hear it. Take heart, though, Miss Stanley. You are vibrant and resourceful. I've no doubt you'll find your way through this. And if it is gossip that is worrying you, don't give it that power. People love to talk about the things that take the focus from their own problems."

"In all the years I've known you, I've never known you to be that way." She pressed her lips together coquettishly before leaning closer and lowering her voice to a whisper. "But now I fear *we* are a source of gossip."

"And why is that?"

She adjusted her gloved hand on his arm and blinked innocently up at him. "That there's an understanding between us, of course. Apparently, our friendship is being mistaken for something more."

Lucas inhaled a deep breath. This was what he had been afraid of. He'd heard of it before—a woman, or a woman's friend or family, starting a rumor that gained traction. Lucas would never compromise a woman's reputation, and yet he'd seen enough examples of how an unsuspecting man would be snared into a position that required him to comply to save the reputations of those involved.

He cleared his throat and banished all hint of good humor from his tone. "I see no reason why that should become an issue. We're friends, are we not? That is all that need be said on the matter."

The current dance ended, and the next dance was called.

She beamed sweetly at him. "Well, as my friend, then, I notice you have yet to ask me to dance. It is dreadfully awful to feel like I'm the woman everyone feels sympathy for."

Annoyed with her veiled attempt to gain his compassion, he pursed his lips. He had no desire to embroil himself in a scandal, but refusing her offer to dance would be even more of an offense.

Soberly, he stretched out his hand toward her.

Her entire countenance brightened, and she placed her gloved hand on his and accompanied him to the floor, where they lined up opposite each other in two long lines of dancers.

The music began, and as they moved through the steps, Miss Brannon entered the chamber alongside Mrs. Milton.

He couldn't recall a single time when he'd felt such a reaction to the mere presence of a person. Her very arrival incited the sensation of elation and affliction at the same time.

He reminded himself that he was dancing with another. He could go to her when the dance was over. But he looked to Miss Stanley, and dread washed over him.

Had Miss Brannon heard this rumor that Miss Stanley claimed existed?

He should not care what she thought. And yet suddenly he did. Very much.

Glittering jewels, hundreds of flickering candles, men dressed in formal attire, ladies in elegant gowns of plum and ivory, jonquil and gold. It was a fairy tale. Never had Olivia encountered such elegant perfection.

"Goodness, but it is hot in here," Mrs. Milton muttered, adjusting the generous length of her gown's taffeta fabric and fluttering a painted fan furiously before her face. "We need to find some air, Miss Brannon."

Olivia was only half listening to her hostess. Mrs. Milton might choose to focus on physical discomforts, but Olivia was mesmerized by the engrossing scene before her.

For this was the dream, wasn't it? Elegance and loveliness, manners and refinement? It was what her mother and father would have wanted for her. But she had to remember—she was not here of her own accord. She was a guest. She might long to participate, but she had to remember her role. She did as bid . . . She led Mrs. Milton to a row of chairs along the wall and sat with her, determined to be grateful and happy to observe.

And she did so contentedly—until she spied Mr. Avery amongst those dancing.

He was partnered with Miss Stanley, whose pretty face was turned up to his adoringly. How elegant and attractive she was, with her titian hair, her warm brown eyes, a silk dress the color of the subtlest celandine green, and a diamond sparkling at her neck.

Olivia had heard the whispers about her lost fortune. Even without the luxury of money, Miss Stanley's charms far outweighed her own. She'd also heard the rumors about Mr. Avery and Miss Stanley, and based on their attentions toward the other at this moment, it was not hard to believe. They swirled and turned, danced and touched palms. It was a lively dance, and they seemed to be enjoying themselves.

Olivia did try to ignore the pang of envy that shot through her. How would it feel to be dancing with him? Smiling. Happy. Her palm pressed against his. The memory of their conversation in the library played out in her mind for the hundredth time since they parted. Even in the midst of the excitement of ball preparations, her heart raced and her hands trembled.

But had she misunderstood the meaning behind his words in the library earlier that day? He'd spoken of mending broken bonds and moving forward. How she longed to believe him, but when she saw him with Miss Stanley, her confidence wavered. Perhaps she'd jumped to a premature conclusion. Most likely he intended the statement professionally instead of romantically. The questions swirling within her almost made her feel ill. Mrs. Milton was right. It was far too warm in here.

Mrs. Milton called to her. While she'd been lost in her own thoughts, a man had approached them and was speaking with Mrs. Milton—a very somber man with mousy hair and a lackluster expression, clad in a coat of very plain, drab wool.

"Miss Brannon, may I present Mr. Foster?" Mrs. Milton's words held authority.

Mr. Foster bowed low. "I'm pleased to make your acquaintance, Miss Brannon. Always a pleasure to have a new face in the area."

She stood from her seat and curtsied in response.

"Would you care to take to the floor for the next dance?"

Mrs. Milton's expectant eyes were on her, and she nodded her graying head encouragingly. Olivia had no viable reason to refuse. She placed her gloved hand atop his and followed him to the floor.

She'd not expected to participate in dancing—she'd fully anticipated acting as Mrs. Milton's companion for the evening. But as the night progressed, Mrs. Milton's introductions to various local men kept her dance card full. Even with the varied company, she had difficulty truly enjoying herself, for the odd sensation of being so physically close to a stranger made her feel clumsy and awkward.

That—along with the fact that she could not keep her gaze from Mr. Avery.

Chapter 31

TATE APPROACHED LUCAS with two drinks in his hand and extended one toward him. "Where have you been? I've been looking for you all evening."

Lucas took the offered drink but did not drink it.

"What's wrong with you?" Tate nudged Lucas with his elbow. "You look miserable."

Lucas checked his words before speaking. He'd spent the better part of the last two hours attempting to speak with Miss Brannon and simultaneously avoiding Miss Stanley. "I fear Miss Stanley has me in her sights tonight. She told me that people are beginning to talk about us."

"And you believe her?" Tate huffed. "The best way to deal with such things is to ignore it. And I don't know what you're complaining about. Look around. The room is full of lovely ladies, and I'm not dancing with a single one. Instead, I'm here talking to the likes of you."

"You could ask Miss Stanley," Lucas quipped.

"Bah." Tate shook his head. "She's far too clever for me. Knowing my luck I'd end up engaged by the time the evening is over and have no idea how it happened."

Lucas chuckled and shook his head. "I've no wish to be cruel, but this is getting out of hand."

"It will blow over."

"Comforting words indeed."

"Isn't that what you come to me for? Comfort and advice?"

And then *she* caught his eye.

Lucas had caught glimpses of Miss Brannon throughout the evening. Dancing with this man. Talking with that one. It was all innocent, he knew—introductory interactions arranged by Mrs. Milton.

But now he saw her walking without Mrs. Milton toward the veranda.

"I'll find you later." Lucas pushed past Tate.

"Where are you going?"

Lucas did not stop.

"Avery!" Tate called. "Where are you going?"

Lucas waved him off and headed toward the veranda. He would not let this opportunity pass.

He quickened his pace until he was outside in the damp night. Other guests had also meandered out into the night's fresh air—an escape from the room's stifling humidity and crowded spaces.

Miss Brannon was standing alone, her back to him, looking out over the black landscape. Her pale gown emphasized her slender form, and the candlelight from the nearby torches highlighted her peerless profile.

His chest felt full, his head light. When had he become like this? How had this woman, in such a short time, affected the inner workings of his heart and mind?

Lucas approached her without entirely knowing what he would say. He cleared his throat and said her name as he drew near. And she turned.

"Miss Brannon."

Olivia did not need to turn around to identify the speaker. Indeed, she'd been hoping, nay, praying, to hear that voice. A smile quirked her lips, and she turned.

Lucas Avery stood just feet from her. The evening wind was catching his hair, and his affable expression was vibrant in the low light. How handsome he looked in his formal broadcloth tailcoat of corbeau green, which emphasized his eyes' verdant hue. He bowed in greeting, clasped his hands behind his back, and glanced over his shoulder. "Is Mrs. Milton not with you?"

"Mrs. Milton would like to return to Cloverton Hall, so she asked me to find Miss Wainbridge since she came in our carriage. I've been looking for her, but I needed a bit of air." Olivia smiled and pressed her finger to her lips in a silent request for him to keep her secret.

"Your secret is safe with me." He stepped closer. "I couldn't help but notice you arrived quite late. I was worried you encountered trouble on the roads."

"Mrs. Milton did not want to travel in the rain, so we were delayed."

"I see. And has Mrs. Milton been introducing you to Yorkshire's finest?"

She laughed at the reference to some of the men she'd been partnered with over the previous hours. How good it felt to laugh. "Mrs. Milton and her friends have introduced me to several interesting people—none of whom compare to the company at Cloverton Hall, of course."

His manner easy, his tone light, he motioned back to the structure behind him. "And what is your opinion of Whitmore House?"

"It's impressive, isn't it?" She looked past him and up to the house's stone facade. "It's not nearly as interesting as Cloverton, at least to me, but lovely nonetheless."

"No dragon statues staring at you?" he teased.

"No, no. Nothing of the sort."

"Just ogling gentlemen and judgmental ladies?" he offered, his gaze unnervingly direct.

So he has been watching.

He leaned next to her against the stone railing. "I've been so preoccupied with the Cloverton collection that I've failed to ask you how the assessment of Mrs. Milton's collection is going. How are you finding it?"

"It's really quite fascinating. I've never seen one quite like it. The number of shells and rocks she has from the Orient is truly incredible. Several I've never seen before, so I'll need to do some more research when I return to London. But in the end, I hope that I'm able to help her. The most difficult part will be getting Mrs. Milton to actually part with them. It can be so hard to assign a monetary value to an item someone holds dear."

"Unfortunately for us, we cannot take emotions into account, can we? The value of these pieces is solely in what they are worth to others, not how much they meant to the owner."

"Very true. Mrs. Milton misses her old way of life. The things just remind her of it."

"It's the same with my mother."

Olivia jerked at the reference to Margaret Avery. How vividly she recalled how his mother and hers had been great friends before their fathers parted ways.

"She hated how Father would clutter the house with things he would bring back from his travels. Now she will not part with a single item."

"And you? Are you a collector?"

His answer came quickly. "No."

She raised her brow, a bit surprised. "No?"

"I'm not a collector, and I never shall be, but I'm admittedly a student of the *art* of collecting. I personally resist the idea of being tied to objects. I suppose it's because I've seen how so much upheaval can be caused when one places all their energy in the amassing of things. Eventually those things become a weight. A burden. Consider Mrs. Milton. Consider Wainbridge. Think of all the turmoil that ultimately could have been avoided."

His words sobered her, and yet the familiarity in them soothed her. She found herself, for the first time the entire day, feeling comfortable, relaxed. Like the charade she'd been endeavoring to play could, for the moment, cease and her true identity could be released.

Over his broad shoulder Olivia spied Miss Stanley through the open doors. The beauty appeared to be searching for someone.

No doubt she was searching for Mr. Avery.

It could not be ignored. "I believe someone might be looking for you."

"Hmm?" He raised a dark brow and turned to follow her gaze, peering over his shoulder. He sighed and raked his fingers through his dark hair.

Olivia waited to speak until the woman was no longer visible through the door. "I feel for her."

"You do?"

"Of course. How awful it would be to think your entire future rested on your ability to marry a certain man." As soon as the words were out of her mouth, she wished she could retract them. "I probably shouldn't have said that."

"You should say whatever you like, Miss Brannon," he encouraged. "And if you'll indulge me, what abilities do you think a woman should rest her future on?"

She blinked at him. Never had she been asked to share her thoughts on such a personal matter. "It depends on the woman, I suppose."

"And you? What do you plan for the future?"

Heat crept up her neck. Their conversation had taken a decidedly personal turn, but she would not shy away from it. How lovely it felt to have real discussions on topics that mattered. "I'm well aware that I'm more fortunate than many women. I have a skill. But whether or not I can make a living with it remains to be seen."

"Then we are in the exact same situation. We are both counting on our skills."

She laughed at the ridiculous comparison.

"But I am curious," he continued. "You spoke of making a living. Don't you think it would be easier if you could share the burden with someone?"

"I've yet to find someone I could trust," she answered matter-of-factly.

He stepped closer, and his scent of sandalwood melded with the honeysuckle and fresh rain, intoxicating and exciting. "Don't forget, Miss Brannon. You accepted my apology. Doesn't that mean you trust me?"

A grin toyed with her lips. "I'm not sure. Does it?"

"I can tell you that I am trustworthy, but what matters is whether or not I can prove it."

Suddenly, they were no longer talking about collections or their business. She looked up into his eyes, their gazes locked, and she was unable to look away.

Could he be trusted as he said?

Could he be trusted . . . with her thoughts? Her confidence? Her heart?

He moved even closer. He was now within arm's reach.

The gathering faded into the background—the voices, the music. It seemed they were the only two people present.

Was he drawn to her in the same manner?

The nearby torchlight flashed on his features that were so attractive to her—his fine, straight nose. His strong jaw. His light green eyes.

He lowered his voice, his tone undeniably intimate. "Another confession."

"My, my." She smiled. "We really must do something about you and your confessions."

"I came out here specifically to find you, hoping you would consent to dance. With me." He offered her his arm. "Will you?"

How strong and confident his arm felt under her gloved hand. She felt safe and secure in a way she had never expected. What would it be like to go through life with this feeling?

As he took her to the floor, all thoughts of Mrs. Milton fled. She felt completely protected. Completely at ease. As if for a moment she could relax into the safety and trust.

Chapter 32

DAWN'S COLORS WERE breaking blue and purple by the time Lucas, Wainbridge, and Tate returned to Cloverton Hall from Whitmore House. The imposing structure slumbered in the pre-morning hours, and Lucas had to admit he was glad to have returned—but he was not tired.

Oh no—his mind was too alive for sleep. Never had he thought of himself as a romantic. The idea of marriage and a family had been one he'd held very loosely—like a distant dream that might or might not materialize.

But now, the entire picture of his future slammed fully into focus, and at the heart was Miss Brannon.

Olivia.

How, in such a short time, had everything he thought he knew about himself changed? Had she really that much power over him?

And yet, instead of fighting it, he found it intoxicating. Never would he have thought such a clever woman, an intelligent woman, a beautiful woman existed. His experience with the fairer sex had been with silly, pretentious girls battling for the most advantageous position. Nothing about it had been real.

Then he encountered Olivia, and an entirely new world—a new way of thinking—opened to him. What was more, she seemed to return the high regard. The manner in which her hand lingered on his arm. Her nearness while dancing.

No, no. There would be no sleep for him for quite some time.

Lucas, Tate, and Wainbridge exited the carriage and entered Cloverton Hall to find the butler waiting for them at the door. His rheumy eyes were wide, his graying hair disheveled. "There is something you need to see in the gallery, Mr. Wainbridge."

"Whatever it is, Gaines, it can wait until morning." Wainbridge extended his black beaver hat toward the butler.

Gaines accepted the hat. "Sir, I really must insist."

Tate, who had overindulged, stumbled toward the attic chamber, but after sensing the urgency in the butler's tone, Lucas remained with Wainbridge and accompanied him up the great staircase. Candlelight glowed from the open gallery doors as they approached, but the sight that met Lucas as he turned the corner chilled his blood.

The Cavesee Vase, the beautiful, large, and extremely valuable piece of chinoiserie, was on the floor in pieces.

Wainbridge erupted in a slew of curses. "What happened?"

Lucas's own steps slowed as he took in the sight before him. He could barely tear his gaze away as Wainbridge peppered Gaines with questions, demanding an explanation.

But the pale-faced butler shook his head. "I've no idea how it happened. One of the footmen noticed it when escorting Mr. Fielding and Captain Whitaker to their chambers and notified me. I am terribly sorry, sir. I have no answers."

Wainbridge, still intoxicated from the evening's events, raged. "Someone *heard* something. Someone *knows* something. No one sleeps, no one rests until I have answers, do you understand?" Wainbridge grabbed at a footman, who had been accompanying the butler, and snatched him by his coat. "You. You go find every single servant who was present while we were gone."

Wainbridge whirled his attention to Lucas. "How much was this worth?"

Lucas stammered, "Without evaluating I-I don't—"

"You have an idea," Wainbridge thundered. "How much?"

"We'd need to consult the original paperwork, but I—"

Without another word Wainbridge flew from the gallery toward the staircase, shouting orders to a footman as he did. Lucas needed to follow him, but before he did, he stooped to pick up one of the pieces at his feet. He rubbed his thumb over the smooth surface. He held it up to the light. He hoped that just maybe this piece was counterfeit and the authentic one was safe.

But his stomach sank.

This was the authentic Cavesee Vase.

It was real . . . and now it was shattered into hundreds of pieces.

Lucas hurried to follow after Wainbridge, his ears still ringing with the shock. He found him in the study, tearing through the stacks of paperwork Lucas had organized.

"Hold on, hold on." Lucas took the files from Wainbridge's hands. He quickly organized the stacks of papers into smaller piles and handed one to Wainbridge. "Search through these and look for the word *Cavesee* in the paperwork. It might be included on a document with other pieces, so look carefully."

Lucas was not sure how much time had passed, but it felt like hours. He'd never seen Wainbridge in such a state, but then again, the man had just lost the most expensive piece that would presumably secure his future. As Wainbridge continued to tear through the papers, a sickening sense of dread trickled through Lucas. There was no way this could end well. It only remained to be seen exactly how extensive the devastating reverberations would be.

At length Lucas picked up a document, and there was the name: Cavesee Vase. The bill of sale. Dated a decade prior. At the bottom was the name of the broker and witness of the sale.

Edward Brannon.

There was no way to keep this information from Wainbridge. Nor should he. But with each second that ticked by, the possible repercussions built.

Wainbridge would see the name.

He'd make the connection to Olivia.

And then what?

Lucas cleared his throat and handed the document to Wainbridge.

Wainbridge snatched it from him, angled it toward the light, and read it hungrily. Frantically. "Yes! This is it." He pointed to the substantial number—an amount that could make or break any man. "This was the purchase price, right?"

"Yes."

"That's what I've lost, then." Wainbridge swore under his breath, sank down into a chair, and leaned his head back.

Lucas shifted, uncomfortable not only with this situation but with the fact that some of the other pieces in the collection were as worthless as the shards of porcelain on the gallery floor.

Wainbridge wrenched his attention back to the paper in his hand, read it further. After several seconds, he jerked his head up. "Who is Edward Brannon?"

Lucas swallowed the lump forming in his throat. He had to answer. He would not lie. "Edward Brannon was an antiquities broker out of London. He is deceased now."

"Connected to Miss Brannon, my aunt's guest, I assume?"

Lucas drew a deep breath. "She's his daughter."

"And you did not think to tell me?" he demanded, his dark eyes wild.

"I didn't think it pertinent."

"Not pertinent?" Wainbridge grabbed another stack of papers and began flipping through them. "Most of these have his name on them! How is it not pertinent?"

"Miss Brannon is not here to evaluate your collection, Mr. Wainbridge."

"And I suppose this has nothing to do with the fact that I saw her trying to climb up to it in the gallery a few days ago?"

"Stay calm. She's here as a guest, and—"

"I will not remain calm! My aunt is a deceiving, conniving woman. Have you not figured that out by this point?"

Wainbridge slammed the papers down on the desk and barged toward the door.

Lucas set down his stack and began to follow.

"Do not follow me!"

Lucas did as bid, and once silence again descended upon the study, he turned to the papers. As he gathered them back into a pile, he reviewed the events of the past several days.

He'd come here with the express purpose of brokering these pieces.

He was not expecting to encounter Olivia.

He'd also not expected to encounter counterfeit pieces.

He certainly wasn't expecting to find the Cavesee Vase in shards on the floor. It seemed with each hour a level of complexity was added to his stay at Cloverton Hall that challenged everything he thought he knew to be true.

Staccato pounding jarred Olivia from sleep.

"Open this door!"

The pounding was not at her door but just outside it. And it did not stop.

Each thud sharpened her senses further, and she jumped from bed. In the purple light of very early dawn, she found her wrapper, flung it about her shoulders, and hurried to pull open her door.

Mr. Wainbridge, wild and frantic, stood in the corridor, hammering his fist against Mrs. Milton's bedchamber door.

"Mr. Wainbridge." She clutched her wrapper around her. "Is everything all right?"

He whirled to face her, red-faced. "You! I—"

Mrs. Milton's door swung open, and he spun back around.

"George!" Outrage colored Mrs. Milton's shocked expression. "What on earth are you doing? Are you aware of the hour?"

"The Cavesee Vase. It's destroyed!"

Mrs. Milton's complexion blanched. "What?"

Mr. Wainbridge spun to face Olivia. "I know who you are. I know who your father was. And I know you're connected with this. How dare you step foot in this house without disclosing the truth!"

Olivia winced. "Sir, I'm not—"

Mrs. Milton pushed past Mr. Wainbridge and rushed down the first floor's long corridor to the gallery entrance. Her hands flew to her mouth. She screamed.

Olivia followed and stopped short and gasped at the horrific sight.

Sobs burst from Mrs. Milton.

Guests, no doubt awoken by the shouts and cries, were gathering in the corridor, still dressed in their nightclothes.

Olivia hurried over and wrapped her arm around Mrs. Milton's shoulder. "Come away, Mrs. Milton, this—"

"And you!" Mr. Wainbridge's attention suddenly shifted to her.

Olivia straightened.

"I know you're involved with this."

The accusation stung. She shook her head. "I wasn't."

Mr. Wainbridge stepped dangerously close. "You will leave Cloverton Hall."

"George," protested Mrs. Milton. "She is *my* guest, and I absolutely forbid—"

"Enough!" He turned the full brunt of his ire on the older woman. "You're no longer the person to decide who is and who is not welcome on this property. *I am.* And I want her gone."

Mrs. Milton's expression shifted as if she'd been slapped. For the first time she did not have a response. She looked fragile. Broken.

Mr. Wainbridge stomped down the corridor before any other words could be spoken.

The stares from the guests bored into her: Mr. Fielding. Miss Stanley. Miss Haven.

She would not appear a victim. Nor would she beg, grovel, or explain. She straightened her posture and returned her arm around Mrs. Milton's seemingly delicate shoulders. "Come, Mrs. Milton. Come away."

After that, no one spoke. For what could be said?

Once Mrs. Milton stood in the threshold to her room, Olivia turned to the Blue Room. Tears blinding her vision, she entered the chamber, but not before she heard the voices from the other end of the corridor explode in harsh whispers. But she heard none of what was said. For she knew the truth—she had gambled that this opportunity would pan out and blossom into an even bigger opportunity. But she had been wrong. And now it was over, and it was time for her to return home.

Chapter 33

RAIN MISTED DOWN, saturating Lucas's formal tailcoat and dripping from the brim of his beaver hat, as if Cloverton Hall itself were commiserating with him regarding the frustration brewing within the walls.

He'd not slept since he returned to Cloverton Hall from Whitmore House. He doubted anyone really had, for shouts, confusion, and angry outbursts had left everyone ill at ease. Even now, he paced the stable courtyard, waiting—determined to speak with Olivia before she departed for London.

Stable hands bustled about him, preparing Cloverton's carriages for the unanticipated departure. Horses stomped and whinnied as if protesting the unexpected morning activity.

Lucas ran his hand down his face to wipe away the moisture. All the options went through his mind, but try as he might, he was unable to make sense of them. No one could have anticipated what happened to the Cavesee Vase, and until there were answers regarding *how* it happened and who was responsible, no one would experience peace.

At length the door from the back conservatory opened. Two footmen exited first, carrying a trunk between them. Mrs. Milton's lady's maid, another servant, Miss Brannon, and Mrs. Milton followed.

He jogged toward her through the rain, mindless of how the mud splashed on his boots. "Miss Brannon, a moment. Please."

She looked surprised, if not startled, to see him. Her eyes, which had been so vivid and bright mere hours ago, had dimmed. Her complexion was cool and pale. She said something to the servant next to her, handed her a small valise, and turned back toward him.

He took her arm and guided her to a sheltered spot just outside the stable to guard against the weather. Sensing he didn't have much time, he forged ahead. "Are you all right?"

Her face was barely visible from beneath her bonnet's broad brim. "I am."

"I'd like to offer my services as an escort, should you feel more comfortable traveling with one." He held his breath, determined that their time together would not end like this. Surely the connection he'd felt the previous few days had meant as much to her as it had to him.

Her distant tone was a knife to his chest. "That is kind but not necessary. The driver will make certain we arrive safely."

He shifted. Why would she refuse? He spied the footman securing her trunk—they hadn't much time. "I can't help but think somehow I could have prevented this."

"How could you possibly have prevented it?"

"Wainbridge saw your father's name on the Cavesee Vase's bill of sale and asked if you were related."

"And I hope you told him I was." She lifted her chin and finally met his gaze.

The fire in her statement encouraged him. "I did."

"Good."

An odd moment of panic seized him. Surely he was overlooking a way to fix the misunderstandings. He had to prevent her from leaving. "What can I do?"

She swallowed hard. "I told you that I came here hoping to prove something, remember? Maybe that was just not meant to be."

Behind him, the carriage was ready. Lucas's time was running low.

"I have to go." She looked over at the carriage, then turned back toward him and offered a hint of a smile. "But how nice it is to know that the Averys are not the monsters I believed them to be."

He would lose this battle—he could not prevent her from going—but he at least had to secure hope that this dreadful morning would not be their final interaction. "Perhaps when I return to London, I could call on you. Would that be permissible?"

She nodded. "Goodbye, Mr. Avery."

As Lucas watched Olivia bid a tepid farewell to Mrs. Milton, doubts stabbed his optimism. Like it or not, he was a different man now. She alone had opened his eyes to what an authentic, pure connection could be, and it was intoxicating—far more intoxicating than any other vice.

He determined in that moment that this would not be the end. This glimpse into what the future could be was realigning everything he thought he wanted out of life. He would pursue Olivia Brannon, for she was taking with her a piece of him that he could not live without—his heart.

———————

It was a miserable day—made ever more miserable by the rain that fell in misty sheets and the damp, bone-chilling wind that seeped in through the space around the doors and windows.

Olivia was not prone to tears. In her experience they'd never been productive or offered any true comfort. But at the moment she was worn. She hadn't slept. She hadn't eaten. The tangle of feelings churning in her was more than mere frustration. It was disappointment over the end of an opportunity. Anger at herself for not being more careful and guarded. More than anything, though, it was overwhelming sadness.

She'd seen the sincerity in Lucas's expression. She believed he was sorry to see her go. How, in such a short time, had Lucas Avery gone from a man she despised to a man who touched her heart? Her soul? She'd been at Cloverton Hall only a week, yet never had she connected with someone so perfectly—felt so understood and seen by another.

But it was likely over now. How could anything come to pass? He would return to his life in London, and his thoughts of her would subside. He'd go back to his existence, and she'd return to hers.

The rain pounded against the window, and a fresh gust of wind pushed against them from the west, swaying the carriage to and fro on the rutted road. She looked over to Tabitha, who was clutching a dark blue shawl about her shoulders and looking out the window, watching the scenery flash by.

Olivia was grateful to Mrs. Milton, for despite her distress, she'd insisted it would be improper for Olivia to travel without at least a maid.

"I am so sorry you were taken away from your routine to stay with me," Olivia said, drawing the young woman's attention.

"No need for an apology, Miss Brannon." Tabitha's smile was oddly bright. "I've only been out o' t' village a couple o' times. I'm excited about it, actually."

In that instance, the similarities between herself and the maid struck Olivia. Their backgrounds might be very different, and yet neither of them had ever been away from home.

"But you will have to travel home alone," persisted Olivia. "Does that not concern you?"

"Not at all! I've known t' driver an' these footmen for quite some time. They know better 'an to bother me. Besides, you're a lady. It would not be seemly for you t' travel alone. I had t' come."

"Oh, Tabitha." Olivia shook her head. "I'm not a lady. Not in the sense that you're referring to."

"Do ye think we'll e'er know what 'appened t' that vase?"

Tabitha's abrupt change of topic unsettled her, and the painful sight of the broken relic flashed in Olivia's mind.

"I 'eard the footmen talkin' 'bout it a'fore we left," Tabitha chattered on. "They said no one 'eard a thing. Isn't that odd? You'd think that when somethin' like that broke, it'd be so loud it would wake t' whole of Cloverton Hall."

Olivia leaned her head back on the tufted seat behind her and closed her eyes, as if to shut the memory out. The Cavesee Vase was an important piece, but it was only part of what made this entire situation so difficult. "I hate to think of the state we left poor Mrs. Milton in. The expression of horror on her face will haunt me, certainly."

Tabitha removed the bonnet from her head and shook out her coppery tresses. "Teague's there for 'er. But Mrs. Milton was already so angry a'fore this even 'appened. I can only imagine it'll be worse now. The sooner she can be away from Cloverton Hall, the 'appier she'll be."

Olivia returned her attention to the dreary, rain-soaked scenery. They would have at least one more full day of travel ahead of them, and how Olivia wished she could accelerate time and forget that this trip ever happened.

But that would mean forgetting about Lucas Avery.

And she was not sure she wanted to do that.

Chapter 34

LUCAS KNELT TO get a better look at the broken shards of cobalt-blue and milky-white porcelain.

The late-afternoon sunlight glinted off the reflective pieces, highlighting their perfect smoothness and beauty. Several large pieces remained intact, but many of the slivers had been reduced to almost a powder. The polished wood floor beneath the largest piece appeared dented, suggesting that the vase had hit the surface with some force.

How on earth would the vase have fallen?

He turned his attention to the shelf on which the piece had been sitting. It was deep. Solid. There was no conceivable way the Cavesee Vase could have just fallen off. Someone had to have tampered with it.

But who? And why?

Holding one of the pieces, he moved closer to the window to take advantage of the light. Over the years he'd thought he'd seen most everything when it came to situations like this. People purposely destroying valuable pieces to prevent someone from possessing them, people hiding items, even stealing or selling them. But this defied logic.

Lucas reviewed the facts once again in his mind. All the house party guests were at the ball, and all the guests' servants were accounted for in their chambers. And if a house servant was involved, why now when they had full access to the piece at any other time?

In that moment, as in so many since Olivia's departure, Lucas wished she were with him. He hadn't witnessed Wainbridge rage at her, but he was told of it, and he'd never be comfortable with how she'd been treated.

Currently, Wainbridge was in his study. Lucas loathed the prospect, but he needed to inform Wainbridge about the counterfeit pieces. Given what had just happened, he could not delay. In the time since Olivia's departure, he had completed his report. He was not entirely done with the assessment but had what he needed for the time being. With the large piece of porcelain in his hand, he made his way from the gallery, down the great staircase, and across the corridor to the study.

Lucas forced lightness to his voice as he entered the room. "I have good news."

Wainbridge scoffed and dropped to the chair behind his desk. "I could use a bit of good news right about now."

"In light of recent events, you and I should discuss the collection's current state. I've composed an initial assessment." Lucas handed him the written report. "I'd like to purchase several of the pieces outright, and the second sheet there is a list of items I believe I can broker sales for you, along with the estimated value

I'd expect them to sell for. You are welcome to entertain second opinions on the items I am offering to buy. These offers are good for a year."

Wainbridge snatched the ledger from Lucas, and his brow furrowed as he read. "This list isn't very long."

"Just as I had good news, I've some bad news as well."

Wainbridge's dark eyes flashed, and his lips flattened in a line as he glanced up from the ledger.

"I need to show you something. Much of Mr. Milton's collection that he was most known for was his blue-and-white chinoiserie. But after examining them closely, it pains me to say that many of the pieces are counterfeit."

Wainbridge scoffed. "What?"

"They appear to be the original pieces that are described in the logs, but they are not Chinese porcelain."

Disbelief reddened Wainbridge's face. "Then what are they?"

"Bone China. It's a ceramic made of bone ash, China clay, and Cornish stone. It has the appearance of Chinese porcelain, but it was made here in England, fairly recently." Lucas handed Wainbridge the piece of porcelain in his hand. "This is a piece of the Cavesee Vase, and it is very much authentic. Feel the weight of it?"

He gave the man a few seconds and then retrieved the counterfeit piece from the sideboard. "Now look at this one. Feel the weight difference? Notice how the coloring and translucency are slightly different?"

Lucas waited for Wainbridge to draw his own conclusion.

After several seconds, Wainbridge lowered the piece back to the table and shook his head. "How is this even possible?"

"I honestly don't know. Normally the bone China would have markings that would indicate where it was made, but none of these do, which makes it difficult to track down their origins."

"Are you telling me that my uncle bought worthless pieces of art?"

"No. I don't believe for a moment that your uncle bought counterfeits. According to these records, many of these were purchased many years ago, before when I suspect these replications were made. Furthermore, these deals were orchestrated by Mr. Brannon. His reputation is solid. He would not have brokered a counterfeit deal. I'd stake my own reputation on it.

"It's much more plausible that someone commissioned these reproductions to make it appear that the collection was indeed intact. Or someone exchanged these for the original counterparts. Truthfully, it is not my place to speculate. All I can do is comment on what I see from a professional standpoint."

Wainbridge blew out his breath in a noisy huff and ran his hands over the dark stubble gathering on his jaw. "Will this nightmare end?"

"I know my assessment is not what you hoped it would be, and I wish there were a way I could make it different, but take heart. There is a great deal of money to be made on what is authentic—the statues. The paintings. The ivory. I've outlined it in the ledger."

Wainbridge tossed the ledger on the table. "I wonder if my aunt knows."

"About the counterfeits?" Lucas shrugged. "That I could not tell you."

"So here we are." Wainbridge threw out his arms. "Are we even better off than when we began?"

Lucas kept his voice steady. "Francis Milton's collection is extensive, and I've merely scratched the surface. More assessments are required, but in light of everything that has occurred, I think it best that I depart for London in the morning. If I may make a suggestion, you should investigate the counterfeit situation further. A great deal of money is unaccounted for. There are individuals you can hire to investigate this matter, and if it would be helpful, I can provide you with some names."

Wainbridge rubbed his palm across his forehead. "I guess it's a start. I need money, so for the time being, this will have to do. I'll review your ledger and call on you when I am in London next."

Lucas bowed slightly as the conversation ended and turned on his heel to leave. This was certainly not the outcome he had hoped for—or expected. And he had no way of knowing if Wainbridge would accept the offers Lucas had outlined in the ledger, but in the end, did it really matter? His experience at Cloverton had opened his eyes to a completely new way of thinking of the future. No, the financial gains he was hoping to realize from this house party would not come to fruition, but he felt as if the true opportunity was only just beginning.

"Why did you not say anything?" Tate prodded, incredulous, as he and Lucas stood in the dining room after dinner, taking their port. "Counterfeit chinoiserie. Who would have thought?"

"You know why I couldn't say anything." Lucas folded his arms over his chest. "I had to find out exactly what I was dealing with. And you may be a friend, but you can't be trusted with confidential matters."

Tate tugged at his cravat, causing it to hang askew. "Bah, I can be trusted."

"You cannot, and you know it," Lucas snipped. "Are you sure you don't want to return to London when I go?"

"I'm certain. I'll stay for the rest of the party. After all, Miss Haven's interest in Wainbridge has suddenly declined, and while I do lament our host's misfortune, there's no reason why I should not take advantage of the opportunity in front of me."

"I'd expect no less."

"But what I really count as an offense is that you kept the truth about Miss Brannon from me for all that time. You sly devil." Tate poked Lucas in the shoulder with his forefinger. "You had the answer to the great mystery and didn't say a word."

"I'd argue that the identity of the person who broke the Cavesee Vase is the bigger mystery of this excursion, but do go on."

"Yes, I suppose you're right." Tate indulged in a long sip. "Any new theories as to who is responsible?"

"No, and I don't intend to propose any." Lucas took Tate's empty glass from him and set it on the table before he could drop it and break it. "If Wainbridge is smart, he'll hire someone to look into it, for something is amiss with this entire situation."

Tate's eyes widened, as if an idea suddenly dawned. "You should stay and find the culprit."

Lucas scoffed. "No. The law on such things is not my forte. I'm an antiques purveyor, not a thief taker."

Tate shrugged. "Maybe I should investigate it."

Lucas laughed—probably the first real laugh he had enjoyed since the discovery of the shattered vase. "That I'd like to see."

When the men joined the women in the drawing room, a shade had been set up, just as it had been a few nights previous, and the ladies were drawing silhouettes. There was no laughter, no chatter—the sedate tone was a sharp contrast to the much livelier events of the past several evenings. In fact, the women barely looked up as the men entered. The only one who took notice was Romano, who abandoned his position by Miss Haven and approached Lucas.

"What an interesting event this turned out to be, no?" Romano said lowly as he stood next to Lucas. "And such a shame our pretty little friend is no longer with us."

There was no need to ask to whom the painter was referring. The party did seem sad without their *pretty little friend*, but Lucas doubted Mr. Romano felt her absence as keenly as Lucas did.

"I could not help but notice the two of you were quite friendly, and I'm told you both reside in London. I hope you will do me a favor?" Romano pulled an item from his pocket. "I finished her portrait last night as best I could from memory, and I wondered if you would be good enough to see it sent to her once you return. I will be traveling north after this party and am not certain when I will be back in London. It would be a shame to let the art go to waste."

Lucas took the small parcel and unfolded the handkerchief around it. There, in a little metal frame, was a small painting of Olivia's face and shoulders, no bigger than the palm of his hand. Romano had re-created Olivia's full florid lips. Her entrancing topaz eyes. The soft dimple in her cheek. Her calm, even demeanor.

"You've captured her likeness incredibly," Lucas responded. "I will certainly see that this gets to her."

Mr. Romano bowed. "I thank you."

Lucas folded the miniature portrait in the handkerchief and tucked it in his coat.

Once Romano returned to the ladies, Lucas assessed the party with a fresh eye. The desire to be back home among what was familiar surged through him. With his work done and Olivia no longer here, the party's allure had diminished. And yet there was one task he needed to do before he departed.

Miss Stanley and her chaperone were standing near the shade, neither speaking nor joining in the activity. She did not look toward him as he approached her, but once he was there, she said, "I heard you're to depart in the morning."

"Yes. Given all that has transpired, it is best that I go."

"What did Mr. Romano give you?"

"He asked that I take Miss Brannon's portrait with me to London to see that she gets it."

"May I see it?"

He took the portrait out and handed it to her.

"She *is* lovely." The sadness in her tone sobered him. She flicked her large brown eyes to him. "You hold her in high regard, don't you?"

Had it been that obvious? Lucas accepted the piece back, wrapped it, and returned it to his coat. "I do."

Miss Stanley folded her arms before her, looked toward the ceiling as one abating tears, and then assumed a smile. "I shall miss you."

It was important to him that he left Cloverton with good rapport with his old friend. "I hope you know how I've enjoyed our friendship over the years. I wish you nothing but the best moving forward."

She sniffed. Redness rimmed her eyes. "Who knows where I'll be this time next year?"

"Who knows where any of us will be in a year's time? But you're intelligent, resourceful, and possess one of the finest wits of anyone I know. It will all be fine in the end."

"Will it?" she asked, turning her warm eyes up to him.

"It will."

As he bowed and left her with her chaperone, fresh eagerness to return to London surged through him. It was true—he had no idea where he would be in a year's time, but if Olivia were a part of his life, it would be well worth the wait.

Chapter 35

THE SUN WAS finally shining on Kingsby Street when the Cloverton carriage turned onto the broad lane. The ever-present blanket of smoke swirled in the humid air, and the noisy sounds of a London afternoon met Olivia when the carriage pulled to a stop. She angled her head to see the shingle boasting the Brannon name through the window. Even though it was nowhere near as lovely as Cloverton Hall, there was something comforting about coming home to what was familiar. Normal life would resume.

"Is this your home?" Tabitha, eager-faced and bright-eyed, leaned forward to see through the mud-streaked windows.

"This is my family's business. We live in the apartments above it."

Memories of how she used to love coming to this shop with her father each day flooded her as her first foot stepped down to the dusty road. And even though she was excited to see Laura, reservation slowed her.

Uncle Thomas had been opposed to the entire endeavor. Russell had tried to talk her out of it as well. And while she had completed her assessment and could provide her uncle and Russell with a thorough report, her professional prospects were no better off than when she left. If anything, she was worse off, for now she nursed a bruised ego and a wounded heart.

Olivia summoned her courage, placed her hand on the receiving room door's brass handle, turned it, and stepped inside. A bell signaled her arrival, and shortly thereafter her uncle appeared from the back room through to the receiving parlor.

"You're back." His eyes held no warmth, his expression no affection. "We weren't expecting you for at least another week."

Russell, no doubt drawn by her uncle's voice, also appeared. "So, how did it go?"

"It went well." She feigned as much enthusiasm as she could. "I've cataloged a number of promising items. The ledger's in my trunk."

"Why are you back so early?" her uncle asked.

"The evaluation went smoothly, like I said, but Mr. Wainbridge wasn't pleased I was there in an antiquities agent capacity. He and Mrs. Milton do not see eye to eye, and when he found out that Father had been the one to broker many of the deals with his uncle, Mr. Wainbridge wasn't comfortable with my presence."

Her uncle turned his attention to Tabitha. "And who is this?"

"This is Tabitha. She works for Mrs. Milton and was kind enough to accompany me on the return journey. The carriage will not return to Cloverton until the morrow, so she'll stay the night here."

"Olivia!"

Laura, bright-eyed and eager, burst down the corridor and through the door and flung her arms around her sister's neck. "I've been dying for you to return!"

When she finally released Olivia's neck, Laura clutched her hands and squeezed. "Come on. You must be exhausted, and I want to hear absolutely everything!"

Olivia looked back at her uncle's somber face and Russell's bleak one. She had no idea how they were going to respond when she shared the full extent of what had occurred, but based on the reception, she was in no hurry to disclose the details.

Olivia placed her candle on the small table next to her bed and turned to draw the curtains over the windows that overlooked Kingsby Street. It really was pleasant to be home. For the first time in days, she could truly breathe deeply and move about completely freely. The familiar feeling of the uneven wooden floor felt heavenly beneath her bare feet, and her favorite wool shawl, although patchy in places, was the most comforting feeling in the world.

Outside the windows, the common sounds of the London evening floated on the breeze: men calling to one another, carriage wheels on the dirt road, a baby crying somewhere in the distance.

It was not perfect, nor was it as fine as Cloverton Hall, but for the time being contentment settled over her.

"I saw the chambermaid in the hall," Laura announced as she entered the room, a blanket in her arms. "She said that Tabitha is all settled downstairs."

"Good." Olivia wished she could have offered the young woman a proper bedchamber, but the only spare bed was with their servant girls. "I hope she'll be comfortable."

"Oh, I'm sure she will," mused Laura as she doffed her dressing gown, donned her sleeping cap, and crawled into her side of the bed. "It's been terribly lonely without you here."

"I thought you said I kick too much," Olivia teased as she moved the candle from the bureau to the small table beside the bed. "I assumed you'd like having the bed all to yourself."

"Sharing a chamber is a small price to pay for having someone to pass the evenings with besides Uncle. He is positively droll."

Olivia laughed at her sister's dramatic description and pulled back her covers. She'd not realized until now just how much she had missed her sister.

"I want to know every single detail." Laura propped herself up on her elbow, her golden eyes wide. "Surely you must have a dozen stories to share."

Anticipation glimmered in her sister's eyes, but Olivia hesitated.

Would she tell her about the beautiful gowns and elegant rooms and dashing gentlemen, or would she tell her about the curious stares, manipulative women, and flirtatious men?

Olivia decided there would be time enough for the world's harsh realities, so she told Laura about the luxurious chamber she'd stayed in. What it was like to have a lady's maid dress her hair. How exhilarating it was to dance at a ball.

"And the gentlemen?" Laura inquired eagerly. "I've yet to hear you mention anyone in particular."

For the millionth time Lucas Avery flashed in her mind.

The memory, however sweet, incited pain. Each time she thought of him, she was reminded afresh that it was simply not to be. "No one in particular, but it was an interesting time. But it is true what they say. Home is the dearest place of all."

"I don't believe you," teased Laura.

"Well, you should." Olivia rolled over, blew out her candle, pulled the blanket over her, and settled against her pillow. "Cloverton Hall was beautiful. It was elegant and pristine. Even the servants were elegant and refined. You would have loved the gardens. But even for all of its loveliness, nothing compares to the comfort of being home."

Chapter 36

A PLAIN MUSLIN day gown. Heavy, scuffed boots on her feet. A cloth tied over her hair. Olivia smoothed over the front of her linen apron. Her attire could not be any further from the finery she wore while at Cloverton. And while she had enjoyed Cloverton's refinement, such attire was not suited to her usual daily tasks.

It would be easy to relive the events of the past few weeks in her mind—to dissect every interaction and reaction—but she'd much rather be up and useful instead of in bed feeling sorry for herself.

After seeing Tabitha safely on the carriage bound for Cloverton Hall the next morning, Olivia found Russell at his desk with ledger and quill in hand. He looked up as she entered and removed the spectacles on his nose. "There you are! Didn't think it would be too long before you were back down here, poking around as you do."

Olivia picked up a stack of unopened letters from the desk and flipped through them. "You know me. I can't abide being idle."

"Yes, I'm aware." He stood, wiped his hands together, and came around the desk. "I don't mind saying that it was not the same without you here every day, nosing in my business. I actually kind of missed it."

"Did you now?" she quipped. "Well, I'm back now, and I fear you will not be rid of me anytime soon." She propped her hands on her hips and looked around the tidy office. "Now, what have I missed? Anything new?"

He motioned toward a shelf on the far wall. "Those are three crates there, just came in on the ships. Haven't gotten around to opening them."

"Are they the ones from Italy?"

"I believe so. The paintings we bought from the Sealborn estate arrived. They are along the back wall. Oh, and we sold the Spanish silver to a gentleman in Austria. It will be going out on the ship next month."

"Very nice." Olivia deeply breathed in the familiar scent of wooden crates, packing straw, and dust. Eager to see the Sealborn portraits, she returned the letters to the desk and headed to the back of the storeroom.

But something she saw on the way slowed her steps.

In a crate on a low shelf, she spied a piece of chinoiserie. She reached down to get a better look.

The strangest sensation crept over her as she lifted the moon flask vase. After the discoveries Mr. Avery had made at Cloverton, she felt unusually sensitive to the feel of Chinese porcelain. Olivia took the piece to the window to examine it more closely.

Her stomach tightened as she ran her finger over the cobalt scene depicting a pagoda and cranes and the two dolphin-shaped handles. She was almost certain that she had seen this exact piece at Cloverton Hall, but the one she saw was not authentic.

Could this be the original?

Certain she was surely mistaken but curious nonetheless, she carried it over to the desk and set it down.

Russell looked up from his ledger. "What's that?"

She'd not told Russell or her uncle about what had happened regarding the Cavesee Vase or the counterfeit pieces. It hadn't felt right. But now, would it be best to divulge what happened?

She tapped her fingers atop the piece. "When I was at Cloverton Hall, a handful of chinoiserie pieces were discovered to be counterfeit. I could almost swear to the fact that I saw one of the replicas there and here is the original."

"Really?" Russell frowned and took the piece from her.

Olivia moved to the files, looked up the number on the tag with the piece, pulled out the papers associated with it, and laid them before her.

"That's odd." She flipped one of the papers over, then returned it to the desk. "There is no bill of ownership, just a transaction history."

Russell moved to read over her shoulder. "You know your uncle. He's not nearly as scrupulous as your father was."

And Russell was right. How many times had her uncle made decisions that should have been passed on or failed to secure the necessary paperwork?

"And the seller, J. Wakes? I've never heard of him before."

Russell scratched his fingers through his curly hair. "Your uncle has taken to going to those auctions at the docks. Might that be it?"

"It hardly seems like a responsible way to do business." She clicked her tongue.

"I don't disagree." Russell replaced his spectacles. "But what's to be done?"

She hid her annoyance. Russell had an irritating habit of agreeing with her, regardless of her stance. She needed a real conversation, not to be told what she wanted to hear.

"I suggest you take the matter up with your uncle," Russell said. "You never said much about your time at Cloverton Hall. How did it go?"

Olivia had tried not to spend a lot of time dwelling on her experiences there. If anything, her visit had opened her eyes to how other people lived. She had felt awe at the beauty surrounding her, she'd received the flirtatious attention of aristocratic gentlemen, and she'd had her likeness painted. But she had also experienced a different side of the higher social strata—one that was harsh and ugly, hurtful and unforgiving.

"It was nice to meet new people, but like I said, I am glad to be home, where things are familiar."

But as she returned the piece to the crate she found it in, a strange twinge pulled at her heart. She had been honest—most of the people were nice to meet, but it was just as easy to forget them. But one stuck with her in the most uncomfortable manner—and she feared it would take her heart quite a while to forget him.

Lucas flipped open his watch—the hour was growing late.

He'd arrived back in London just that afternoon, and already he'd called on his mother. This time she'd refused to leave her bed, and Mrs. Smith had shared that she'd spent nearly every hour of the last week in her chamber. Even so, he spent an hour with her and told her all the details of Cloverton Hall, but he stopped short of telling her about Miss Brannon. He was unsure how she would react to that particular link to the past.

He was not nearly as selective about what he shared with Night when he went to the shop.

Lucas filled his agent in on every relevant detail of the event, from the counterfeit pieces to Miss Brannon's presence, to the haphazard paperwork, to the fate of the Cavesee Vase. Wainbridge had permitted him to bring one of the counterfeit pieces—a small bowl—back to London to show his agents with the hope that one of them recognized it.

"This is impressive, isn't it?" Night exclaimed as he lifted the piece to examine it more closely.

"I'm ashamed to say that I didn't even realize it wasn't authentic until I held it," Lucas admitted. "Cloverton was full of them."

"I'll share it with the others and see what they can find out." Night tucked it under his arm.

Once he was satisfied that his men had the information they needed to continue with their work, Lucas had one more thing to attend to. He patted his pocket and felt the miniature portrait that Romano had given him.

The walk from his shop to the Brannon shop was a short one. He had no qualms with Russell Crane, but he'd never interacted with Thomas Brannon and had no idea how the man would receive him. He also had no idea if Olivia had told them about encountering him.

Memories flared as he approached the modest door. This was the building his father had shared with Edward Brannon all those years before their partnership dissolved. Lucas and Olivia had spent hours in the warehouse with their fathers, learning and playing. They'd been very young, of course, but he still remembered. Olivia was a few years younger than he. Were her memories as vivid as his were?

When Lucas opened the shop door and entered the receiving parlor, a bell chimed at his arrival. A few seconds later, Russell Crane, with his curly blond hair and heavy leather apron, stepped through a connecting door.

"Mr. Avery!" he exclaimed, his light blue eyes widening with surprise. "My word. This is unexpected."

"Good day, Crane. How are you?"

"Fine, fine. A bit surprised to see you here, though." He propped his hands akimbo. "What can I help you with?"

"I'm here to speak with Miss Brannon."

"Olivia?" Crane's brows drew together in confusion.

"Yes."

"Of course. Wait here."

Lucas paced the small, plain receiving room until at last a distant door opened and footsteps approached. His heart leapt in his chest at the sound, and he turned toward the corridor.

But instead of Olivia, Thomas Brannon entered.

Lucas was struck at the sight. It had been months, if not years, since Lucas had spoken with the man. He bowed.

No friendliness or warmth marked Brannon's expression as he wiped his hands on a rag. "I was not aware you were on such friendly terms with my niece."

"I had the pleasure of renewing my acquaintance with Miss Brannon while at Cloverton Hall. I was there to assess the Cloverton collection, and she was there with Mrs. Milton."

"She failed to mention it."

Normally, Lucas had no problem conversing with anyone, but something about Thomas Brannon sat ill with him. Furthermore, he wasn't sure how to interpret the fact that Olivia had not mentioned their meeting to either her uncle or Mr. Crane. Had it not been significant enough to her to mention? Or did she think her family would oppose such an interaction?

He pushed his thoughts aside. "I've been asked to deliver something to her that was left behind at Cloverton Hall."

But he did not need to say any more, for just as the last words were out of his mouth, he heard the rustling of fabric just beyond the door, and Olivia appeared.

His chest tightened at the sight of her.

Beautiful.

She was not attired as she had been at Cloverton, in silks and lace, with her hair dressed in curls and pins. A simple gown of sage gingham, protected by a khaki linen apron, adorned her frame, and her chestnut tresses were secured at the base of her neck in a simple plaited chignon.

He'd clearly interrupted her work. The sleeves of her gown were rolled up to her elbows, and she rolled them down as she stepped through the threshold. And yet a genuine smile dimpled her cheek. "Mr. Avery! I was not expecting to see you. What a pleasant surprise."

Chapter 37

HER HEART THUDDED an erratic cadence in her chest, making her head light and her breathing shallow.

He was here. Mere feet away from her.

As soon as her uncle quit the small receiving room, she inched closer to Mr. Avery and lowered her voice. "How surprised I am to see you! I assumed you'd remain at Cloverton Hall for the duration of the gathering."

A grin tugged his mouth. "In light of all that happened, I thought it best to return to London."

She swiped long wisps of hair from her face, wishing she'd had a chance to tidy it before he arrived. "I confess I have been thinking a great deal about Cloverton Hall lately. How did you leave things there?"

He lowered his beaver hat to his side and raked his fingers through his hair. "I departed the day after you did. But after you left, the entire atmosphere was quite somber. The discovery of the Cavesee Vase's destruction dampened the whole party."

The events—and the feelings she experienced as a result—raced through her mind. "It's all so unbelievable. Were they able to learn any more about what happened?"

He shrugged his broad shoulder. "As of the time I left, it was still a mystery. But I can confirm that the piece was the authentic Cavesee Vase."

She drew a deep breath and exhaled slowly. "It just doesn't make any sense, does it?"

"Something odd is happening at Cloverton Hall. The entire situation is problematic. I advised Wainbridge to engage assistance to look into the matter further. I hope he does."

"And Mrs. Milton? How was she faring?"

"I didn't see her at all after you left. She'd confined herself to her chambers and refused to speak with anyone."

Their conversation slowed. How handsome Lucas looked in his crisp midnight-blue tailcoat and maroon waistcoat. She noticed the careless manner in which his sable hair fell over his forehead, and the bright light filtering through the front windows emphasized the mesmerizing hue of his eyes. She felt like a schoolgirl, enchanted and hopeful, and it was an intoxicating, liberating sensation.

Lucas glanced toward the door before leaning a bit closer toward her and lowering his voice. "I understand that Wainbridge treated you horribly the night the Cavesee Vase was discovered, and it was shameful. You deserved none of it."

Olivia rubbed her hand over her arm. "Mr. Wainbridge was shocked and upset. I understood his frustration—really, I did. I assure you, no harm has been done."

"Oh, I almost forgot. I have something for you that you left behind at Cloverton." He reached into the inside pocket of his coat and then extended a folded handkerchief toward her.

Curious, she accepted it and unfolded the cambric kerchief to reveal the painted miniature of her likeness. A giddy laugh bubbled from her. "Why, this is amazing! What a talent Mr. Romano has. It is like looking in a small mirror."

He leaned his head closer to her and looked at the painting. "It's very beautiful, but I daresay it is because of the subject matter, not the painter."

Heat rushed her cheeks at the compliment. How easy it would be to fall back to that place of infatuation with him—that feeling of elation at just being in his presence. But she had to be realistic. She now knew he called on her for a specific reason—to give her the painting. It would serve no purpose to jump to conclusions. She would not let her heart build up something that might or might not exist between them.

She sobered, recalling her discovery earlier that morning. "I want to show you something. Wait here." Olivia tucked the miniature portrait in her apron pocket, hurried back to the store-room, retrieved the chinoiserie piece she had discovered earlier that morning, and brought it out to him. "I came across this in our inventory earlier today."

He took it from her, frowned, and assessed it for several moments. "This is a match of one of the replicas at Cloverton. Isn't it?"

"Exactly what I thought." She nodded, eager to discuss it further. "And it's authentic. According to our records it was purchased three years ago, but the only documentation I could find was a bill of sale from a seller named J. Wakes."

"I've not heard of him."

"Neither have I. But my uncle has taken to attending the auctions for the unclaimed items at the docks. I can't figure out how this would have gotten there. Surely it's connected. Don't you think?"

He returned the moon flask vase to her. "I'll talk to my agents. They are more familiar with those auctions than I am, and they might be familiar with this Wakes fellow."

Thumping sounds and a crash emanated from the storeroom, and they both turned to look that direction.

Lucas chuckled a bit and adjusted his hat beneath his arm. "I don't think your uncle and Crane are too pleased with my presence here. And I can tell you are busy, so I won't keep you."

Olivia's heart dropped. She didn't want him to leave. In fact, this visit had given her the first real sense of happiness since she returned.

"But before I leave," he said, "I was hoping I could beg a favor. A personal one."

She raised her brow. "Oh?"

"My mother and your mother were friends."

"The very best of friends, so I've been told," she added.

"Since my father's death, things have been quite difficult for her. I thought that maybe if you were to call on her, it might bring her a measure of happiness—a way for her to connect with the past but also see how life does go on."

His words struck her—how familiar the sentiment was. "I know that sadness. My father suffered from it after my mother died. It is a cruel pain."

"Our families have had difficult times. I would like to think that if we can heal from that, perhaps we would all be open to new things."

She smiled. "I'd like that. Perhaps I will bring Laura. She has few memories of Mother. A visit would help her as well."

"She'd be more than welcome. Perhaps next Thursday? I could send our carriage for you."

After the visit arrangements were made and Lucas bid his farewell, Olivia watched him through the window as he turned down the street. Her head felt light. Her heart felt full. How would she ever return to work after this visit?

Before her time at Cloverton Hall, Olivia had never really noticed just how noisy London was at night. With the exception of the chatter from the other guests or the occasional hoot from an owl in the nearby trees, Cloverton slept in silence. London, in comparison, seemed wild and unruly.

The street outside her window was never still. Voices, movement, calls, and shouts—it was a lullaby she'd not noticed until it was absent. And now that it was back, she found it difficult to ignore and it kept her awake. Nearly a week had passed since she'd returned, and she still hadn't readjusted to the nightly noises.

Next to her, Laura's rhythmic breathing confirmed she was sound asleep, and the ticking of the mantel clock marked the lateness of the hour.

Olivia surrendered to the sounds. She stood from the bed, lit a candle, and made her way to the kitchen to make tea. Knowing that the servant girls slept on the other side of the kitchen wall, Olivia did her best to be quiet.

Once in the kitchen, she heard voices. At first she thought it nothing more than the maids engaged in a late conversation or the sounds of the street filtering through the windows.

But then it sounded as if the noises were coming from the storeroom.

Concerned, she tiptoed from the kitchen into the corridor and listened.

There could be no mistaking it—the voices came from behind the door.

Her heart began to race within her chest. No one should be in the storeroom at this hour. She extinguished her candle and moved to the door, held her breath, and listened.

She recognized Russell's voice first. "I got your letter. What were you thinking coming here again? It was bad enough you were here at all."

"I couldn't help that," responded a heavily accented feminine voice. "Mrs. Milton made me."

Olivia froze.

Tabitha!

But how? She'd left nearly a week prior.

Why would Tabitha be talking to Russell? She hadn't even spoken to him while she was a guest in the house.

Olivia pressed her lips together in concentration as Tabitha resumed talking.

"Besides, I had to. Time's runnin' out. Mr. Wainbridge is takin' t' lot o' them t' London soon. I 'eard 'im say as much t' Mrs. Milton two days ago. If ye want t' switch 'em out, ye need t' be quick 'bout it."

"When?"

"From what I 'eard, a transport with guards an' t' like is comin' within the fortnight."

Olivia froze. Could she be hearing this correctly?

"How would I even know if the pieces are ready yet?" snapped Russell. "These things don't just appear out of thin air."

"Don't I know that?" she hissed back. "But ye need t' figure it out. Our time's comin' t' an end, an' fast."

"All right, all right," came the hasty reply. "When?"

"Mr. Wainbridge an' 'is sister'll be at an engagement next Wednesday—another party at t' Whitmore House. Mrs. Milton too. Cloverton'll be empty."

"You're certain no one suspects anything?"

Tabitha scoffed. "If t' debacle with t' vase didn't incite anythin', I think we're clear."

Olivia felt sick. Tabitha was referring to the Cavesee Vase— there was no other explanation.

Russell muttered, "It'll cost us a pretty penny to make up for that. Wakes will demand payment for his work. He doesn't care if we got the original out or not."

Wakes! Surely it was not a coincidence that his name was on the paperwork.

"I knew it was a bad idea t' trust Billy t' get the vase. This whole mess is 'is fault. 'e dropped it—said it were 'eavier than 'e expected, and it fell when he was gettin' it down. Broke into a 'undred pieces."

"Why did you even bring him into it? You should have just done it yourself."

"It was clear up on t' shelf! You know full well I couldn't get it down."

"Where's Billy now?"

"Got spooked. I doubt we'll ever see the likes of 'im again."

The pieces fell together quickly in her mind—a disastrous, messy puzzle.

Russell already knew about the counterfeit pieces, because he knew Tabitha.

At first the connection was ludicrous. Then it made sense. Russell had been a part of their business and Milton's dealings for over a decade. He knew everything. And then when her father had died and their uncle took over, the discipline was lax, which gave him the perfect opportunity to do whatever he liked. It explained why the original moon flask vase was in their storeroom.

"Can ye get t' Wakes in time?" Tabitha continued.

"Yes. I'll have to, won't I? I can't be sure he'll come, though."

"'e must. And *you* must get 'im there. I'm tellin' ye, this is our last chance. Now that Wainbridge knows, they'll be watchin' things awful carefully."

"We could have another problem on our hands," Russell added. "Olivia was down here earlier and saw the original pieces we are storing here. She said she thought they might be a part of the Cloverton collection. I was able to cover for it, but if she suspects something, we could be in trouble."

"Best not let John know that. Ye know 'ow 'e is. I 'ate to think what 'e'd do to her if 'e thought she knew somethin'."

The threat of violence in Tabitha's words stunned. Would someone be willing to harm her over this? Or worse?

"I'd best be gettin' back. I—"

Olivia wanted to hear no more. She made her way back down the corridor. There was no time to be shocked. To be angry. She didn't know who Billy was. She didn't even know how or why Tabitha was here. She'd seen her leave herself.

She had this information about criminal activity. The important thing was how to act upon it.

Chapter 38

THE NEXT MORNING Olivia donned her straw bonnet and stepped into the humid morning. She'd not slept a wink since overhearing the midnight conversation in the storeroom. Her mind was alive with all she'd heard, and she'd spent every moment attempting to complete a picture of exactly what had been happening.

The stale air caught the folds of her light wool pelisse as she rounded the corner from the shop's alley to the main street. She wound her way through the business district's crowded streets. Milliners and haberdashers, banks and grocers were all opening for the day, and busy chatter and the crunching of carriage and cart wheels echoed from the structures lining the road.

After a short walk she arrived at the Avery shop—a smart, clean storefront with large, bowed, multipaned windows and a deeply set door painted a vivid yellow. She'd walked past this place numerous times, but never would she have dreamt of setting foot inside.

But today was different. Many things were different.

Olivia paused in front of the door.

It was bold—brazen, even—to call on a man.

True—he'd called on her first, and as the only one who could truly understand the significance of what she'd overheard, he needed to know this information. Even though her singular goal for the last several years had been independence and self-reliance, it didn't feel like she was going to Lucas for help. She was going to him to collaborate. Nothing in his manner suggested that he looked down on her or her abilities. And that fact attracted her to him even more.

Summoning fortitude, Olivia straightened her shoulders and opened the shop door, which triggered a bell, and entered. The musty scent of dust and antiques tickled her nose, and light from the front windows landed on an assortment of displays—a collection of Turkish urns on a velvet patterned rug, an assortment of oil paintings on a wall papered with Chinese wall coverings. Several Persian rugs of vibrant greens and blues covered the planked wooden floor.

Movement at a curtain near the back of the room captured Olivia's attention, and she turned. A tall, wiry man with wispy white hair and eyebrows stepped through.

"Welcome to Avery's, miss. Is there something I can assist you with?"

Olivia tightened her grip on her reticule as the nerves fired through her. "I would like to speak with Mr. Avery, please."

"Mr. Avery is engaged at the moment." The man lifted his pointed chin, doing little to hide his assessment of her. "Are you sure there is nothing I can—"

"It is very important that I speak with him," Olivia blurted. "Is he on the premises?"

The man's bony jaw twitched. He lifted his chin. "I'll see if he's available. The hour is quite early yet, though. May I tell him who wishes to speak with him?"

"Miss Olivia Brannon."

The clerk's sparse brows jumped. "A moment, please."

She stood completely still until the clerk disappeared through a door. She didn't have to wait long before the sound of footsteps clipped a nearby floor, and then the curtain again pulled open.

At the sight of Lucas, Olivia's trepidation fled.

"Miss Brannon," Lucas exclaimed, his customary smile inciting her to smile in return. "What a surprise to see you this morning."

Olivia flicked her gaze toward the clerk, who'd followed Lucas in. "I must speak with you. Privately, if possible."

Lucas motioned for the clerk to leave, who did as instructed, but only after casting a suspicious glance in her direction.

Refusing to be dissuaded by the skeptical glance, Olivia waited until all was again silent. "I'm sorry to bother you like this, but I've learned something quite unnerving, and I didn't know who else to come to."

His brows drew together in concern, and he folded his arms over his chest. "What's the matter?"

Olivia lowered her voice and conveyed every detail she'd overheard the previous night—from Russell's involvement to Tabitha's betrayal. To the time and date they planned to meet on Cloverton's property and to the fact that the man named Wakes might be willing to harm anyone who knew of their deception. The words rushed out, and as they did, relief filled her.

"From what I can surmise, this arrangement—or whatever it is—has been going on for quite some time, and it affects both of our businesses. In good faith we cannot just stand by with the knowledge that this is happening."

Lucas's sober expression did not change. "Does your uncle know of this?"

She shook her head.

"You did not tell him?" Lucas's brows rose.

Olivia drew a deep breath. Sharing details about her personal life—and her relationship with her uncle—would give Lucas more insight into who she was, which made her more vulnerable. But what choice did she have? She needed help, and he was the only one who could give it. "My uncle cares very little for the business. To him, it is simply a living that fell into his lap."

"Do you think he's involved in this as well?"

When Olivia did not answer, Lucas rubbed his chin. "If there is a craftsman who makes such impressive replicas, then we'll face this issue again and again. After all, if this crew was able to affect the Milton collection, who knows who else might have been affected? But we must inform Wainbridge. As the owner of the stolen pieces, legally he is the one to bring in the proper authorities for any real investigation. The burden of proof would lie entirely with him."

"Would he be willing to get involved?" she asked.

Lucas shrugged. "He's lost a great deal of money. I'm sure he would. But what of Mrs. Milton? Tabitha is her maid, isn't she? Do you think she's aware of what is going on?"

The conversations she'd had with Mrs. Milton, combined with her possessiveness and protectiveness over the pieces, ran through Olivia's thoughts. Could that be why she was so opposed to Lucas's presence? "Honestly, I don't know. My instincts tell me no, but clearly I have misread several situations as of late."

He inched closer to her, and the light filtering through the front windowpanes fell across his face, highlighting the straightness of his nose and giving his pale eyes the appearance of glass.

Her breath shuddered within her. How would she ever be able to balance these feelings—this sensation of needing him to help her but also wanting to revive the tension that had simmered between them at Cloverton?

"Wainbridge is to call in a few days to discuss the sale of some of his items. I'll speak with him then and we'll figure out a plan of action."

Lucas's suggestion seemed solid. It made sense that he would be the one to speak with Wainbridge, especially given the manner in which he expelled her from Cloverton, but she didn't want to be left out of this process. It was too important. "You must promise to inform me of the outcome. This has serious implications for my business as well, for if Russell is selling stolen items from our shop, then I must know."

His eyes locked with hers. "I have a better idea. Perhaps you should join us when Wainbridge calls. We should be doing this together, you and me."

Olivia felt as if the air had left her lungs. It might have seemed a simple request to him, but to her, it was a testament to the fact that he viewed her as a professional—an equal. "I—I would appreciate that. Thank you."

"I'll send you word as soon as I hear from Wainbridge."

The conversation had reached a natural end, and her entire reason for being at the Avery shop was complete.

Yet she hesitated. For she simply did not want to leave.

She liked the feeling of being close to Lucas—of collaborating with him. His easy manner and quiet strength were a balm to her agitated thoughts. In his presence she felt respected. Admired. Seen.

Perhaps he shared the sentiment, for the somber expression had faded into one much more informal. "I'm by no means happy about this development, but seeing you is certainly a pleasant way to start the day." He looked down at her hand. Slowly, he reached out his own toward it.

Almost through no power of her own, she lifted her hand in response. He took it with his fingertips—so lightly, so gently, that his touch sent a bolt of fire surging through her.

He held her gaze as he lifted her hand higher and grazed the top of it with a fluttery kiss.

If only they could stay here, together, in this moment when only the two of them existed, when everything else subsided. But as lovely as it was, she had to remember who she was. Who he was.

As reason slowly won the battle, Olivia begrudgingly eased her hand back.

"I must be going," she managed to say. "They'll miss me if I'm gone much longer."

"I'll escort you." He released her hand and straightened his posture.

"Thank you, but it is probably best if I return alone."

"I understand," Lucas conceded. "I'll send word about Wainbridge as soon as I can."

As she turned to leave, a crooked smile crossed his face. The pragmatic air that had directed their conversation up until this point began to evaporate. His playful expression, which she had grown so accustomed to at Cloverton, was beginning to return. And she liked it.

"Good day, Olivia."

The use of her Christian name slowed her steps. "Good day, Lucas."

Chapter 39

HOW AWFUL IT was to be so suspicious of someone she thought she knew so well. All afternoon, Olivia worked alongside Russell as she normally would, but mistrust tightened her stomach, making her feel nauseous and unsteady.

For she *had* trusted Russell. Implicitly.

The idea that he'd been lying to her for possibly years repulsed her.

"You've been quiet all day." Russell placed a crate on the floor in the middle of the storeroom. "Is something wrong?"

"I'm tired, is all." Careful not to let him suspect she knew anything about his connection with the counterfeit chinoiserie, she forced herself to look at him, and then to the crate he'd brought in. "What are you doing with that?"

"Remember that set of silver French candelabras your uncle bought at auction last year at Flanner's? An inquiry to purchase came in while you were at Cloverton, and I'm taking them to a fellow in Harlow."

"Anyone we know?"

"Nah. Fellow by the name of Herman."

Normally, Olivia would not think twice about such a trip, but now her skepticism flared. He'd made dozens of such trips over the course of the past several years. Had his purpose behind those trips been sincere, or had they been made with nefarious intentions? "Will you be gone long?"

"Not sure. Thought I'd stop by the docks over in Brighton and along the coast while I'm there. Make the most of the effort." He glanced up at her and paused his action. "What's the matter? You look angry."

"Angry? No, of course not." She forced a smile. "It's just that I'm trying to familiarize myself with all that happened while I was gone."

"Think you'll be fine without me?" He grinned.

Olivia leaned her side against the doorframe. The inflection in his voice, which had been so commonplace and typical for so long, now rang with incongruity. "I'll be perfectly fine."

Later that night, after everyone else had gone to sleep and Russell had departed for Harlow, Olivia crept to the storeroom. She'd never be able to sleep—not with her newfound knowledge and her conversation with Lucas racing through her mind. There had to be something about Russell she was missing—and she was determined to find it.

Russell's bedchamber was just off the storeroom. He'd lived with her family for as long as he had worked for her father, and in that time she'd never been to his chamber.

She hesitated before entering. The door was not locked, but then again, she'd be surprised if it were. The thought of intruding into someone's personal space unsettled her, but what choice did she have? If she was going to accuse Russell of something this serious, she'd need substantial proof.

She lifted her candle higher and stepped inside his room. The windowless chamber was long and narrow, and it consisted of a bed in the corner, a table and chair on the opposite wall, a wardrobe, two stacked chests, and a trunk.

Wasting no time, Olivia placed the chamberstick on the table and moved to open the wardrobe door. Inside hung hats and clothing, and shoes lined the shelf across the top. Nothing seemed suspicious, so she abandoned the task and moved to the chests. Slowly, quietly, she opened the top one and drew the candle closer. Letters, handwritten notes, and small boxes cluttered the interior. Methodically she pored over them, careful to remember the location of each. With each word she read and each box she opened, fresh guilt heaped heavy on her. So far, everything seemed completely harmless.

After she returned the items the way she'd found them, she moved to the leather trunk at the foot of his bed. She crouched next to it and pushed the unlocked lid open. Inside were more letters, linens, and various pieces of clothing. She placed each piece on the wooden floor next to her as she continued her examination. She was about to return the items to their original places when she lost her balance and fell against the trunk.

The trunk did not move. In fact, it was far heavier than an empty trunk should be.

She removed the remaining articles and reached inside, and when her hand scraped the bottom of the wood, a hollow sound echoed. Alarm flaring, she used her weight to pull the trunk on its side, and as she did, a false bottom fell forward and a bound volume and a secured portfolio tipped out.

She snatched the book and opened it.

Inside was documented a series of transactions. The words made no sense, as if they were written in a code, but the numbers were clear and large. The corresponding dates were only recorded by the quarter of the year, but further exploration revealed the earliest recorded dates were from the year her father had died.

She unwound the twine securing the portfolio and opened the flap. Banknotes fell out. Lots of them.

Heart racing, she left her perch by the trunk, hurried to the office to retrieve a paper and pencil, and returned to make notes about everything in the ledger, paying particular attention to the items she believed could have possibly been some of the pieces in the Milton collection. With each discovery, each nugget of information, her determination to uncover the truth intensified. She refused to give in to the sense that she'd been taken for a fool. Instead, she determined to be meticulous in her search for details.

She would unearth the truth and uncover how these odd pieces were connected. She owed it to her father's legacy. She owed it to her clients. She owed it to herself.

By the time Olivia returned Russell's room to the state in which she'd found it, the long clock in the corridor had chimed the three o'clock hour. She expected to return to her bedchamber and find Laura sleeping, but upon approaching it, she saw a candle's glow flickering from behind the ajar door.

Concerned, she slowly approached and peered inside. Laura was sitting up in bed, her knees drawn up to her chest. In that moment, even with her chestnut hair woven in a long plait and wearing her nightdress, she no longer appeared as a child. The very mature expression of definite disapproval tightened her expression.

The slender young woman straightened as Olivia entered, and for several seconds, neither spoke. It was only after Olivia placed the candle on the table next to the bed that Laura blurted, "Where have you been?"

Olivia shook her head and attempted to mask her discomfort with a laugh. "I couldn't sleep."

Laura tossed the blanket away from her. "It's the middle of the night. Why are you still dressed in a gown?"

Taken aback by the forcefulness in her sister's tone, Olivia stiffened. It was becoming increasingly difficult to conceal the truth about so many things from Laura. She was clever. Perceptive. Their personalities could not be more different, and yet respect existed between them that demanded honesty or, at the very least, an explanation.

Before Olivia could formulate a believable response, Laura swung her legs over the side of the bed and stood. "You have been acting strangely ever since you returned from Cloverton Hall. Something must have happened."

Olivia's cluttered mind struggled to come up with a response that would satisfy.

When she didn't reply soon enough, Laura shook her head vehemently. "Perhaps you forget how well I know you. I know the difference between when you are tired and when you are worried and when something is bothering you, so you might as well tell me what it is, for I'll not let you rest until you do."

Laura's genuine concern touched her. How could Olivia tell her sister what she knew? How could she help Laura make sense of what was going on around them when she herself could not?

Olivia drew a sobering breath, closed the door, and sat on the bed next to her sister. "Like I said, a great deal happened at Cloverton Hall. A very great deal. I'm perfectly fine, but it was an eye-opening experience—about how abominably people treat each other and the great lengths to which others are willing to go to advance themselves."

"And Mr. Avery?" Laura lifted her brow as she turned to face Olivia. "I heard from Russell that he was here. I thought you hated the Averys."

There was no reason to hide her true feelings from her sister. "You're right. I did dislike them. But so much time has passed, and after spending time with Lucas, I learned that he is much more like us than I ever would have expected."

"Lucas?"

Olivia locked gazes with her sister. She'd let his Christian name slip from her lips.

"I-I mean Mr. Avery. We became friends during our time at Cloverton, and I believe we both want to continue that friendship now that we are home. But there is a great deal to consider."

Laura's eyes widened. "As in a beau? As in—?"

Olivia held up her hand. "Let's not get ahead of ourselves, but I do think—I hope—we will see more of Mr. Avery in our future."

As if satisfied with the answer, Laura sat back down on the bed. "Just please promise me you will not move on without me. You are my only family. If I didn't have you, I wouldn't have anyone."

Olivia sat next to her sister, put her arm around her, and kissed her head. "We will always have each other. On that you have my word."

Chapter 40

WHO EXACTLY WAS John Wakes?

The question had nagged Lucas ever since Olivia had said the name. Two days had passed since she brought him the list she'd copied from the ledgers hidden in Russell's chamber, and ever since, he and his men had been dedicated to tracking down any pieces they possibly could.

But they'd found nothing.

What was more, Olivia had heard Tabitha say that this man could be dangerous, and the idea of someone harming Olivia fanned the fire beneath him.

Lucas waited just outside the rear entrance to their shop, where Olivia was supposed to meet him. He spotted her as she crossed the road, and he straightened. Thoughts of porcelain and thefts fled.

The early afternoon sunlight fell over the crowded street, and the resulting shadows highlighted her slender form and played against the wisps of hair visible from beneath her straw bonnet. The skirt of her empire-waisted peach-hued gown swayed with each determined step, and the ribbons securing her bonnet danced in the breeze. But it was more than her beauty that captured his imagination. Her every motion exuded a refreshing confidence that he was not sure he'd ever seen in a woman before. None of the other women at Cloverton would dare be seen on a public street without a companion or at least a maid. But Olivia did things her own way. She thought differently. She challenged what was considered feminine. And yet she *exuded* femininity.

As she drew nearer to his shop, he jogged and met her half-way in the crowded road. "There you are! I wish you would have permitted me to send my carriage for you."

She beamed at him before they fell into step with each other back to the shop's rear entrance. "The offer was kind, but it would only make my uncle suspicious."

Once inside, she removed her bonnet and brushed her hair away from her brow. "I've been eager to hear if you've been able to find anything more on John Wakes."

"No, I haven't. You?"

She hung her bonnet on the hook just inside the door. "I spent all morning looking through records and couldn't find a thing."

He motioned toward his office. "Wainbridge is here already. He's in my office."

Olivia jolted, and her forehead furrowed. "I thought he wasn't supposed to arrive for another half hour."

"He's early. I've managed to put him off for a bit. I told him someone knowledgeable on the topic would be joining us."

"Did you tell him it was me?"

He chuckled. "No."

She expelled a nervous laugh and fussed with the fichu about her neck. "I suppose I can understand why."

"Don't worry. All will be well. Wainbridge is a reasonable man. Mostly."

Together they made their way to the office, and Lucas opened the door and paused for her to pass before him.

Almost immediately, Wainbridge jumped to his feet from where he'd been sitting near the desk. His appearance had much improved from the wild version she'd encountered the morning she'd left Cloverton. He was once again the immaculately dressed, clean-shaven man she'd met that first day of the house party, but instead of his customary grin, a disapproving scowl darkened his visage. "Miss Brannon. I was not expecting to see you here."

"I asked her to join us." Lucas raised his hands, as if soothing a spooked stallion. "Before we discuss your collection, she has something you must hear."

Wainbridge's irritated expression hardened. "With all due respect, Avery, I don't think so."

Lucas maintained a firm tone. "She has news that impacts all of us. Like it or not, your collection is at the center of a larger issue."

After Wainbridge's expression softened and he relaxed back into his chair, Olivia calmly informed him of what she'd learned over the last several days—about Tabitha, Russell, and Wakes. About the ledgers and the midnight conversation, the planned meeting, and the authentic piece at her shop that, in all likelihood, belonged to him.

When all again fell silent, Wainbridge pushed his fingers through his dark hair and shook his head, as if shaking himself out of a stupor. "I see."

Recognizing that Olivia's words were gaining traction, Lucas added, "We must act upon what we know. As the owner of the pieces, you are the only one with authority. Based on what Miss Brannon overheard, there's an exchange planned for Wednesday night on Cloverton property. If these thieves are to be brought to justice, the three of us must work together."

"The three of us?" Wainbridge raised a thick eyebrow. "With all due respect, Miss Brannon, I—"

"I take this very seriously"—Olivia's impassioned tone was steady—"and I'm the one who overheard the conversation and found the original piece in the storeroom. I can answer questions that no one else can."

Lucas moved to stand next to her. "We should have no problem keeping any plans from Crane since he's away from London, but ensuring that Tabitha doesn't suspect anything is imperative."

"Very well," Wainbridge acquiesced at last. "Isabella and I will be returning to Yorkshire in two days' time. You're welcome to share our carriage, and we can sort the details from there. Will we be able to recover the stolen pieces? Or the money at least?"

Lucas shrugged. "That's the goal. I suggest you inform your solicitor of our suspicions before you leave London, and we'll want to speak with the magistrate in Yorkshire, but recovering the money will depend on whether the authentic pieces have been sold or not. Crane is well-connected in the antiquities world, but so are Miss Brannon and I. Hope is not lost, but you must trust us."

Olivia never failed to impress Lucas.

She'd been articulate. Confident. And doggedly resolute. Even as she leaned to see out the office window, her golden eyes were wide and eagerly intent. "How do you think that went?"

Lucas stood next to her as they watched Wainbridge's carriage disappear around the corner. "He's agreed to help. That's a start, isn't it?"

Once the carriage was completely out of sight, she dropped the edge of the curtain and moved back to the center of the office. "He still doesn't trust me. I can tell."

"Well then, you'll just have to prove yourself," Lucas offered encouragingly. "Just as you have been. I only hope you proceed with caution."

"Meaning?"

"Meaning this entire situation could be very dangerous. These people aren't the sort of people we usually interact with. You even said that Tabitha suggested Wakes could be violent."

She drew a deep breath and folded her arms. "I know, but we can't let them succeed. Especially Russell. They may have stolen from the Cloverton collection, but Russell also took something from my family. He betrayed my father's legacy and took advantage of his good name. He must be held accountable for that."

Lucas recognized the fire and need for justice in her words. He wanted to do something that would protect her and rectify the injustices she faced, but he also suspected that doing so would almost be an insult to her. She was composed and clever, and she possessed more aplomb than anyone he knew. Her inquisitiveness and poise would be the envy of most men.

No, she did not need him.

But maybe—just perhaps—she *wanted* him.

"This isn't going to be easy. If you need my support, you have it." He moved toward her. "And you will always have it."

She noticed the small rendering of the Avery boys on the desk and lifted it to get a closer look at the drawing his brother had made all those years ago. "I wonder what our fathers would say if they knew we were working together like this."

"My father would be relieved," Lucas offered. "I know he always regretted the way things turned out between them."

"I think my father would too. We have all seen how life is too short for holding on to grievances."

He took another step in her direction until he was quite close.

Her curls sparkled in the afternoon sunlight. She lowered the drawing back to the desk and turned to face him.

Emboldened by the solidarity deepening between them, Lucas smoothed an errant lock of hair away from her face. He was close enough to see the golden flecks in her eyes that captivated him so, breathe the scent of rosewater that always wafted off her, and feel her warmth. "I don't know about you, but I hope this is the first of many endeavors we undertake together."

A playful smile curved her lips. "What else did you have in mind?"

He lowered his hand to her shoulder. She swayed subtly toward him, and it was all the encouragement he needed. He took her in his arms, relishing her softness. She melted against him, and in that moment no more words were needed.

He lowered his lips to meet hers, and the tender passion he found there, the earnest return of his affection, confirmed that in the midst of searching for the success he'd thought would make him happy, he'd found the *person* who would not only make him happy but make him complete.

Chapter 41

"LAURA. LAURA." OLIVIA touched her sister's shoulder. "Wake up."

Laura stirred under her covers, opened her eyes, and squinted in the faint light of dawn. "What time is it?"

"I need to talk to you."

Confused, Laura pushed herself up on her elbows. "Is something wrong?"

"No, nothing's wrong," Olivia whispered. "But I am leaving for a few days."

"What?" Suddenly fully awake, Laura sat upright. "What are you talking about?"

"Shh! I need to return to Cloverton Hall."

"Cloverton Hall! Why?"

"Nothing to worry about, just something I need to see to. I'll be back within the week."

Laura pushed her blankets away, her movements now alive with alert energy. "No, no. This is not right. Surely you—"

"Shh. Laura, I must go. Please believe me when I say that this is what I need to do for both of us. I've left a letter for

Uncle, and I promise I'll explain everything to you upon my return."

Laura's gaze fell to Olivia's traveling cloak. Her packed valise. "But what am I to say if he asks about you?"

"Tell him the truth. Tell him I said I had to leave on an errand."

"I don't like this, Olivia. This is not like you."

"But do you trust me?"

Her sister nodded slowly.

"I love you, and I'll be back as soon as I can."

Olivia pressed a kiss to her sister's forehead before donning her traveling cloak and securing her bonnet. Nerves fired through her as she prepared to embark on her second journey to Yorkshire, but this time, instead of wide-eyed optimism and the mere hope that everything would simply go as planned, her goal was finite: She *would* see that the thieves were brought to justice, and this time, she would not hide her identity or purpose. She would prove herself capable, one way or the other.

A steady morning rain fell over the gloomy London streets when Olivia joined Mr. Wainbridge, Isabella, and Lucas in the carriage bound for Cloverton Hall. The windy gusts carried an early autumn chill, and despite the carriage's elegance, the rutted roads promised an uncomfortable drive.

Throughout the first day of the journey, Olivia and Isabella shared the seat across from Mr. Wainbridge and Lucas. Olivia longed to discuss the entire situation with Isabella and rectify any lingering misunderstanding, but an unwieldy tension permeated every interaction. The air sizzled with unspoken explanations and sentiments, yet very little conversation occurred among the four travelers. To add to the strain, the memory of the galvanizing kiss she had shared with Lucas competed with almost every thought that crossed her mind. It was not until they'd reached the coaching inn and Olivia and Isabella were settling into their chamber that Olivia finally felt at liberty to address the situation at hand.

When Isabella's maid, who'd been traveling outside the carriage with the driver, had gone to procure tea, Olivia's pent-up words rushed out before their traveling cloaks had even been shed. "I've been waiting for a chance to speak with you. I owe you some explanations for what happened at Cloverton Hall."

Isabella shook her head slowly, removed her bonnet, and lowered it to the room's only table. "There's no need for explanations. What's done is done."

But Olivia forged ahead, determined to right any wrongs and clear up any misconceptions from her time at Cloverton Hall. "While we were at Cloverton, you asked me several times about my relationship with Mrs. Milton, and I never answered clearly. And I've felt guilt about that ever since. You were so kind to me, and you deserved to know the truth."

"Oh, Olivia." Isabella removed her damp cloak and hung it on a hook just inside the door. "My aunt did explain everything to me, and honestly, my heart broke for you. How terrible that you had to pretend to be someone you were not."

"But ultimately it was a deception," clarified Olivia. "And I do apologize."

"If you feel the need to apologize for deceiving another, then we all would, would we not? Every woman in attendance, myself included, was wearing a mask of sorts, presenting only the parts of themselves that they wanted to be seen."

Olivia removed her own cloak and hung it on the hook next to Isabella's. "I hope that in spite of everything, you and I can start our friendship anew. I should like to know you—the real you—and I should like for you to know the real me."

Isabella tilted her head. "I would like that very much."

The door creaked open, and the maid returned with a tray. After changing to dry night clothing and pouring tea, Isabella and Olivia sat on two wooden stools next to the small fire, warming themselves.

"And what of Mrs. Milton?" Olivia inquired, inching closer to the fire to take advantage of its warmth. "How is she faring in the midst of things?"

Isabella indulged in a dainty sip and lowered her cup. "She's always been a difficult person, but she's growing all the more contentious. The discovery of the counterfeit pieces has sent her on a rampage, and she has been accusing every member of the staff of involvement. It has been quite challenging."

Olivia cringed. Mrs. Milton had trusted Tabitha implicitly. How would she react to learn that her chambermaid was involved? "I feared as much. I wrote to her upon returning to London but have not received a response."

"Come now. All of that has been such unpleasant business, and it will be ready for us to deal with tomorrow. So let's talk of something more pleasant. I have a question of my own for you."

Olivia raised her brows at the spritely tone.

Isabella's words rose barely above a whisper. "Mr. Avery."

At the mention of Lucas's name, heat inched up Olivia's neck.

Isabella took another long sip of tea, as if enjoying the discussion very much. "You two seem as if you've been working closely together."

"W-we are in a similar business," Olivia stammered.

A knowing grin curved Isabella's lips, and she tilted her head to the side. "Many people are in a similar business, but may I point something out? They do not look at each other the way Mr. Avery looks at you."

Chapter 42

HAD IT REALLY been three entire days since they'd left London?

Lucas made his way down the high street of the small village just outside of the Cloverton estate, where he—not to mention Olivia—would be lodging until the issues surrounding the counterfeit pieces were resolved.

Lucas and Wainbridge left the meeting with the local magistrate—a nearby landowner by the name of Arthur Cunningham. All the planning, all the waiting, was coming to a head. Together the men had formulated a plan, and if everything went according to that plan, in mere hours the three people behind this enterprise would be arrested.

Lucas turned from the village's high street and headed toward the inn when a man on the far side of the road caught his eye. He squinted to ensure that the overcast sky and misty fog weren't obscuring his vision, but there was no denying it.

He recognized the tight, curly hair and pale skin: Russell Crane.

The muscles in Lucas's neck and jaw tightened. Crane was speaking with another man. Could it be Wakes? At first glance the conversation appeared quite casual, but upon closer inspection, the stance of both men suggested urgency, and the sudden jerk of the other man as he looked over his shoulder suggested he was far from being at ease.

Lucas lowered his hat to obscure his face as much as possible and made his way to the inn's main entrance. If Crane recognized either Olivia or him, their entire plan could be in jeopardy. What was more, Tabitha had indicated that Wakes was violent. He didn't fear for himself, but Olivia's safety was another matter entirely.

He found Olivia at a table in the dining room, where they'd planned to meet following his interview with the magistrate and Wainbridge.

She smiled warmly, even affectionately, at him as he approached, but the expression quickly faded as he sat opposite her.

"What?" A frown creased her brow. "What is it?"

He glanced around the dining room. "You must go to your chamber. Without delay."

"But why? I—"

"Go up," he urged in a low tone. "I'll be up in a minute to explain."

She pressed her lips together and wordlessly complied, and Lucas did not move from his spot until he was certain that Russell Crane had not noticed him or followed him in. After a few minutes, he made his way up the inn's narrow wooden stairs and down the paneled corridor, then tapped his knuckles against Olivia's door.

The lock clicked. The door opened.

He quickly stepped inside and shut the door behind him.

"What's the matter?" she whispered, her hazel eyes wide.

"Russell Crane is here." He swept his hat from his head and combed his fingers through his hair. "I saw him on the street just outside."

Her eyes grew even wider, and her hand flew to her mouth.

"We shouldn't be surprised," he added quickly to calm her. "We knew he'd be here. If anything, this validates our suspicions."

She lowered her hand and toyed with the coral necklace about her neck. "Was Tabitha with him?"

"No, but when I spoke with Wainbridge earlier, he confirmed that he saw her at Cloverton. There was a man with Crane. I'm assuming it was Wakes."

"Did you and Mr. Wainbridge meet with the magistrate?"

"We did. His name is Arthur Cunningham. He owns the estate directly to the east of Cloverton. We explained the entire situation, and he has agreed to assist us. He said he will round up some constables to help."

"That's a relief." Her shoulders slacked slightly. "So what is the plan?"

"Later this evening we'll meet the magistrate and constables at the cottage at dusk and wait for Crane and his associates to arrive. The constables on hand will apprehend them. Wainbridge has also engaged additional guards to be aware of any other unusual comings and goings on the property. The magistrate will be there to observe, which will give him eyewitness proof for the legal proceedings."

"Good." Enthusiasm brightened her tone. "When are we going?"

We?

He paused, taking in her earnest expression. She wanted so much to be a part of the arrest. Given her role thus far, she had every right to be. Reason urged him to forbid her to accompany them. The plan seemed straightforward, but the potential for danger was high, and despite her determination to uncover answers and to right wrongs, she was petite. Delicate. If the situation were to become perilous, would she be able to protect herself?

But she had been the one to uncover this entire plan—the one to bring Lucas in. She had as much to risk as anyone.

As if sensing his skepticism, she entreated, "I'm not reckless, Lucas, nor am I ignorant. I fully understand the potential danger, but I am a part of this. Can you see that? I have my future to think about. Laura's future. Please do not omit me. Perhaps it's not conventional, but I—"

"Olivia."

The use of her Christian name silenced her racing words. She snapped her mouth shut and pressed her lips together.

He placed his hands gently on her shoulders and inched closer. "Over the past few weeks I've watched you. Learned from you. I see your determination, and I'd not dampen that for anything. But as someone who cares deeply for you, I must protest. It could be precarious, and if anything were to happen, I'd never forgive myself for not doing more to protect you."

She seemed stunned.

Could she really be that surprised?

"But I—I—"

He took her hand in his. "I've never encountered anyone quite like you. I understand and adore your passion and ambition and would not change it for the world, but that does not change the fact that this is dangerous. I want to protect you."

"If you understand it, as you say, then you understand why I must be there," she retorted, her tone unyielding.

The words hung between them.

He studied her—really studied her.

What other woman would be willing to risk her safety for something she believed in? What other woman did he know who cared about principle and truth to the degree he did and was willing to put her dedication into action?

It was that very enthusiasm that made her *her*—that set her apart from other women. To squelch it or to deny Olivia would be to silence her uniqueness.

"Russell has abused my family. My father's memory," she argued, her tone sharp and steady. "Yes, I want him found out and I want justice rendered. But I need to be there for myself. I owe it to my father. You would not stand by and let someone else handle this. Why should I? This business is all I have of my father, Lucas. I have to see this through."

He felt her ardent words as keenly as if they'd been his own.

He wanted to soothe her. Encourage her. Join her on a journey they both could find peace and purpose in. But she was right—she needed to see this through for herself.

And he'd not stand in her way.

"My dear Olivia." He brushed a lock of hair away from her face and let his finger linger on her cheek. "You are stubborn."

She gave a little laugh and impatiently swiped at the moisture pooling in her eyes.

"I'll not stop you, nor will I forbid you to come. I don't think you'd listen to me anyway. But you must let me make one request. Don't you dare do anything too dangerous. I don't think I could bear it if I lost you."

Chapter 43

ARTHUR CUNNINGHAM LOOKED nothing like Olivia expected him to. He was small and gaunt, and deep lines creased the skin around his eyes and mouth. His thick white hair hung disheveled from beneath his wide-brimmed hat, and he walked with a limp, as if in pain.

How on earth was this man supposed to apprehend a criminal, especially if he tried to escape?

Judging by the hard glare he fixed on her, she didn't meet his expectations either.

Mr. Cunningham jerked his thumb in her direction and turned to Lucas. "Who's this?"

Lucas, with exaggerated manners, pivoted toward her. "Miss Brannon, may I present Mr. Cunningham, the magistrate of this area. And, Mr. Cunningham, may I present Miss Brannon of Brannon Antiquities and Company."

At first neither moved as they all stood in the shadowed stable just outside of Stoat Cottage. Even in the lantern's faint glow, Cunningham's disapproval burned as bright as fire.

Lucas must have sensed it, too, for he continued, "Miss Brannon personally overheard the conversation between Russell Crane and

Mrs. Milton's maid, and she is well acquainted with the porcelain pieces in question."

Mr. Cunningham looked back to the four constables behind him with a grunt before returning his attention to her. "With all due respect, Miss Brannon, these constables can take it from here. You'll be safer in the village. Mr. Avery will stay to aid us, and one of the constables will escort you back to—"

"If it is all the same to you," interrupted Olivia abruptly, "I believe it's best for me to remain here."

Mr. Cunningham raised a shaggy eyebrow and noisily cleared his throat. "Perhaps I should rephrase that. One of my men *will* escort you back to town. You will be notified as soon as the situation is in hand."

She lifted her chin and obstinately shook her head. "That simply will not do, Mr. Cunningham. Mr. Crane has been in my family's employ for over a decade. I'm not afraid of him, and I want to see with my own eyes that he is brought to justice."

Mr. Cunningham scoffed, and he looked toward Lucas as if seeking reinforcement. But Lucas gave none. Instead, he shifted the topic. "When I returned from our meeting earlier today, I spotted Crane in the village. He's close, so I believe our time would best be spent making sure we all understand the task at hand instead of debating where Miss Brannon should be."

Olivia jutted her chin up in the wake of Lucas's words.

Mr. Cunningham narrowed his eyes at the subtle reprimand and mumbled under his breath before continuing. "I've given these men an overview of what we are expecting tonight, but, Avery, share with them what you know."

Lucas turned to the four darkly clad constables. "Russell Crane is an antiquities agent out of London. John Wakes is a ceramist, as far as we know. Tabitha Martin is a lady's maid at Cloverton Hall. The three have been working together to swap out pieces from the Cloverton collection and replace them with replicas."

"Right." Mr. Cunningham pivoted to face the constables behind him. "And the easiest way to have charges brought against them and make sure they are enforced is for me to personally see the illegal activity occur. Altogether, there will be us six men. Since the meeting is expected to take place in the cottage, Avery, Patterson, Brown, Miller, and I will wait in the cottage's loft. Armstrong, you will stay at the door in the back, just in case."

"What about me?" Olivia blurted.

Cunningham groaned. "You'll stay here in this stable in case anyone comes in here."

"But I—"

"I'm in charge here, Miss Brannon," warned Cunningham. "What I say is how it will be. Are we clear?"

She pressed her lips together.

Mr. Cunningham tore his eyes away from her. "As I was saying, I've inspected the cottage, and there's not much to it. The five of us will wait in the loft until the three offenders are present. Then, on my signal, Avery and Patterson will subdue Crane. Brown and I'll subdue Wakes. Miller, you subdue the woman. When we have them, we will use the rope to secure them so I can question them, and then we will transport them in the wagons. From there we will take them to the jail, and if the weather's too murky for transport, Wainbridge said to hold them at Cloverton. Any questions?"

Questions?

Olivia could scream with frustration. Yes, she had questions. Many questions.

Mr. Cunningham extinguished the lantern, and darkness filled the stable. As the men started to exit the small building and head toward the cottage, Lucas touched her arm and whispered, "It will all be fine. Just stay here, all right?"

Olivia huffed.

No, it would not be all right. But she didn't really have a choice.

So she begrudgingly leaned against the door to wait.

Lucas shook his head at the recollection of petite Olivia Brannon standing up to Arthur Cunningham. She may not have gotten her way in that instance, but she'd caught the magistrate off guard. And Lucas was not surprised one bit.

He trudged through the wild, unkempt grass outside the cottage with the other men. The moorland night was dark and thick, and murky fog hugged the uneven landscape. Barn owls hooted in the distance, and the wind barreled in from off the moor, whistling in the grasses and rustling the leaves of the nearby copse of trees.

Cunningham had been right—there wasn't much to the cottage. The magistrate used a pocket tinderbox to produce enough light for the men to climb the ladder to the loft, and when he did it shed light on two tables and a handful of chairs. Nothing else was in the cottage.

Once they were up in the narrow loft, minutes rolled into an hour, and Lucas wondered if perhaps they'd been mistaken in their assumptions. But then the faint sound of distant wooden wheels rolling over wet ground echoed in the blustery night.

Lucas licked his lips in anticipation. Never before had he found himself in such a volatile situation, but now, as the possibility of every outcome raced through his mind, his senses were alive with expectation.

Cunningham whispered an order for silence.

Lucas's heart beat wildly in his chest.

At length, the front door creaked open and scraped loudly against the cottage's dirt floor. A rough male whisper uttered, "You said she'd be here at nine."

"And she will," responded Crane's voice. "Will you relax?"

"'Relax,' he says," grunted the first voice, who could only be Wakes. "They know 'bout the counterfeits, Crane. I'll not relax 'bout nothin' 'til this is done."

"We've got no choice but to stay the course, do we?"

Footsteps sounded outside, and then the door rasped open once more.

"What took you so long?" Crane sneered.

"I did m' best," a feminine voice hissed. "If ye think it's so easy t' sneak these out o' t' 'ouse wit' no one seein' ya, then ye try it."

"No sense getting all worked up." Crane sniffed. "Do you have it all?"

"It's 'ere. Take it." Some sort of fabric rustled, and the sound of porcelain clinking captured his attention. "'ere are t' originals for t' ones ye brought, and 'ere is t' next piece for you to replicate."

"I thought we said no more," Crane growled. "This stops now."

"I can make that," Wakes said after several moments, ignoring Crane's comment. "I'll need a drawing."

Light emanated from the floor below and cast shadows on the ceiling as a candle was lit. Lucas listened intently as Crane outlined the specifics of the piece that would need to be forged—the details of the images. The size of the handles. The thickness of the rim.

Motion caught Lucas's attention from the corner of his eye. Cunningham gave the signal.

It was time.

Lucas and the constables flooded from the loft, and havoc erupted.

"Listen up!" shouted Cunningham over the confusion. "You are under arrest for larceny and conspiracy to commit fraud."

Men shouted. Tabitha screamed. Porcelain crashed.

Using all his weight, Lucas rushed into Crane, pushing him back against the wall. The constable named Patterson lunged forward and slammed his fist into Crane's jaw.

Somehow in the midst of the shuffling and shouting, shoving and heaving, Lucas braced his knee against Crane's back on the ground, and the constable bound his hands behind his back.

Chest heaving from exertion, Lucas looked over his shoulder to see Wakes in a similar situation.

Then someone shouted, "Where's the girl?"

Olivia paced the damp, dark stable. With each step her boots sank farther into the soggy mud. She grimaced at the strong scent from the constables' horses, which were secured behind her, and rain dripped on her from a hole in the ceiling's thatch.

She'd agreed, reluctantly, to remain in place. But how could she possibly do that? She'd heard the wagon wheels approach. She'd observed a glow coming from behind the cottage's thin window covering. She'd heard voices blurred by the night's wind.

But nothing was happening.

Minutes slid by at such a glacial rate that she completely lost track of time, and frustration at not being included pressed her. Of course she understood Mr. Cunningham's reasoning behind making her stay in the stable. She was not daft. If the altercation became physical, she had little hope of defending herself against a man. But here in the stables doing nothing, Olivia felt helpless.

She hated it.

Yet in the very same heartbeat, she also knew she wasn't helpless. What was more, she knew she wasn't alone. She did have a partner . . . in Lucas. She trusted him, more than she had trusted anyone since her father. Had he not proven that he believed in her, that he valued her?

Her own reservations were crumbling. Her stubborn desire to become completely self-reliant was diminishing, and in its place blossomed a dream of building a future with Lucas. But even though she cared for him, and she knew he cared for her, she did not want him to fight her battles for her.

She paused again in front of the window and peered out, fully expecting to see naught but darkness. But this time, the glow coming from the window was brighter, and shadows darted wildly behind the thin curtain.

She hurried to the door and flung it open. Cold gusts and bits of rain met her, and she squinted to see in the distance.

Indecipherable shouts carried on the wind. A woman's scream.

Then, as quickly as the clamor had started, a door opened and a figure ran out, with hair streaming and a woman's cloak billowing behind her.

Tabitha.

The maid ran out of the cottage at an angle, toward the open moor on the other side of the stable. Alarm flared. No one was following her.

Olivia did not think. She only acted.

She burst at a full-speed run toward Tabitha.

Tabitha, no doubt distracted by the commotion Olivia had created, looked over her shoulder. As she did, she tripped and, with a cry, tumbled to the ground.

Olivia lunged at her and, with her own body, pinned the girl to the ground.

Tabitha flailed. Fought. "Get off me!"

Never in her life had Olivia physically tried to hold someone, but she employed every bit of energy to prevent the young woman from rising to her feet.

Tabitha pulled at Olivia's hair. Grabbed Olivia's arm and tried to push it back.

But Olivia held firm. She might not have been allowed to help the men, but this was her contribution, and she'd not fail.

Voices and harried shouts approached from behind them, and strong arms pulled her away just as two men yanked Tabitha from the ground.

The entire episode seemed to be over before it started, and Olivia gasped for air. She turned to who had pulled her up, and Lucas was just behind her. Dirt smeared across his cheek. His hair hung in damp, haphazard clumps.

But he was the most wonderful sight she'd ever seen.

Chest heaving, she lifted her gaze over Lucas's shoulder, and in the faintest bit of moonlight she could make out Russell and another man being bound, and the constables' wagons being pulled from the stable to transport them.

"We did it," she gasped, pausing a moment to allow air to reenter her lungs and her breathing to properly resume. She returned her attention to Lucas. Upon closer inspection she saw that a scratch marred his cheek. "Are you all right?"

"I'm fine." He lowered his voice. "But I'm a little worried about you. Did I really just witness you accost that woman?"

Olivia gave a little laugh, breaking the night's heavy tension. "I suppose it was not a very ladylike thing to do."

"Well, it worked." He draped his arm around Olivia's shoulder.

Tabitha's shouts of protest carried on the night wind, and the constable's harsh instructions should have given Olivia more delectation than they did. It would be easy to think they'd accomplished their goal. But now the three culprits would have to answer for their criminal actions. She would undoubtedly speak to Mrs. Milton again. And she would likely come face-to-face with the memories of her past and her father.

As they walked back toward the stables, she tucked her hand in Lucas's.

At least she would not have to face it alone.

Chapter 44

NOT EVEN HALF an hour after Russell, Tabitha, and Mr. Wakes were apprehended, Olivia found herself back in Cloverton's Blue Room. She'd experienced a wide range of emotions while standing in this room on previous occasions, but none matched the vexed urgency that plagued her in this moment.

She needed to hurry.

Because a heavy fog had descended on the moors, Cunningham had brought the prisoners back to Cloverton Hall instead of to the village for questioning. Mr. Wainbridge, Isabella, and Mrs. Milton were still away at the Whitmore House dinner as planned, but they were expected to arrive at any moment.

Isabella's maid had loaned Olivia one of her mistress's gowns, and with the woman's help she quickly changed from her mud-caked, rain-soaked gown to a warm wool one, washed her face and arms, and brushed her hair. As soon as she was ready, she descended the great staircase and headed to Mr. Wainbridge's study, where the men had gathered.

She hesitated outside the door. On the other side of it were people she'd once trusted and even counted as friends. Not only had they betrayed her, but they had betrayed many others as well. She was nervous to face them, but she also knew that Lucas was inside.

She placed her hand on the brass handle and opened it.

Heat from the large fire in the grate rushed her as she entered, and the plethora of candles added light to the cluttered chamber. Several crates had been placed on a table in the center of the room, revealing an assortment of chinoiserie. Tabitha, Russell, and Mr. Wakes were each seated in a chair with their hands tied behind them. Lucas, Mr. Cunningham, and two of the constables were also present.

Immediately, she caught Russell's eye.

He did not look away. Instead, he fixed his hard, angry gaze on her.

Years of shared experiences flashed before her. Up until now he had been an important figure in her life—a constant when so many other things had shifted.

And then she looked to Tabitha. As odd as it seemed, this betrayal stung more. Tabitha's cheerful friendliness had been a safe harbor during her uneasy time at the house party, but looking at Tabitha now, she could scarcely believe any softness resided in her. Her wet copper hair was plastered to her forehead and the side of her face, and the moisture in it made it appear that much darker. Her skin was ghostly white, which emphasized the dark shadows beneath her lower lashes, the smattering of freckles on her upturned nose and cheeks, and the purplish-red hue of her eyelids.

Olivia moved wordlessly next to Lucas, who stood just next to the fire, but as she did, footsteps and cries echoed from the hall, followed by panicked voices. Mr. Wainbridge, Isabella, and

Mrs. Milton all bustled in, still clad in their fine attire from their evening at the Whitmores' home.

In the midst of all the confusion, it was Mrs. Milton who drew Olivia's attention, and her heart ached for the older woman. Horror and distress at seeing Tabitha tied up with the men suffused her face. No doubt she was putting the pieces together.

Mr. Cunningham raised his hands to quiet the chatter. He fixed his glare on the three perpetrators, and his voice echoed hard and deep. "Do any of you three want to start by telling me what exactly is going on here?"

No one moved or spoke.

"If no one's going to respond," Mr. Cunningham continued, "I'll tell you what I observed with my own eyes. I saw this maid bringing items from Cloverton Hall to an old cottage on the moor. And I saw that these two gentlemen brought exact replicas of the pieces. Now, why would that be?"

The three thieves remained silent.

"It wouldn't be that you were going to swap them out, thinking no one would be any the wiser, would it?"

When they failed to respond again, Cunningham leaned a few inches in front of Tabitha's face. "Maybe I am not being clear. I'm asking you questions. Did you steal these items?"

Fresh tears streamed down her already tearstained cheeks, but instead of remorse, hardness settled over her features. She whirled her head to face Olivia. "Ye know me, Miss Brannon! Ye know I'm no thief."

Olivia shook her head. "No, I don't know you, Tabitha. I thought I did, but I was mistaken."

"These things, all of 'em, should belong t' me." She fought against the ropes, then spun to face Mrs. Milton and pinned a hard, hateful glare on the older woman. "Either you tell 'em, or I will."

All color drained from Mrs. Milton's face. Her cheeks shook. Her hands trembled.

Olivia feared Mrs. Milton might faint.

Tabitha jeered toward Mrs. Milton. "Francis Milton was me father. Wasn't 'e, *Mrs. Milton?* Ah, ye can be generous t' me and hide me away, pretend it's not so, but ye know I'm right. Those things are me birthright. And so I took 'em."

She swung her head back to face Olivia. "Did ye not wonder why Mrs. Milton was so kind t' me mother? 'Twas 'er 'usband what took advantage of 'er. 'er 'usband who ruined me mother's life. And instead of throwin' me mother out, she used 'er—an' me—t' make Francis Milton pay for 'is sins every day of 'is miserable, deplorable life."

Mrs. Milton, in a display much more fitting to the woman Olivia had gotten to know, slammed her hand down on a nearby table, rattling the chinoiserie. Olivia anticipated yelling, shouting, but instead the woman's eyes narrowed. Her voice tightened. She locked eyes on Tabitha. "Is this really what you've come to? No allegiance? No loyalty? No friendship?"

"'Twas *yer* 'usband," Tabitha hurled, her face pale, her eyes wide. *"Yer 'usband* who is responsible for all o' this."

"Oh yes, my husband made mistakes," admitted Mrs. Milton, her gumption strengthening. "But I treated you with nothing but kindness and respect. And this is how you repay me?"

Tabitha scoffed, even as fresh tears raced down her round cheeks. "Don't ye dare use me t' ease yer conscience. You're just as bad as 'e was, because ye 'id it from t' world. Your 'usband ruined me mother and ultimately killed her."

The hatred, the anger in Tabitha's voice, shocked Olivia. Never would she have thought the girl so capable of vengeance.

But whereas Tabitha seemed to be crumbling, Mrs. Milton seemed to be garnering vigor. "No, Tabitha. No. You chose this path. And I cannot, I will not, help you. Not anymore."

"I've had enough of this," Cunningham interrupted, refocusing the interrogation. He pointed a finger at Tabitha. "You will answer my questions and only my questions, are we clear?"

Mrs. Milton spun and hurried from the room.

Everything in Olivia wanted to hear the excuses and the reasons from Russell and Tabitha as to why they'd betrayed her. But Lucas was present to hear it, and at the moment, she suspected Mrs. Milton needed her more than Arthur Cunningham did.

Olivia left her place at Lucas's side and found Mrs. Milton in the drawing room, which was lit only by the fire in the hearth. She was seated on the sofa, still in her elegant finery from the Whitmore dinner, staring into the fire. She was not crying, but her hands were shaking.

Olivia was trying to determine what she should say when Mrs. Milton beat her to it. "You'd best go, Miss Brannon. You'll miss the questioning. I'm not entirely sure what has happened here tonight and what exactly it is that Tabitha and those men have done, but since you and Mr. Avery have returned and there is a pile of porcelain on the table, I can only assume you have business to tend to."

"The constables will take care of it." Olivia sat next to Mrs. Milton. "Right now I'm more concerned with you than the questioning."

Olivia took Mrs. Milton's hand in her own, and they sat in silence for several moments. At length, Mrs. Milton heaved a shallow sigh. "I thought I'd take that secret with me to the grave."

Olivia squeezed her hand. "It must have been a very difficult secret to live with."

Mrs. Milton sniffed and impatiently swiped at the moisture in her eyes. "It was, at the beginning. I was so angry with Francis. And Tabitha was right. I did want to make him pay and regret his actions. But time has a way of softening such intentions. I forgave him. In fact, I never thought of Tabitha as his child. I considered her a friend. I was able to separate them in my mind. I thought Tabitha did as well. Clearly, I was mistaken."

"I know Mr. Milton was very dear to you."

"He was. But as dear as he was to me, he was often foolish, often selfish. Francis made several questionable decisions when he was young, but he was still my husband, and I had a choice to make. I could forgive him and do my best to move on, or I could stay in a place of anger. Those were the only two options, and I chose the one I thought I'd be able to live with."

There was a soft, sad wistfulness to Mrs. Milton's tone that Olivia had not heard before. "You cannot control what your husband did, any more than you can control what Tabitha did."

"It turns out I was the fool. I had no idea she felt this way. All these years, and I had no inclination."

"You're not a fool. The way I see it, you made the best decision you could with the information you had and chose to take Tabitha at her word. You did not waver."

Silence once again fell over them, and Mrs. Milton patted Olivia's hand this time. "Where do I go from here, I wonder."

"That is the beauty of it. You get to start fresh. A brand-new story waits for you, Mrs. Milton, and I, for one, can't wait to see where it takes you."

Had it really only been a couple of weeks ago when Olivia was here for the house party? When Mr. Romano painted her portrait, when she first tried champagne, and when she reignited her relationship with Lucas?

Life had resumed in the ensuing weeks, but in truth, it wasn't the life she'd known. Something in her had changed during her time at Cloverton Hall. She'd arrived here with no other focus than to further her prospects and prove herself self-sufficient. That was still important to her, but now the future she saw for herself was shifting. She no longer saw only a future where she was responsible for herself and Laura. Her future now included Lucas.

Footsteps sounded, and Lucas appeared in the doorway. And he looked tired. His tousled brown hair was brushed carelessly to the side. He wore no tailcoat, his neckcloth was loosened about his neck, dried mud speckled his breeches and riding boots, and his shirtsleeves were rolled to his elbows.

Even after all that had happened, he offered her a lopsided grin as he entered the room. "What an ordeal that was. I'd have never thought Crane had that sort of fight in him."

"I guess you would, too, if you'd just found yourself caught in illegal activity." She motioned for him to join her on the sofa. "What do you think will happen now?"

"They've taken them out to the stables to guard them there for the night. The fog is too thick to travel to the village now, but tomorrow Wainbridge will bring charges against them. Tabitha has all but confessed, and even if Crane does not say a word, there's a paper trail. After all, you have his ledger, and we will be able to match that up against the counterfeit pieces. What's more, Wainbridge is paying to have a constable go to Wakes's house and buildings. They will inevitably find evidence. Maybe they will find leads on other collectors he has deceived."

"Wakes had such talent as an artist. Imagine being able to create such beautiful things. It is such a waste."

"Ah, you know how it is, Olivia. Some collectors value antiquities because of what they represent. Others value them because of what they are worth. It's a delicate balance . . . one that he obviously tried to manipulate." Lucas wrapped his arm around her, and she leaned against him. He kissed her forehead. "It's after midnight. You should go to bed."

"How could I possibly sleep?"

"Well then"—he settled in, tightening his arm around her—"tell me what happened with Mrs. Milton."

She leaned her head against his shoulder and lifted her face to his. "It's heartbreaking, Lucas. She did confirm that Mr. Milton was Tabitha's father, and yet she really did love him. She wanted to preserve what she believed was his legacy, and yet it was that very legacy that caused such turmoil and brought his past back to haunt him."

"I always find it ironic when we encounter situations like this. These chinoiserie pieces are so valuable, and yet they are no substitute for those we love." He traced his finger down the side of her cheek, letting it linger on her chin. "I really am proud of you, you know. You're brave. In fact, it's almost scary how brave you are."

She laughed. "It's not bravery. I fear it is stubbornness. Or perhaps a reaction to injustice."

"Whatever it is, it's quite unusual."

"Speaking of unusual events, I'm ready to put all of these unusual happenings and events behind us and return to what is normal."

"My dear Olivia," he teased, "nothing about my life has been normal since the moment I saw you walk into Cloverton Hall."

She raised a brow. "Are you sorry, then?"

"Not sorry at all. I wouldn't have it any other way. Which reminds me. I have another confession."

The reprise of their secret joke brightened their conversation. Olivia straightened and turned to face him. "What, another one?"

"Yes. Another one." He took her hands in his and leaned close. His gaze met hers so fully that it was as if he could see into her very soul. "I confess that I am hopelessly captivated by you. And if this past month has taught me anything, it's that love, and love alone, makes life worth living. So that is why I ask you, Miss Olivia Brannon, if you will do me the honor of becoming my wife."

She didn't want to break his gaze. The girl who had arrived at Cloverton Hall desperately seeking approval was now a woman who'd learned that strength came through love and acceptance. And it was beautiful.

She reached up, placed her palm on the side of his face, and looked deep into the green eyes of the man who had helped her find such truth. "Mr. Avery, I would be honored to become your wife."

Epilogue

LONDON, ENGLAND, SUMMER 1819
BRANNON & AVERY ANTIQUITIES

OLIVIA AVERY STOOD next to her husband on the bustling London street and faced the storefront with her eyes closed.

Lucas moved his hands on her shoulders and adjusted the angle at which she was standing. "Open your eyes and tell me what you think."

She opened her eyes, and the new shingle hanging outside the shop door, fresh with bright and shiny gold paint, boasted the words *Brannon & Avery Antiquities*.

She clasped her hands before her. "Oh, Lucas, it's beautiful!"

He put his arm around her waist and pulled her tightly to his side. "Are you happy?"

"I could not be happier." She flung her arms around his neck and kissed his cheek.

"Now it's official," he bantered. "You can teach me everything you know about antiquities and all things unusual and ancient."

She placed her hand on his chest and leaned toward him. "We can teach each other."

Lucas looked back to the building, and his expression sobered. "I'm only sorry we were unable to secure your father's building. I know it would have pleased you."

Olivia's heart tightened. Upon learning about Russell's betrayal, Uncle Thomas cut Olivia and Laura out of the business and sold everything—the building and the inventory—and left for America.

At first the news stung, but time and her new circumstances were softening it. "Whether we like it or not, Father left his part of the business to his brother, not me. It was his to sell or to do with it as he liked. Besides, I think this is what Father would want for me. A fresh start. A new beginning."

"And me?" Lucas asked. "What would he have thought of me as your husband?"

"I'm sure with a little coaxing he would have come around eventually." She smirked. "But I do think this change has been good for Laura. She seems so much happier living with us than she ever did on Kingsby Street."

"And for my mother as well. She and Laura have become quite good friends, haven't they? Laura even got her to go out on a carriage ride. I've been trying to do that for months."

Tate, who'd stopped by to see the new addition to the building, exited the shop, let the door slam loudly behind him, and turned to the shingle. "Look at you two. So in love. And to think, none of this would have happened if it wasn't for me."

Lucas scoffed. "And how do you figure that?"

"Isn't it obvious?" Tate propped his fists akimbo. "*I* introduced you to Wainbridge. *I* secured the invitations to Cloverton Hall, at which point you connected with your lovely future bride. And if it weren't for that, none of this would have been possible."

"You're ludicrous," Lucas observed.

"Perhaps. But I'm right." Tate's expression shifted, and he shook his head. "As exciting as this all is, it is also a pity. Your focus will change entirely. No more carousing for us. I hate to think all our adventures will be coming to an end."

"Who says the adventures will be coming to an end?" Lucas retorted. "Olivia and I have the whole world to explore."

Tate stepped closer to Lucas and stood with him shoulder to shoulder as they assessed the shingle. "Speaking of the world, when are you leaving for Egypt?"

Egypt.

A thrill surged through Olivia at the very word. It was to be her wedding present—a trip, a dream come true.

"We leave next April. But before we go, we will oversee the auction for Mrs. Milton's collection. We've already found buyers for the bronze pieces and every one of the shells, and inquiries are coming in for the gems and other pieces. I expect it to do very well."

"Ah yes. And how is Mrs. Milton?" Tate asked. "Still cantankerous?"

"Yes," Lucas blurted.

Olivia swatted playfully at his arm. "Don't listen to him, Mr. Tate. She is not nearly so much now as she was during the house party. She and Mr. Wainbridge have come to an understanding of sorts, and he has sold her a cottage on the grounds. It's not entirely ideal, but it seems to be working at the moment. In fact, she's here in London now. Laura and I are to have tea with her and Miss Wainbridge tomorrow if you'd care to join us."

"Tea with her *and* Miss Wainbridge? I thought they didn't like one another."

"They've been spending a great deal of time together. I think it's a positive development. They are family, after all."

"Family, eh?" Tate lowered his voice. "Speaking of family, whatever happened to the girl? The illegitimate daughter?"

Olivia sobered. The last time she'd seen Tabitha, not to mention Russell, was the night at Cloverton when they were apprehended. "Tabitha. She is in prison and will be for some time. As are Mr. Crane and Mr. Wakes."

Tate clapped his hand on Lucas's shoulder. "Well, I'd love to stay and chat more about all of these happy developments, but I'm off to meet my father."

"You'll have to tell him that we send our regards," Lucas offered.

"I fear this is not a social call. Oh no. No, no. You know my father, all seriousness, all the time. He says he has a few *concerns* he would like to discuss with me." Tate jerked his head and an exaggerated expression crossed his features. He then smiled, bowed toward Olivia, and tipped his tall beaver hat at Lucas. "I'll be off, then."

Olivia and Lucas bid their farewells and then turned back to the shiny gold paint on the shingle. Lucas took her hand in his, and together they made their way back into their store, back amongst the valuable vases and paintings and statues.

She moved to go back through the office, but he caught her hand and playfully pulled her close to him. "A moment before we do, if I may."

She giggled and allowed herself to be drawn into his embrace.

He kissed her, and she wrapped her arms around his neck.

"Promise me, my darling," she said softly, "that we will always be this happy."

He lifted his hand and brushed a lock of hair from her face. "You have my word."

He kissed her again, and she surrendered to it, resting in the fact that there was nothing she needed to prove. She was loved and respected for who she was. She had found the person who not only viewed her entirely as an equal but also challenged her to continue chasing her dreams and following her passions. What was more, they could do it together.

She had found her home in Lucas Avery's arms. It was a beautiful place to be.

Acknowledgments

JUST AS EVERY novel is full of twists and turns, so is the writing process! I learn so much with every book I write, and I'm so grateful for the people who support and encourage me along the way.

To my family—I am thankful every day for your unending love and encouragement.

To my agent, Rachelle Gardner—I can always count on you for the best advice around!

To my editor, Becky Monds, and to my line editor, Julee Schwarzburg—I appreciate how you two always challenge me and support me. To the rest of the team at HCCP—thank you for all you do.

Last but not least, to KBR and KC—I can't wait to see what the next decade brings!

Discussion Questions

1. For Olivia, growing up around antiquities influenced her passions as an adult. Did you grow up around certain items or skills that influenced your activities or passions later in life?

2. If you had to pick three words to describe Olivia's character, what would they be? What words would you use to describe Lucas?

3. How is Olivia different at the end of the book than she is at the beginning? What about Lucas?

4. Let's discuss Mrs. Milton. Do you think Mrs. Milton changes at all throughout the course of the story? Why or why not?

5. If you could give Olivia one piece of advice at the beginning of the story, what would it be? What advice would you give her at the end?

6. Did you have a favorite character in the story? If so, who was it, and what drew you to them? Who was your least favorite?

7. What lessons can a reader take away from *The Cloverton Charade*?

8. It's your turn! What comes next for Olivia and Lucas? If you could write the sequel, what would happen?

LOOKING FOR MORE GREAT READS? LOOK NO FURTHER!

THOMAS NELSON
Since 1798

Visit us online to learn more:
tnzfiction.com

Or scan the below code and sign up to receive email updates
on new releases, giveaways, book deals, and more:

@tnzfiction

About the Author

Photo by Emilie Haney
of EAH Creative

SARAH E. LADD is an award-winning, bestselling author who has always loved the Regency period—the clothes, the music, the literature, and the art. A college trip to England and Scotland confirmed her interest in the time period, and she began seriously writing in 2010. Since then, she has released several novels set during the Regency era. Sarah is a graduate of Ball State University and holds degrees in public relations and marketing. She lives in Indiana with her family.

Visit Sarah online at SarahLadd.com
Instagram: @sarahladdauthor
Facebook: @SarahLaddAuthor
X: @SarahLaddAuthor
Pinterest: @SarahLaddAuthor